"Am I the father of your baby?"

Grace knew the answer Ethan wanted. It was in his scowl, his clenched hands, the sinking feeling in her stomach. It was foolish to be disappointed. She was twenty-five, a woman on her own, about to become a single mother.

There was no room in her life for daydreams or fantasies, no chance that a charming rogue might turn into her very own Prince Charming, no chance at all that something special could develop out of a one-night stand. Yes, he'd come back upon learning that she was pregnant, but only because he wanted her to deny that he was the father.

"No," she said softly, feeling the ache of the lie deep inside.

He looked startled, then relieved, then suspicious. "No, what?"

"You're not the father."

His gaze narrowed, sending heat flushing through her face.

"You're lying. It's my baby, isn't it?"

Dear Reader,

Once again Intimate Moments is offering you six exciting and romantic reading choices, starting with *Rogue's Reform* by perennial reader favorite Marilyn Pappano. This latest title in her popular HEARTBREAK CANYON miniseries features a hero who'd spent his life courting trouble—until he found himself courting the lovely woman carrying his child after one night of unforgettable passion.

Award-winner Kathleen Creighton goes back INTO THE HEARTLAND with *The Cowboy's Hidden Agenda,* a compelling tale of secret identity and kidnapping— and an irresistible hero by the name of Johnny Bronco. Carla Cassidy's *In a Heartbeat* will have you smiling through tears. In other words, it provides a perfect emotional experience. In *Anything for Her Marriage,* Karen Templeton proves why readers look forward to her books, telling a tale of a pregnant bride, a marriage of convenience and love that knows no limits. With *Every Little Thing* Linda Winstead Jones makes a return to the line, offering a romantic and suspenseful pairing of opposites. Finally, welcome Linda Castillo, who debuts with *Remember the Night*. You'll certainly remember her and be looking forward to her return.

Enjoy—and come back next month for still more of the best and most exciting romantic reading around, available every month only in Silhouette Intimate Moments.

Yours,

Leslie J. Wainger
Executive Senior Editor

Please address questions and book requests to:
Silhouette Reader Service
U.S.: 3010 Walden Ave., P.O. Box 1325, Buffalo, NY 14269
Canadian: P.O. Box 609, Fort Erie, Ont. L2A 5X3

MARILYN PAPPANO

ROGUE'S REFORM

Silhouette®

INTIMATE™ MOMENTS®

Published by Silhouette Books

America's Publisher of Contemporary Romance

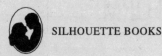 SILHOUETTE BOOKS

ISBN 0-373-27073-9

ROGUE'S REFORM

Visit Silhouette at www.eHarlequin.com

Printed in U.S.A.

Books by Marilyn Pappano

MARILYN PAPPANO

After following her career navy husband around the country for sixteen years, Marilyn Pappano now makes her home high on a hill overlooking her hometown. With acreage, an orchard and the best view in the state, she's not planning on pulling out the moving boxes ever again. When not writing, she makes apple butter from their own apples (when the thieves don't get to them first), putts around the pond in the boat and tends a yard that she thinks would look better as a wildflower field, if the darn things would just grow there. You can write to Marilyn via snail mail at P.O. Box 643, Sapulpa, OK 74067-0643.

IT'S OUR 20th ANNIVERSARY!
We'll be celebrating all year,
Continuing with these fabulous titles,
On sale in May 2000.

Romance

 #1444 Mercenary's Woman
Diana Palmer

#1445 Too Hard To Handle
Rita Rainville

 #1446 A Royal Mission
Elizabeth August

#1447 Tall, Strong & Cool Under Fire
Marie Ferrarella

 #1448 Hannah Gets a Husband
Julianna Morris

#1449 Her Sister's Child
Lilian Darcy

Desire

 #1291 Dr. Irresistible
Elizabeth Bevarly

 #1292 Expecting His Child
Leanne Banks

#1293 In His Loving Arms
Cindy Gerard

 #1294 Sheikh's Honor
Alexandra Sellers

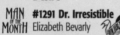 **#1295 The Baby Bonus**
Metsy Hingle

#1296 Did You Say Married?!
Kathie DeNosky

Intimate Moments

 #1003 Rogue's Reform
Marilyn Pappano

 #1004 The Cowboy's Hidden Agenda
Kathleen Creighton

#1005 In a Heartbeat
Carla Cassidy

 #1006 Anything for Her Marriage
Karen Templeton

 #1007 Every Little Thing
Linda Winstead Jones

 #1008 Remember the Night
Linda Castillo

Special Edition

 #1321 The Kincaid Bride
Jackie Merritt

#1322 The Millionaire She Married
Christine Rimmer

#1323 Warrior's Embrace
Peggy Webb

 #1324 The Sheik's Arranged Marriage
Susan Mallery

#1325 Sullivan's Child
Gail Link

#1326 Wild Mustang
Jane Toombs

Prologue

It was a slow night at the Pirate's Cay. Some joker in the corner had spent the last two hours playing every Jimmy Buffett tune on the jukebox, and two of the worst pool players on Key West were playing a game of eight ball that was never going to end the way they were going at it. The few regulars who had wandered in had wandered back out before long, leaving Ethan James with no one interesting to watch but the redhead alone at a table for two.

He had a weakness for redheads—had ever since he was sixteen and had hitched a ride across Texas with a redhead five years his senior. She'd shown him the sights at damn near every stop, and he'd developed a fine appreciation for flaming hair and fiery passion along the way.

The redhead at Pirate's Cay was looking at him as if she could show him a few things, too. On a slow night, with nothing else, he was sure he would enjoy the ride.

As he finished wiping down the bar, the owner of the Cay came out of her office, took a look around, then joined him. "Life in wild, wonderful Key West. I don't know how we survive it." She tossed two envelopes onto the bar between them. "Here. Happy payday."

"What's the other?"

"Letter came for you today. I put it with your check so I wouldn't forget, and then I forgot." She glanced up at the clock on the wall, then swiveled her stool around. "Last call, folks. We close in ten minutes."

No one showed any interest in more drinks. The redhead waited until he was watching her, then stood up, smiled and sauntered to the door. If he were a betting man, he'd give himself better than even odds that she'd be waiting in the parking lot when he walked outside.

Actually, he *was* a betting man, though it was one of many vices he'd been working at giving up. He'd achieved a higher degree of success with some than others. He'd stopped stealing and drinking, and was honest more often than not. Staying away from the gambling was harder, but he told himself when he slid that at least it was better than earning his money by conning innocent dupes out of theirs. He'd cut back on indiscriminate sex, but he couldn't give it up completely. Hell, he had to have *something* to make life worth living. He damn sure didn't have anything else…except a drop or two of self-respect. He doubted anyone else would be proud of the changes he'd made, but he was, and that was almost enough.

Setting the envelopes aside, he began closing up. By the time he finished, it was only two minutes past closing time and everyone but him and the boss was gone. She didn't have far to go—through the storeroom door and up a flight of stairs to her apartment on the second floor. His own apartment was a few miles farther in a neighborhood significantly shabbier. He had five hundred square feet over a two-car garage that took too much of his paycheck, but he had nothing else to spend the money on. No family who wanted anything to do with him. No girlfriend. No future besides trying to stay out of trouble.

He waited for the boss to walk him to the door so she could lock up behind him. "See you tomorrow, darlin'," she murmured as he left.

He responded with a nod and a wave, then glanced at the letter as he started for the parking lot. The postmark was illegible, the handwriting familiar, the return address even more so. His sister-in-law Olivia was the only member of the family who kept tabs on him—whether out of affection or self-protection, he didn't know. He suspected the latter.

She'd gotten the Cay's address from the birthday card he'd sent his brother Guthrie last December, and in return, she'd signed Guthrie's name to a Christmas card, along with an invitation to spend the holidays with them. He'd ignored the invitation, knowing he was about as welcome in Heartbreak as a prairie fire in a drought, but he'd kept the card, and the two she'd sent him since.

As he turned the corner into the parking lot, he saw the redhead draped over the hood of a sharp little ragtop before turning his attention back to Olivia's letter. He tore a jagged strip from one end and slid two fingers inside to pull out a photograph with a yellow sticky note covering its subject. In Olivia's elegant hand was a short message: *I thought you should know.* Know what? he wondered as he peeled the note off.

The answer stopped him in his tracks.

The snapshot had been taken in a parking lot on the main street of Heartbreak. The day had been sunny, the sky barely blue, but he would know it was cold even if the woman hadn't been wearing a coat, scarf and gloves, even if her breath hadn't crystallized in the air the instant the photo was taken.

Just as he'd known her instantly, without the long, wild curls, the sexy, tight clothes or the husky, seductive voice.

Just as he'd known that night seven months ago that rowdy bars weren't her usual hangouts, that no-good con artists weren't her usual companions.

He steadied his hand to stare at the photo. She wore no makeup, and her thick brown hair was pulled back in a ponytail. She was turned slightly away from the camera to avoid a direct shot. Instead of drawing attention to her face, the stance drew the viewer's eye lower. To what Olivia wanted him to know. To a not-so-small detail the too-big and unstylish clothes she wore couldn't disguise.

She was pregnant. About seven months so.

After a long, stunned moment, he returned the photograph to the envelope, then carefully folded it to fit in his pocket. As he walked past the convertible and the beautiful, sexy redhead, he knew there was only one thing for him to do.

He had to go home.

Chapter 1

As towns went, Heartbreak, Oklahoma, wasn't much, Grace Prescott thought as she walked briskly along the sidewalk. The buildings in what they laughingly called the business district were old and shabby. The sidewalks were cracked, the streets needed repaving, and too many of the parking spaces downtown had been empty for far too long. The ranchers and farmers for whom the town existed had always been in a tough business, and it had become even more so in recent years. Economic prosperity wasn't even a pipe dream for the stores in town. The reality for most of them, her own included, was mere survival.

But she couldn't think of anyplace else she'd rather be, of any other neighbors she'd rather have. In the last few months, she'd found a satisfaction in Heartbreak that she'd thought she would never know. For the first time in her life, she fit in. She had friends. She *belonged*.

And all it had taken was getting pregnant by a stranger and, when her father found out, a punch to the jaw. One moment of pure pleasure leading to a moment of pain, and the end result was this—freedom. Happiness. A bright future, no matter how bleak it might sometimes look.

"Hi, Grace." Trudie Hampton greeted her as she unlocked the insurance agency door. "It's a bit chilly this morning for your usual walk, isn't it?"

"I'm not cold," Grace said, though it wasn't true. This morning's forecast had called for a wind chill of eighteen degrees, and she was pretty sure they'd reached it. In spite of all her cold-weather gear, her reflection in the plate-glass window showed that her cheeks were ruddy. Her nose was sniffly, and her breath puffed into the air like smoke from a signal fire.

"They're saying we'll have snow before evening."

"Really? I didn't hear that."

"Not on the radio. The old hens at the café. Bill Taylor says the creaking in his bones means there's a snowstorm headed our way."

"I thought it meant rain."

"Aw, it means whatever suits the old goat's fancy. I imagine he took one look at that cold gray sky and decided the rest on his own." Trudie peered inside to make out the clock high on the wall. "I'd best get this place opened up, and you need to get inside before you freeze that young'un's little toes off—to say nothing of your own toes. Have a good one."

"I will. You, too." As Grace walked on, she considered the truth of her statement. Lately she'd had nothing but good days. Sure, she was living on a tight budget and working longer hours at the hardware store than the doctor wanted her to. And, yes, there were still people trying none too subtly to discover the identity of her baby's father. She had no insurance to cover the prenatal care and delivery of the baby, and no family to turn to for help. Some days she was convinced that she couldn't possibly be a good mother, others she mourned the fact that there was no father, and too much of the time she was just plain scared by it all.

But they were still good days. Living on a budget was a piece of cake when you'd never before had a dime to call your own. Long hours at work for her own benefit was a lot different from long hours for someone else's benefit. She had no family—her mother had fled Jed Prescott thirteen years ago, leaving Grace and Heartbreak behind—but for the first time in her life she had friends.

Also for the first time she'd found peace. She was no longer suffocating under her father's rigid control, no longer living in fear that her most innocent action might send him into a rage. She no longer felt like an inmate in the grimmest of prisons.

She was a person with opinions to express, with value beyond the long hours she could work for free, and she felt like it.

Prescott's Hardware, her destination, was located in the middle of the next block. All the other buildings on the block were boarded up and empty, giving her store a rather lonesome air, she thought fancifully as she unlocked the glass double doors. Inside the place smelled of metal and chemicals, with the pleasant aroma of sawn lumber drifting in faintly from the back. A serious builder would have to go to the big lumberyards and home centers in Tulsa or Oklahoma City, but Prescott's provided everything necessary for the small jobs.

She turned on the lights, flipped the Closed sign on the door to Open, then headed for the counter back in one corner. Conscious of her tight budget, she turned the heat on only high enough to take the edge off the chill, then turned on the radio that sat on the file cabinets. Music, in the store or anywhere else in her life, had been against her father's policy, so now that he was gone, she defiantly kept the radio playing all day and into the night. She even sang along, though her voice was rusty and always a half note off-key.

By the time she'd shed her winter garments and gotten a pot of coffee perking, the first customer had arrived. Actually, though he made regular purchases, he was more visitor than customer. Reese Barnett was the sheriff and, in some private little place deep inside, her hero. He'd been in the store the day her father had realized that she was pregnant. It was Reese who'd pulled Jed away after he'd hit her, who'd taken her to see Doc Hanson, then helped her settle in at the little house Shay Stephens had left when she'd married Easy Rafferty. It was Reese, with help from Heartbreak's only lawyer, who had more or less intimidated her father into giving everything to her—the house and the store, though precious-little money—when he'd left town a few weeks later. He'd taken to looking in on her regularly ever since.

"I didn't see your car in the parking lot," he commented as he leaned one hip against the counter.

"I walked." She watched as the last of the coffee dripped into the carafe, then poured a cup and handed it to him, her fingers brushing his, sending a tiny shiver down her spine. She could never admit it to anyone but herself, but she had a bit of a crush on Reese. It wasn't just that he was incredibly handsome, capable and strong, though he was all three and then some. No, those weren't necessarily qualities to admire. When her father had been Reese's age, he'd been handsome, capable and strong, too, but none of that had stopped him from constantly abusing and tormenting his family.

She liked Reese because he was kind. Sympathetic. He genuinely cared about others. He was noble and honorable and decent. He had character, and she admired men with character.

Even though *this* man viewed her as a very young sister

who needed looking after. Right now he was frowning in disapproval at the answer she'd given him. "You shouldn't be walking that far."

"It's only one and a quarter miles each way, and Doc Hanson says walking is good exercise for pregnant women."

"It's too cold."

"I dress warmly."

"It's supposed to snow late this afternoon. Then what will you do?"

"I'll walk faster," she retorted, then pointed out, "It's not as if I'm the only one who travels that road. Someone always comes along." That *someone* was often him—when it was raining or on the few other occasions this winter when it had snowed. If the snow materialized before closing time, he probably would, too.

He looked annoyed but dropped the subject. Leaning against the counter, he let his gaze slide across the room. "How's business?"

"Steady. Up a bit over this time last year."

"Because Jed's not here," he replied derisively, then belatedly glanced at her. "Sorry."

"No need to be." She'd been afraid of her father for as long as she could remember. Sometimes she'd felt sorry for him. Always she'd wanted to please him. But she couldn't remember ever feeling what a daughter should feel for her father. She wasn't sorry he'd left, or for the names he'd called her or the curses he'd heaped on her before going. She wasn't the least bit sorry that she would probably never see him again, and she was downright grateful that her baby would never know him.

Reese drained the last of his coffee, then threw the foam cup in the trash. "I guess I'd better head to the office. Don't walk home if it snows."

"I won't," she replied, and they both knew she wouldn't

get the chance. If it was snowing, come six o'clock, he'd be parked out in the side lot. The knowledge brought her a sweet, warm feeling, along with a pang that his concern wasn't likely to ever be anything but brotherly. She wondered idly as the door closed behind him if any man would ever feel anything but brotherly toward her.

There'd been nothing brotherly about Ethan James's feelings.

Usually she kept the memories of that night locked away where they belonged. For weeks after her own personal Independence Day last July, she'd fantasized about her hours with him during the day and fallen asleep at night to the memory of his arms around her, his mouth on hers, his body inside hers. They'd been the sweetest dreams and had kept her going at times when she'd thought living with her father might drive her mad.

Then she'd discovered she was pregnant, a development definitely not in her plans. She hadn't been able to take precautions herself, but she'd ensured that Ethan had each time. She'd thought she was safe, in every way, until the home pregnancy test her friend Ginger had sneaked to her had confirmed what her body had already told her.

Then Ginger had thought to mention the fact that no birth control was a hundred percent foolproof. Then, when the information couldn't help Grace one bit.

To Ginger the pregnancy had been no big deal. Get an abortion or give the baby up for adoption—or, hey, novel idea, have it, keep it and raise it. End of crisis. Of course, Ginger hadn't lived twenty-five years under Jed's iron rule. She hadn't been treated to a lifetime of warnings on the dangers and consequences of becoming a tramp like her mother. She hadn't watched her very life drain away under his oppression until there was nothing left but a sad little mouse, afraid of everyone and everything. A pathetic creature pitied by some, unnoticed by most.

Unnoticed by Ethan James for the sixteen years they'd lived in the same town, the ten years they'd gone to the same school. With the school's mixed grade policy, she'd sat a few seats behind him in biology, across from him in Spanish and had waited on him a time or two in the store. Once, when she'd dropped her books between classes, he'd helped her pick them up, had handed them to her with a careless "There you go," but he had never even looked at her. He'd had eyes for practically every girl in the school, but he'd never known she existed.

One stifling hot Saturday night last summer, he'd learned…sort of. For the first and only time in her life, her father had gone out of town, leaving her on her own for a full twenty-four hours. It had taken about two heart-stopping seconds to decide what to do with her unexpected gift of freedom.

Go out. Have a drink. Meet a man. Maybe get a kiss, maybe a whole lot more.

Pretend for one night that she was a perfectly normal twenty-five-year-old woman. Experience enough of life in those few hours to sustain her in her prison for the next fifty years.

For help, she'd turned to the friend she'd made behind her father's back at the grocery store. Thanks to Ginger's cosmetic expertise, when she'd left the house that night, she'd looked nothing like the real Grace. She'd had rinse-out red highlights in her mousy brown hair, and long heavy curls that had corkscrewed in every direction. Tucking her glasses into her bag, she'd sacrificed seeing for looking good, but Ginger had assured her that the makeup job was flawless, making the most of her lamentably plain features. As for the clothes…she'd never worn a skirt so short or a top so tight in her life, and probably never would again.

But once had been enough. It had gotten Ethan James's attention, and he'd finally known she existed.

As a rather mysterious redhead from someplace else named Melissa.

She'd crept out of his bed the next morning while he slept, hurried home and showered to scrub away the makeup, the curls, the fake color. The scents of sex, of a man. She'd half feared her father would look at her and know, would sniff the air when she walked by and recognize the cologne she was forbidden to wear, the aftershave she would never wear. He hadn't.

And she hadn't seen Ethan since. She hadn't tried to locate him—hadn't asked his half brother, Guthrie Harris, where he was, hadn't told his pregnant sister-in-law Olivia that their babies would be cousins. Frankly, she wasn't sure they would believe her. For a time the father's identity had been a popular topic of conversation. Everyone had had theories, ranging from the truth—someone she met in a bar—to the obscene observation that her father *was* the only man with whom she'd spent time. No one had ever guessed Ethan. No one ever would.

It was her own little secret. And since Ethan wasn't likely to return to Heartbreak for another several years, and would neither recognize nor remember her when he did, no one else would ever know the truth.

Which was exactly the way she wanted it.

The sky was a dull, relentless gray when Ethan passed the sign marking Heartbreak's town limits. It was hard to believe that, night before last, he'd been in sunny, warm Florida and now he was right back where he'd started from. Back where all his troubles had begun. Where they certainly weren't going to end.

He hadn't needed a map to find his way back to Oklahoma. In all the endless miles he'd traveled, all the big cities and dusty towns where he'd stayed until he wore out his welcome or an impending arrest sent him on his way, he'd always known how to get back home.

At the same time, he'd never known.

He'd started running away from Heartbreak when he was barely fifteen. He was just like his father, his mother had always said with exasperated affection. Gordon James had done more than his share of rambling. In fact, he had rambled so often and so far that one time, when Ethan was ten, he'd never come back.

He *was* just like his father, Guthrie had always agreed, and with no affection at all. It was common knowledge that Guthrie thought his stepfather was no good, lazy and worthless. It was one of Ethan's greatest regrets that his brother thought the same of him, and one of his greatest shames that he'd done his best to live down to Guthrie's opinion. In fact, he'd done his father one better. He'd added *crook* to his litany of sins. Liar, thief, gambler, con man.

And, coming soon, father-to-be.

His fingers clenched the steering wheel spasmodically as anxiety tightened his chest. He'd always sworn he'd never bring a child into the world. He was indisputable proof that some men had no right passing on their genes to innocent babies. His father had been a loser, and he was a loser, so the odds were good that any child of his would also be a loser. Even if that wasn't the case, any kid deserved better than him for a dad. He knew nothing about fatherhood, about responsibility or maturity or setting a good example.

He wasn't sure he could learn. Not if he had to do it in Heartbreak, where Guthrie would be watching and judging his every move.

But he had to do something. He'd learned from his own experience that even a father who made nothing but mistakes had to be better than a father who didn't care enough to even come around. At least he would be trying. Surely that would count for something with his kid. With Guthrie. With pretty Melissa.

Flipping the visor down, he pulled the snapshot free of the rubber band that secured it. If he knew where to look for her, he would go straight there, but the photo gave no clues. After studying it a while, he'd recognized the parking lot as belonging to the grocery store. Since it was the only one for twenty miles, that told him nothing about who she was, where she lived, where he might find her.

In their long, sweet night together, she'd told him nothing, either. It had been the perfect one-night stand.

Except for the baby.

He'd used protection—had never had sex even once in his life without a condom. His dependability on the issue was the one thing about him that Guthrie had approved of. Well, that, plus the fact that every time he'd come back to Heartbreak, he'd always left again.

Not a bad run of luck. Too bad it hadn't held.

As he slid the photo back under the strap, the road curved and the few blocks that made up Heartbreak proper came into view ahead. He turned onto the first side street and followed a meandering back route to the dirt road that led to the Harris ranch, where they wouldn't be happy to hear he'd come home again. Where Guthrie would be seriously dismayed that this time he intended to stay.

Provided Melissa would let him.

He'd seen the ranch just seven months ago, but it looked different as he turned in the gate and drove across the cattle guard. The house had a fresh coat of paint, and a wreath of flowers and vines hung on the front door. The flower beds had been cleaned out and mulched for winter, and the yellowed yard looked as neat and trim as it ever had when his mother was alive.

They were Olivia's changes, Ethan knew. Guthrie had neither the time nor the energy for purely cosmetic work.

He had his hands full taking care of three hundred acres of land and a couple hundred head of cattle. There'd been a time, after their mother's death, when he'd wanted Ethan to share the responsibility with him, and Ethan had tried, he truly had, but he'd only lasted a few months. He wasn't cut out for ranching, for working from sunrise till sunset, for pinching a penny until it squealed, for dealing with cattle and horses, droughts and floods, fluctuating market prices, luck and bad luck.

He'd sneaked away in the middle of the night to avoid seeing that look on Guthrie's face—that long-suffering, no-surprise, Ethan-never-could-do-anything-right look. He'd wanted to avoid hearing Guthrie say, "You *are* just like your father," and know it was the worst insult his brother could give.

So instead he'd faced the look and heard the insult in his dreams every night for months.

He parked beside Guthrie's pickup and simply sat there for a time. In spite of the cold, his palms were damp and sweat beaded his forehead. He was twenty-eight years old, he thought with disgust, and scared spitless by the idea of seeing his brother. Worse, he couldn't remember the last time he hadn't been scared of Guthrie, scared of disappointing him. Of letting him down yet again.

He drew a frigid breath, then opened the door. He wasn't a lonely little boy anymore. Guthrie's approval was no longer the most important thing in his life. Belonging someplace—to someone—didn't matter, except with his baby.

He crossed the frozen ground to the porch, then rapped on the door. He could wait until the count of ten, or maybe five, then assume that no one was home, and he could leave while telling himself that at least he'd tried—

The lock clicked, then the door swung open and his heavily pregnant sister-in-law was greeting him with a surprised smile. "Ethan! Oh, my gosh, you came! I was hoping you would, but…it's so good to see you! Come on in. Let me get you some coffee to warm up.''

It was a warm welcome from a woman whose husband he had once ripped off. Come to think of it, in that one scam, he'd cheated both her husbands—the one who'd died and left her penniless, and the one who'd taken her in last summer and given her a place to live before falling in love with her. She had good reason to hate him. He wasn't sure he trusted the fact that apparently she didn't.

The welcome got warmer as soon as he closed the door behind him, when she caught him in an unexpected embrace. He held himself stiffly, well aware of what Guthrie would think if he saw his precious Olivia in his brother's arms. When she stepped back, with relief he put some distance between them, then nervously glanced down the hall and up the stairs. "Is…he around?"

"Guthrie? No, he's out checking the herd. We're supposed to have snow tonight. He's getting ready for it." She started toward the kitchen, then turned back when she realized he wasn't following. "I have coffee left over from breakfast, or the fixings for hot cocoa, or there's iced tea and cold pop. Take your coat off and come on back. We'll talk."

He didn't want to obey her, didn't want to walk through the house he remembered so well but rarely with fondness. He'd lived in it for the better part of eighteen years, but it had never truly been home.

From the time he was a little kid, he'd understood without being told that the house belonged to the Harrises, not the Jameses, just as he'd understood that Vernon Harris had been twice the man Gordon James could ever hope to be. A better rancher, better neighbor, better husband, better father, and he'd turned out a son who would be all those things, too.

Better. Leaving Ethan to be not good enough.

When he finally forced himself down the hall and through the double doors into the kitchen, Olivia was bent inside the refrigerator. She came out with a carton of whipped cream and a pecan pie, then flashed him a smile. "What would you like to drink?"

"Coffee'll be fine."

"Sit down. Take your coat off."

He slid out of his denim jacket and hung it on the back of a chair, then cautiously sat down. He wouldn't get very comfortable, wasn't sure that was even possible when Guthrie could come through the door at any minute.

She dished up two slices of pie, poured coffee and milk, then took the seat opposite him. "When did you get in?"

"This morning. I came straight here."

She buried her pie in whipped cream, then took an extra spoonful for good measure, licking it clean with slow, savoring gestures. When she realized he was watching her, she smiled without embarrassment. "I've had terrible cravings lately for whipped cream. Since the rest of the family thinks my eating it on bread is yucky and gross—" she said the last words in a fair imitation of her six-year-old twins "—Mary's been bringing over freshly baked pies every couple of days."

"When…" He thought of the photo in the truck, of Melissa, with her stomach almost as distended as Olivia's, and swallowed hard. "When is the baby due?"

"Next month. Elly says I'll be as big as a heifer carrying twins before I drop this young'un."

Elly, he remembered from the few hours he'd spent here last summer, was the older of her daughters—the tomboy, sassy and too smart for her own good. The younger daughter was Emma, sweet, quiet, demure. As different as day and night. As Guthrie and Ethan.

"What does Guthrie say?" he asked, his voice thick and hoarse.

"He says I've never looked more beautiful." Her smile was broad, a bit wicked and full of womanly satisfaction. "My husband's no fool. He knows better than to get on the wrong side of a woman who hasn't seen her own feet in months."

He wondered if there was anyone around to tell Melissa that she looked beautiful. He'd wondered a lot about her since getting the photograph—whether she wanted him to take responsibility for his part in creating their child. Whether she had simply wanted him to know that he was about to become a father. Whether she wanted money, or if she hoped to gain a real live, equal-partners, here-and-now father for her baby.

He wondered if she had a father just waiting for the chance to make the scoundrel who'd taken advantage of his little girl pay. If her family was helping out or if they'd been disappointed enough to turn their backs. He wondered if she even had a family, or if she was as alone in the world as he felt.

Feeling Olivia's gaze on him, he looked up to find her watching him. "Have you seen Grace?" she asked in a quiet, just-between-us sort of tone.

"Grace?"

"Grace Prescott." Seeing the blankness in his expression, she impatiently added, "You remember—short, slim, brown hair, thick glasses. The mother of your child. The reason you're here."

Melissa. So she'd lied about her name. And why shouldn't she? New hair color, new style, new clothes and new behavior all deserved a new name, something prettier, less old-ladyish than Grace. Melissa was a hot redhead offering to fulfill wild fantasies in a bar. Grace was an old maid, waiting in vain for that first second look from a man on the prowl.

Olivia's expression bordered on scandalized. "You didn't even know her name?"

He didn't offer a response. What could he say that wouldn't reflect as badly on Melis—Grace as on him? "Grace Prescott...should I know that name, other than the obvious?"

"She's lived here forever. You must have gone to school with her. For years her father had owned the hardware store on Main."

The clues didn't help him remember Grace, but Jed Prescott... Oh, hell, yeah, she had a father just waiting to make him pay, but there'd be no talk of a shotgun wedding or accepting responsibility. With a well-documented reputation of being the meanest bastard in the county, ol' Jed would be more likely to take him out and shoot him than to allow him within a mile of his daughter again. Better to have an illegitimate grandchild than to have that worthless James boy for a son-in-law.

But once the shock passed, Olivia's words sank in. Jed *had* owned the hardware store, she'd said, as if he didn't own it now. "So..." His voice was the slightest bit unsteady. "What does old Jed think of becoming a grandfather?"

Olivia took her dishes to the sink and rinsed them before turning back. "I don't imagine he thinks too highly of it, since he left town as soon as he found out and hasn't been heard from since." She folded her arms, resting her hands on her stomach. "Don't you have any questions to ask about *her?*"

Only about a thousand, but he'd rather get the answers to most of them from Grace herself. "Why did she ask you to tell me? Why didn't you just give her my address and let her write?"

She looked as if she wanted to fidget, but she didn't. "She didn't exactly ask me to tell you."

The hairs on the back of his neck stood on end, and his palms got sweaty again. "What exactly did she ask you to do?"

"Exactly? Um…nothing. You see, she hasn't told anyone who the father of her baby is, but—but she always gets this guilty little look whenever your name comes up, and Shay noticed it, too, and we got to counting, and…it seemed likely, so…"

"So you brought me halfway across the country on the off chance that I could be the father of her baby."

"We figured if there wasn't a chance, if that photograph of her meant nothing, then you wouldn't come. But you did come, because it is possible, isn't it?"

Oh, it was more than possible. It was damn near guaranteed…for whatever it was worth. He'd come back thinking that Melissa wanted him here when the truth was that Grace didn't have a clue that he was even in the state. She'd known for seven months that if she wanted to find him, Guthrie and Olivia were the place to start, but she'd never told them anything. She'd kept her involvement with him a deep, dark secret. Because she was ashamed of it? Because she didn't want him around? Or because she didn't want her child to bear the burden of having him for a father?

Probably all of the above. And he couldn't even blame her. If he had a bad reputation, he had no one to blame but himself. When his name was a burden that even he didn't want, how could he blame her for not wanting it for her baby?

It would be better all around if he just climbed back into his truck and left the state again. He could head out west, or maybe go south into Mexico, and this time he could stay gone long enough that no one would ever connect his name to Grace's, not even remotely.

But he knew without considering it that he couldn't do

it, not without seeing Grace first. If she didn't want him around, if she truly thought that the best thing he could do for his kid was disappear, then he would do so. He would feel like a bastard, but he'd do it.

And if she thought the best thing he could do was stay here, make a respectable name for himself and pass it on to the kid? He'd do that, too. At least, he would try.

And he would ignore the fact that almost everything he tried failed. He'd give himself maybe thirty-seventy odds of succeeding.

If he was a gambling man.

Chapter 2

Because she worked such long hours, Grace was under doctor's orders to spend much of the day with her feet propped up, which was easier than a person would suspect, given the nature of folks in Heartbreak. Most of her customers had been customers so long that they knew their way around the shelves and were perfectly willing to help themselves. They would even make their own change from the antique cash register if she gave them the chance. Last week old Pete Davis had brought her a thermos of his granny's famous chicken soup because he'd thought she looked a bit peaked, and Mavis over at the five-and-dime had brought her a puffy quilt to warm up under on dreary, gray days like this.

But she rarely felt the need to stretch out with her feet up. In fact, she'd had more energy in the last few months than ever before. Doc Hanson said it was because she walked every day. Callie, the midwife who would deliver the baby when it was time, credited the primarily vegetarian diet she'd started Grace on.

Personally, Grace believed it was her father's absence. Living day in and day out with overwhelming bitterness and anger could suck the life force right out of a body. Life without Jed not only *was* different, but it felt different. Even the very air smelled different. And Callie swore her aura was totally changed, too.

Life was darn near perfect.

While the store was empty, she dragged a stepladder out so she could combine straightening the shelves with taking inventory. Jed had always insisted on doing inventory on the last day of the month, so Grace spread it out over several days at the beginning of the month. He'd made her sweep the floors first thing in the morning; now she did it last thing at night. He'd never extended a penny's credit to anyone in his life. She offered it to everyone.

The further her pregnancy progressed, the harder taking inventory got. Not because she had a problem, but because people fussed at her for climbing ladders, lifting boxes, being on her feet. She'd learned to do it in quick snatches when the store was empty and liked doing it that way. It gave her time to wonder over the fact that all this was hers—well, hers and the suppliers'. She, who'd grown up with constant reminders that she owned nothing, not even the clothes on her back, owned this store. She marveled over it every day.

She was standing on the top step of the ladder when the bell over the door dinged. "I'll be right with you," she called as she quickly sorted and counted the boxes used to restock the shelves below.

Footsteps crossed the store and came around the corner into her aisle as she made notations on her clipboard. "Take your time, Melissa," a quiet voice said, then deliberately added, "Or should I call you Grace?"

Ethan James. She froze in place. She hadn't heard his voice in seven months, but she would have recognized it after seven years. A woman who'd lived her life without affection, without even a kind word from anyone else, wouldn't soon forget the first voice to call her darlin', or to tell her she was beautiful.

She would never forget the voice of the man who'd fathered her child.

Her hands were trembling as she carefully laid the clipboard and pen on the shelf, then turned on the narrow step to face him. He'd stopped ten feet away and was watching her with a totally unreadable expression.

He looked more handsome than ever, with unruly blond hair and wicked blue eyes, with a stubborn jaw and cover-model-perfect features. Every young man in the state owned the same outfit—faded Wranglers, a white T-shirt, jeans jacket, scuffed work boots—but he wore them with more ease than she imagined anyone else could. Snug and comfortable, like a second skin.

As she looked at him, appreciating the sheer beauty of him, he looked back. Was he disappointed, she wondered uneasily, that the wild, curly red hair, the sexy clothes, the lovely woman on the make—Melissa in her entirety—had all been an illusion? Was he dismayed that he'd spent a good part of a long summer night naked and hot with her? Was that why his features were schooled into such blankness? Why his blue eyes were so cold? Why his voice had been so flat?

She wished she had the nerve to lie, to swear that he was mistaken, that she didn't know him. But, except for that night, she'd never lied, and she didn't have the desire to start now. Slowly she came down the ladder, relieved when she felt the floor solid under her feet.

Folding her hands tightly together behind her back, she said in the calmest voice she could muster, "I...didn't expect to see you." *Again. Ever.* She didn't add the qualifiers, but he heard them. It showed in the tightening of his jaw.

"You can thank Olivia and Shay Stephens for it. They thought I should know—" his gaze raked her up and down "—about you."

"Rafferty," she said nervously.

"What?"

"Shay Stephens. Rafferty. Easy came home last fall, and he and Shay got married in November…or maybe October. I'm not sure. It was before he started buying the horses for his ranch but after her birthday. October, I think, but—"

"Forget Shay," he said sharply, and she sucked in whatever rambling words she might have spoken with a startled breath. He gave her another hard look up and down, one that made her fingers knot where he couldn't see them. "Olivia tells me I'm…responsible for this."

In Heartbreak *responsible* was not a word people used in reference to Ethan James. *Ir*responsible, yes. Trouble. Lazy. Dishonest. Disloyal. Selfish. She could stand there the rest of the day, listing every negative quality she could think of and still not cover all the failings attributed to him.

But he was waiting for a response to his comment. Which did he want—yes or no? How did he feel about being a father? How did he feel about fathering a child with *her?*

He was here. That said something, didn't it? He'd come back to his least-favorite place in the world because he'd been told his one-night stand had produced an eighteen-year commitment. Surely that meant he wasn't totally averse to the idea.

Unless he'd come back to buy her silence. To give her some reason not to make demands of him. Maybe he wanted her to continue to keep his identity secret. After all, he had a reputation to protect. Charming rogues like Ethan James did not get suckered into one-night stands with plain Janes like Grace Prescott. Or maybe he'd settled down somewhere, with someone special, and didn't want word of an illegitimate child leaking out to tarnish his future.

"Well?" Impatience colored his voice and gave her the courage to shrug carelessly and start toward the counter.

"I never mentioned you to Olivia or anyone else."

"That's not what I'm asking." He leaned on the counter as she circled to the other side. "Is that— Am I—" He dragged his fingers through his hair, muttered a curse and tried again. "Did we…?"

After studying him for a moment, she knew the answer he wanted. It was in his scowl, his clenched hands, the sinking feeling in her stomach. It was foolish to be disappointed. She was twenty-five, a woman on her own, about to become a single mother. There was no room in her life for daydreams or fantasies, no chance that a charming rogue might turn into her very own Prince Charming, no chance at all that something special could develop out of a one-night stand. Yes, he'd come back upon hearing that she was pregnant, but only because he wanted her to deny that he was the father.

"No," she said softly, feeling the ache of the lie deep inside.

He looked startled, then relieved, then suspicious. "No what?"

"You're not the father."

"Who is?"

"That's between my baby and me."

His gaze narrowed, sending heat flushing through her face. "You're lying."

"I don't lie."

"Everything about the night you spent with me was a lie," he said scornfully.

The heat intensified. Did the fact that it was a necessary lie count for anything? It was a simple truth that without the makeup, the clothes, the hair, she never would have found the nerve to walk into that bar. It was another truth that without the makeup, the clothes and the hair, he never would have looked twice at her.

She had desperately needed for someone to take a second look at her.

"It's my baby, isn't it?"

She thought of all the emotions she'd experienced since finding out she was pregnant. Shock. Panic. Dread. Fear. Heartache. And, finally, joy. She'd had such dreams, made such plans. She'd fallen in love with her daughter—she liked to think it was a girl—soon after learning of her existence. She couldn't imagine anything more wonderful, any gift more precious, than the one she'd been given.

"Do you *want* a baby?" she asked, hearing the wistfulness in her voice. It would be an even more precious gift if he answered yes honestly and sincerely. Even if she was the last woman he would choose to play the role of mother, she would be forever grateful if he could truthfully say yes, he wanted their baby.

For a moment, he couldn't say anything at all. He opened his mouth twice, then closed it again. Finally, with a stiffness that vibrated the air between them, he said, "It's a little late to be considering what I want. This baby's going to be here in two months, whether I want it or not."

"But you don't have to be here in two months."

Once again she'd startled him. He blinked, then refocused on her as she continued.

"I do want this baby. It's the best thing that ever happened to me. I want to change diapers and have 2:00 a.m. feedings and teach her to walk and talk and ride a bike. I want to be such a good mother that she'll never miss having a father." In spite of the awful examples her parents had set for her, she knew she could do it. She had more love to give than any little girl could ever need. She could easily

be mother and father both, especially when the father she
was replacing had no desire to be a father.

"So I'm not needed here. That's what you're saying."
Ethan heard the bitterness in his voice, felt it deep in his
gut, but didn't understand it. He should be grateful. She
was offering him the opportunity to walk away and never
look back. She didn't want his name, his money or his
presence. Hell, she didn't want anything to do with him.

He should be used to it by now. He'd been living with
it most of his life. His mother had loved him, but she'd
loved Guthrie more. His father hadn't loved him at all, and
Guthrie had wished that he'd never been born. Now he was
neither needed nor wanted in his kid's life.

"You don't want to be here," she said quietly. "You
don't want to be a father."

The truth, plain and simple. And not so simple. It was
true that he'd never wanted kids—but that was speaking in
terms of possibilities, prospects, somewhere down the line.
This baby wasn't a prospect. It—he or she—existed, a real,
live part of him and Grace. It wasn't fair to apply theoret-
ical ideas to reality. Whether or not he wanted to be a father
didn't matter, because the simple fact was, in another eight
weeks, he would be one. Wanting or not wanting couldn't
change that.

Realizing that his hand was cramping, he slowly eased
his fingers flat against the counter. He didn't know what to
say. Obviously she would be happy if he accepted her offer
to give up any claim he had on her baby and left town, but
he knew instinctively that he would regret it if he did. Leaving would only prove that he was no better than his own
father. Guthrie would never forgive him. His child would
grow up to hate him. He'd have no choice but to hate himself.

And if he stayed? Maybe the kid would still hate him.
He wasn't exactly prime father material. He'd made too

many mistakes, disappointed people too many times. No matter how hard he tried, he would never be a father to make a kid proud.

Across the counter, Grace shifted uneasily, drawing his gaze that way. She looked so different from before. Truth was, if he'd met her without meeting Melissa first, he wouldn't have paid her any attention. He wouldn't have sat down at her table, bought her a beer, asked her to dance. He certainly wouldn't have taken her to the motel next door.

And it would have been his loss.

The hair that had been gloriously red and wild that night was really brown, pulled straight back from her face and braided to her waist. The brown eyes that had seemed so soft and hazy then had actually been unfocused. Judging by the thickness of the lenses in the glasses that kept slipping down her nose, she'd been damn near blind that night. That explained why she hadn't run the other way when he'd approached her.

She wore no makeup, not even lipstick, and her dress was shapeless except where it draped over her belly on its way to her ankles. The sweater she wore over it was equally shapeless, with sleeves that fell three inches past her wrists.

She wasn't pretty, and she wasn't homely, either. She was just plain. And yet it had taken him mere seconds to recognize the lovely, sexy Melissa in her.

But Melissa, who had wanted him, didn't really exist, and Grace, who did exist, didn't want him. At all.

She fidgeted under his gaze, drawing the front edges of the sweater together and holding them with her arms folded tightly over her chest. "Listen, Ethan," she said, and he recognized sexy Melissa in the way she said his name. "You came back, you did what was right. You can go now. I'll convince Olivia and Shay they were wrong. No one will hold it against you. No one will ever even know."

And because he was irresponsible, worthless, no good, that was supposed to satisfy him. It was supposed to ease his conscience, assuming he had one, and get him back on the road out of town.

He gazed away from her to the dusty plate-glass window that looked out on the parking lot and wondered if his mother had ever encouraged his father to go away and stay away. There was no doubt that Nadine had regretted her marriage to Gordon James. That last time he'd left, she'd waited only days—ten, maybe fourteen—to file for divorce, and though she'd never changed her name legally, she'd gone back to using Harris again. Being ten years old and stupid, he'd asked if he could use the Harris name, too. After all, they were a family, right? And families should have the same last name. But Guthrie had objected, and their mother had made some excuse about needing his father's permission, and he'd known then that he wasn't *really* part of the family.

Now it was payback time. He'd wanted to give up his father's name, and now his own child was never going to be allowed to know *his* name. Grace and the baby were one more family that he wasn't welcome in.

Unless he changed her mind. Unless he proved to her that he was fit to be a part of their lives. The hell of it was, he didn't know that he *wanted* to be a part of their lives. He didn't know if he could live up to the responsibility, or if he would run true to form, disappoint them and run away. Like he always did.

Hell, if he couldn't trust himself to stick around, how could he ask her to?

He glanced at her but didn't make eye contact. "I...I don't think I can do that, Grace."

He could tell by her voice and no more that she was alarmed. "Why not? You've been doing it for years."

"I don't know. I just can't... This is different. Before it

was always people I walked out on—adults who didn't want me around, anyway. This is a baby—''

"*My* baby," she interrupted sharply.

"And mine." He felt the bitterness swell until it threatened to choke him. "Don't worry. I won't tell anyone that. I'll keep your little secret. But I'm not leaving. Not until I figure some things out." Like what he wanted, and why, and whether he had a right to want anything at all.

He took a few steps toward the door, then turned back. "Olivia has offered me use of the cabin out at their place, if Guthrie doesn't throw me out. I'll be around."

Before she could respond or react in any way, he turned and walked out.

So much for the creaking in Bill Taylor's bones.

Grace stood at the window in her dark, still bedroom, wearing a nightgown of flannel and wrapped in a quilt, staring out into a quiet, cold and incredibly clear night. She should have been asleep hours ago, but her mind wouldn't stop spinning long enough to let sleep creep in. She'd prayed for snow all the way home in the Blazer that served as Reese's sheriff's car, for the rare kind of blizzard that Oklahoma never saw that would bury her house to its eaves and leave her safe and protected from the world—from Ethan—until the spring thaw.

But there was no snow. No protection, either.

Expect the worst, her father had always preached, and you won't be disappointed. Never trust anyone, never take chances, never count on someone doing what he should. She'd always thought it was a sad way to live, so sad that she'd gone a hundred and eighty degrees in the opposite direction. Her motto, since his leaving, had been simpler. *Don't Worry. Be Happy.*

She'd thought years would pass before Ethan's next return, had thought he'd never recognize her as Melissa, and even if he did, he would never have any interest in playing daddy to her child. After all, he *was* the irresponsible one, the immature one, the selfish one out for himself and to hell with everyone else. Like everyone else in town, she'd been so convinced of it that she almost felt cheated that the image wasn't entirely accurate. He had a conscience. He felt some sense of obligation, some duty.

How long would it last? A few weeks? A few months or, heaven forbid, a few years? There was no way of knowing. Long enough, though, for everyone in town to guess the truth. Long enough to saddle her child with the burden of the James name, the James reputation.

Long enough to put Grace herself at risk. She'd proven her susceptibility to daydreams and fantasies. Lord knows, she'd lived enough of her life in them. She'd already proved her susceptibility to handsome con artists. Toss in the idea of creating a family—husband, wife, child, in-laws, nieces, maybe soon a nephew—and in a blink of an eye, she just might forget all about her hard-won independence.

But Ethan James wasn't a family sort of man. He'd been running away from his own family for half his life. He wasn't likely to accept any ties that might hold him down. Sure, he felt some sense of obligation, probably some unresolved issue from his abandonment by his own father, but it would never be enough to keep him here. At best, he'd stick around just long enough to screw up everything, and then he would leave Grace and their daughter to deal with it while he went on to greener pastures.

Sighing, she turned away from the window and faced her room instead. Until her father had found out she was pregnant and thrown her out, she'd slept every night of her life but one in this room. She'd huddled in the closet over there, hands over her ears, to block out the sounds of her parents' fights. She'd curled up in the rocker and dreamed about catching the eye of someone at school. Boy or girl, it hadn't mattered, just someone who would be friends with her and make her feel less desperately alone. She'd lain awake nights in that cramped little bed, lamenting the healthy, normal relationships missing in her life— the boyfriends, the dates, the little intimacies—and she'd wondered if anyone would ever truly love her.

Now, she thought, patting her stomach reassuringly, she had an answer.

And she had Ethan James to thank for it. Even if she did wish she had never seen him again. Even if some traitorous little part of her hoped to see him again and again.

Suddenly chilled, she returned to the bed, snuggled in under layers of blankets and closed her eyes for a series of deep-breathing exercises. She kidded herself that simply relaxing, resting and breathing were almost as good as sleep, which she certainly wasn't going to get tonight. She was too wide awake, too worried.

But the next time she opened her eyes it was morning, and the sun was shining brightly in the east. Refusing to think about anything other than her normal routine, she got ready for work, cooked and ate her breakfast, then began dressing in the layers necessary for the walk to the store. It was just another day, she told herself. Like the last ninety or so, nothing special, nothing to be dreaded.

Maybe saying it made it real. Her walk was uneventful, even a bit boring. The usual vehicles were parked outside the Heartbreak Café, where Shay Rafferty gave her usual wave through the plate-glass window. Trudie Hampton called a hello as she unlocked the insurance agency door and commented on the cold temperatures and toes freezing off. The store looked exactly as it had when she left the day before.

Life hadn't changed. It was ordinary. Routine.

Until 10:32 a.m., when Ethan walked through the front door.

She was busy with customers when the bell rang. She didn't glance up. She didn't need to, thanks to their murmured comments.

"Well, look at that. When do you suppose he came back?"

"Better question would be *why* do you suppose he came back."

"Y'think Guthrie was expectin' him?"

"Sure. Guthrie always expects trouble. 'Least, from that one."

At that, Grace didn't even try to resist looking at Ethan. He was in the last aisle before the far wall, pretending interest in a display of dead-bolt locks, his head ducked so that all she could see was tousled blond hair and a denim collar. No doubt he knew he had everyone's attention. She hoped he was smart enough to stay over there until the others were gone, but she wouldn't hold her breath.

She rang up the sale, took the cash, made the wrong change, then corrected it. She bagged the purchase in a sack large enough to fit it five times over, then dropped it on the counter instead of handing it to the customer. When they left, she straightened the few items on the counter, breathed deeply and straightened them again, then summoned the nerve to approach him. Before she'd taken three steps, he started toward her.

He was dressed much the same as the day before, but somehow he looked even better. Sometime in the last seven months she'd forgotten just how gorgeous he was. Looking at him now, she was amazed that she'd been able to catch his eye, even dressed up in Ginger's flashiest clothes. He could have crooked his finger at any woman in that bar and she would have gone running, but he'd chosen *her*. The fake. The fraud.

He was disappointed that she wasn't pretty. She'd read that in his expression yesterday. Part of her felt insulted.

They were adults. They were supposed to prefer things like character, honesty and personality over good looks. And part of her couldn't blame him. Was it so wrong to want the character, honesty and personality wrapped up in a pretty package? Would she honestly have been so quick to go to the motel with him that night if he hadn't been drop-dead gorgeous?

Well…yes. But she'd been desperate, remember?

Finally he stopped on the opposite side of the counter. ''Hey.''

''Hi.'' Her gaze settled on his hands, resting on the scarred countertop. They were bigger, longer, than hers, but they could manipulate a deck of cards or remove a woman's clothing with smooth, easy grace, never fumbling, never making a mistake. They were so strong, so certain of every move. And soft, like silk against her skin. Capable of seducing a never-been-kissed virgin right out of her clothes and her fears. Talented enough to make her thank him when it was over.

Her face grew warm, and she had to clear her throat before she could speak. ''I take it Guthrie didn't throw you out.''

''Only because Olivia talked him out of it. He knows better than to get on the wrong side of a woman who hasn't seen her own feet in months.''

Grace's smile was small and tentative. She liked Olivia Harris a lot, but that didn't stop her from also envying her. Olivia had everything Grace had ever wanted. Her husband worshiped the ground she walked on, and no one could love her daughters more than he did. Their baby, due a month before hers, would receive a warm, loud and enthusiastic welcome into the world, and he—for Olivia insisted it was a boy—would know from his first breath how dearly loved he was.

On the other hand, Grace's daughter would likely have

no one but her, and she was no prize under the best of circumstances. Just ask Ethan.

Her smile fading, she turned away from the counter to the desk behind her. "I thought you might have left." It was a lie, although she'd certainly *hoped* he would leave, taking her secret with him. She'd known it wasn't likely, though. He hadn't come from—well, wherever he'd come from, only to take off again immediately. That wasn't the way he worked. According to rumor, he never left without stirring up trouble of one sort or another. This time that trouble would surely involve her.

Ignoring her comment, he looked around. "Do you work alone?"

"Yes."

"Must be tough."

She shrugged. "I'm a hard worker."

"That can't be good for..."

The baby, she silently filled in. Just say it. The baby. But instead he merely gestured toward her middle, as if the words were too difficult. Too damning. "Doc Hanson says I couldn't be healthier. Callie agrees."

"Who's Callie?"

"My midwife."

That brought his gaze to her face. "You're seeing a *mid-wife?*"

Grace eased into the wooden chair behind the desk, propped her feet on the stool underneath the desk and folded her hands over her belly. "She's going to deliver the baby."

"Why not let Doc Hanson? He's been doing it for fifty years."

"Precisely why he's not doing it anymore. He's turned that part of his practice over to Callie."

"So why not go to Tulsa or Oklahoma City?"

"Why would I do that when Callie is right here in

town?'' A scowl knitted her brows together. ''She's not some old granny that country folk turn to because they don't know better or can't afford a real doctor. She's an R.N., a nurse-midwife. She practices in Doc Hanson's clinic.'' She paused before adding the one comment that would make a difference to him. ''She's delivering Olivia and Guthrie's baby.''

It did make a difference. She could practically see the change in attitude. *Oh, well, if Guthrie says it's all right, then it must be all right.* On the one hand, it annoyed her. It was her baby, her delivery, and if she said it was all right, it was. On the other, it was touching that, despite all the trouble between them, he obviously still had a great deal of respect for his brother.

But all that respect hadn't stopped Ethan from fraudulently selling Guthrie's ranch out from under him a year or two ago. Though the very idea of it was amazing, if pressed, she would have to admit that it was a good thing he had. Otherwise, he never would have developed a guilty conscience, he wouldn't have come back last summer to undo his wrong, and he wouldn't have been in that bar on her first night of freedom. She wouldn't have such sweet memories, her friends, this business, the house or, most important, her baby. She owed a lot to his disreputable ways.

Still, ''disreputable'' didn't come high on her list of qualities desired in her baby's father.

Hands in his pockets, he came around the counter and circled the small space that served as her office. He glanced out the window at her view—the dock where customers backed up their pickup trucks to load lumber and wallboard—then thumbed through a catalog offering every hand tool known to man before finally speaking. ''Tell me something. What was Jed Prescott's little girl doing in that bar dressed like a—'' He broke off, then substituted a less-harsh description, she suspected, than what had initially come to mind. "Like a woman looking for a good time?"

"If I'd gone in there dressed like this, I wouldn't have gotten the same response."

The hint of a smile crossed his face, then disappeared. She remembered his smiles best of everything about him. They'd come so quickly, so easily, from sweet, gentle smiles to broad, oh-so-cocky grins. She'd thought halfway through the evening how incredibly wonderful it was to spend time with a man who expressed pleasure so naturally. Her father was not a smiler. Living with him, she hadn't been, either.

Finished with the office, he turned and leaned back against the counter. "No," he agreed. "Going in looking like that—" once again he gestured toward her stomach "—would have scared all the men away, including me." Crossing his ankles, folding his arms across his chest, he waited for the real answer to his question.

She considered ignoring it, and him. She had end-of-the-month invoices to prepare, a couple of orders to call in, tax records to update, inventory to finish. If she chose, she could find any number of excuses for not answering, and she couldn't think of one single reason for telling him.

So she told him, anyway. Go figure. "Do you remember me?"

He gave her a puzzled look. "From...?"

"High school. Middle school. Grade school. Church, when my father still let me go. When your mother still made you go." She shrugged. "From growing up two years apart in the same small town for sixteen years."

Ethan didn't need to think about his answer. For all he remembered, she could have sprung into existence full-grown yesterday, with absolutely zero contact between them before then. He didn't offer the response immediately, though. It seemed cruel to be so quickly certain that she hadn't existed in his world—in their mutually shared world—for all those years.

But finally he couldn't delay any longer, and so he shook his head. "No, I don't. I'm sorry."

"I'm the most forgettable person in Heartbreak. People who have known me all my life don't know my name. My own father called me 'girl' rather than make the effort to remember 'Grace.'" Her smile was thin and bitter. "He called his dog 'girl,' too. He took her with him when he left."

For a moment she seemed lost in that thought. Missing the father who'd apparently never loved her? Maybe regretting all the years she'd spent with a man who'd walked out when she needed him?

At least it gave them something in common—they'd both had lousy fathers. And they both wondered whether he could do better. And she had good reason to think her child would be better off with no father at all.

"That day last summer was the first time in my life that I was free of his control."

It was an outrageous statement, but she said it so flatly that he knew it was true. Ethan couldn't imagine living a life so restrictive. From the time he was fifteen, he'd taken such freedom that his life had been virtually without rules. Sometimes he'd wished his mother would put her foot down and hold him to the same rules she'd held Guthrie to. He'd figured that she thought he wasn't capable of living up to them, so why even try.

"So you transformed yourself into someone else—" beautiful, sexy, sultry Melissa "—and determined to live all you could in that one day." How many firsts had she experienced? First bar, first drink, first dance? Definitely first kiss. Sweet, a bit awkward, as if she'd expected their noses to bump or their mouths not to fit. It had taken only one kiss to convince her that wasn't the case. The next had been sweet and steamy, full of promise, and at the motel, virgin or not, she'd delivered on that promise.

And he had definitely been her first man. Her only man, he suspected. There was something old-fashioned and satisfying about that knowledge.

"And that's why you disappeared in the middle of the night."

She shook her head. "Not in the middle of the night. Early, just before dawn."

She was right, of course, Ethan thought, because in the middle of the night, they'd been making love again. She'd liked it better the second time. He'd fallen asleep wondering how much more she was going to enjoy the third time, only to awaken alone. The only thing she'd left behind was the faint scent of her cologne perfuming the sheets wrapped around him.

It was the first time in years that the roles had been reversed. He was the one who woke early and slipped away. He was the one who didn't want to face goodbyes, demands, recriminations. He was the one who kept his sexual encounters as anonymous and short-term as possible.

And Grace had shown him how it felt to be the one walked out on.

"So...I woke up alone, and you...?"

"Went home. Washed the color and the curls out of my hair. Scrubbed the makeup off. Gave the clothes back to my friend. Put away the memories and prepared to convince my father that I'd been a good girl while he was gone."

"And he believed you."

"For a while. One day I was over there—" she gestured to the shelves that flanked the side windows "—getting something off the top shelf for Miz Walker and...I don't know. The light was right. My clothes were a little snug. Something about the way I was standing... He realized I was pregnant.'' She lowered her hand to her stomach in a touch that Ethan suspected was totally reassuring. ''A few weeks after that, he left town. But before he left, he signed the store and the house over to me.''

There was more to the story than that. Ethan was sure. Jed Prescott never gave anyone anything but grief. He wouldn't have spit on his neighbors if they were on fire. He wouldn't even call his only child by her name. He certainly wouldn't have voluntarily given her everything he'd worked a lifetime for, especially after she'd disappointed him.

But if she wanted to leave it at that, who was he to push it?

Just the only man she'd ever been intimate with.

The father of her baby.

A virtual stranger.

''So, how's business?''

Her gaze narrowed. ''Fine for Heartbreak.''

''I—'' His face flushed hot, and he turned away, pretending interest in the store to hide it. ''I have some money set aside if...''

''No, thank you.''

Something about the prim tone of her voice raised his defenses and made him face her again. ''It's not tainted. I didn't steal it or win it in a crooked card game, or scam some poor sucker out of it. I earned it at an honest job, tending bar in Key West. I've been working since I left here last summer, and I've saved everything I didn't need to live on.''

She looked embarrassed, too. ''I didn't mean—I'm fine right now. I don't need money.''

''What *do* you need?''

She thought about it a moment, then shrugged. ''Nothing.''

That sounded damn near perfect, he thought bitterly. That was all he was, and all he could offer. *Nothing.*

The bell over the door rang, drawing their attention that way. The man who came through the door was white-haired and stoop-shouldered, and though Ethan hadn't seen him in ten years, he would have recognized him anywhere. It wasn't easy to forget the man who'd laid his mother to rest a good fifty years before Ethan was ready to let her go.

"Pastor." Grace eased to her feet, pulled her sweater tighter across her front and went to stand at the counter. If Ethan were asked, from a purely analytical standpoint, he would say she was trying to hide her pregnancy from the old man. But seven months was a lot to hide, especially on someone as delicate as she was. "What can I do for you?"

"Mama wanted me to pick up two gallons of paint, and she wants it to match the green on this paper." The old man laid a swatch of wallpaper on the counter between them. "She's redoing the guest room again. Our son and his wife are coming for a visit next month to help us celebrate our forty-fifth anniversary, and she seems to think the house needs to look different every time they come."

"I'll mix this up for you," she said with a flash of a smile before grabbing the paper and walking off with it.

Pastor Hughes turned his attention Ethan's way. "Ethan." He bobbed his head in a disapproving nod. "I heard you were back. It's been a long time."

"Not long enough, from what I understand."

"What brings you home this time?"

Ethan shoved his hands into his jeans pockets, then lifted his shoulders in a shrug as he parroted the preacher's words. "It's been a long time."

"I didn't realize you and Grace were friends."

Not friends. Not even acquaintances. Just accomplices in a night's sins that had changed both their lives. But of course he couldn't tell the preacher that. "We went to school together. I couldn't come back and not say hello."

Pastor Hughes looked as if he didn't quite accept the explanation, but he didn't look as if he suspected the truth. No, that would surely widen his old blue eyes with shock and distaste, with a self-righteous *This-is-no-more-than-we-expect-from-you* for Ethan and a dismayed *How-could-you-with-him* for Grace.

"Where have you been this time?" Pastor Hughes asked.

"Florida."

"I understand it's warm there this time of year. Too warm, perhaps?"

Ethan felt the damned guilty flush start again. "I wasn't run out of town, if that's what you're asking. I left on my own."

"And how long will you be staying?"

"That depends." He watched Grace set two paint cans on the counter in the distant corner. With quick, efficient movements, she pried the tops off the cans, then began measuring in tints. He would offer his help for no other reason than to get away from the preacher, but he couldn't help her. He knew nothing about mixing paints or matching colors. He knew nothing about anything but causing trouble. Certainly nothing about making it right.

"I assume Grace has told you about her predicament."

Afraid of what might show in his face if he continued to watch her, Ethan turned his gaze back to the preacher. "Her predicament? You mean being pregnant?"

"And unmarried. Abandoned by both her own father and the baby's father. Left to suffer the consequences alone."

He hadn't abandoned her, he wanted to protest. He knew too well how that felt, had been through it with his father, with Guthrie, even with his mother. God help him, he would never do it to someone else.

But Grace had made it pretty clear that neither she nor

her baby needed him, that she didn't want him. So if he left again, that wasn't abandonment, was it? Even if it felt like it?

"She can't be the first unwed mother Heartbreak's ever seen," he said, injecting a touch of scorn into his voice to cover his guilt.

"No, sad to say she's not. Which doesn't make her situation any less fortunate."

Her misfortune was not running the other way when she met him that night. It was not telling him to go to hell when he'd invited her to the motel. It wasn't the baby. She insisted she wanted the child, even though it was *his* child, and he believed her.

He *wanted* to believe her.

Before the pastor could say anything else, Grace returned with the paint. She rang it up, then waited while the old man wrote out a check. As soon as he was gone, she let out a long sigh.

"I know the good pastor doesn't think highly of wayward sons. I take it he's not much kinder to unwed mothers," Ethan said flatly.

She tilted her head side to side, stretching the muscles in her neck. "Actually, he is. He sees me as an innocent victim, taken advantage of and betrayed by some unrepentant scoundrel." Abruptly, her gaze widened, as if she'd belatedly seen the insult in her words, and she opened her mouth to apologize.

"I'll admit to the scoundrel part," he said, his tone more casual than his emotions. "But I've always been repentant."

"Just not enough to stop being a scoundrel."

"Not until recently."

"Why recently?"

"It was time," he said with a careless shrug, but that wasn't the real answer. He'd started trying to change because one morning he'd awakened from a three-day drunk and realized that he'd *sold* his brother's ranch—his livelihood, his family history, the one thing Guthrie loved most in this world. The fact that land fraud was taken seriously in Oklahoma ranching country hadn't concerned him, nor had the fact that he could go to prison for it. He'd been in jail before. It hadn't been his favorite place, but truth be told, it hadn't been his least favorite, either.

It was the idea that he'd committed the ultimate betrayal against Guthrie that had sobered him. Virtually anything else in the world could eventually be forgiven, but stealing his brother's land was unforgivable.

He'd thought he might have a chance to set things right without Guthrie even finding out, and so he'd headed for Atlanta to find David Miles, the smug businessman who'd been one of the easiest marks Ethan had ever fleeced. He hadn't had much of a plan—to admit that the sale was fraudulent, return what was left of the money and face whatever consequences Miles wanted to dish out.

In Atlanta, though, things had gone from bad to worse. He learned that Miles had been killed in an accident, leaving his wife and twin daughters penniless and homeless. The last anyone had heard, they were on their way to Oklahoma to claim the only thing left them—the ranch. Guthrie's ranch.

Ethan remembered sitting in a seedy motel on the outskirts of the city, trying to gather the courage to pick up the phone and call his brother. But his hands had trembled and his throat had closed off. Even if Guthrie would have talked to him, *he* wouldn't have been able to say a word.

And what words could he have offered? I'm sorry? I didn't think you'd ever find out? I'll never do it again? He'd said them all so many times before that they didn't mean a thing.

In the end, it had worked out well, for Guthrie, Olivia

and the girls, at least. They'd turned tragedy into triumph—had fallen in love, gotten married and created a new family that was a million times better than the old families that had let them down.

Maybe it had worked out well for Grace, too. Instead of making that phone call from Atlanta to Heartbreak, he'd made the drive, arriving in time to catch the last few minutes of Guthrie and Olivia's wedding. He'd given Miles's money to Olivia, given Guthrie the deed to the portion of ranch that had been his for a time, then left them to celebrate their wedding with their friends while he sought the comfort of a few beers and a willing woman in the bar in Buffalo Springs. And there he'd met Grace.

In the end, everyone involved—Guthrie, Olivia and Grace—had gotten the one thing they valued most. A family. Someone to love, someone to love them.

That was the one thing Ethan had always wanted, too.

It was the one thing he didn't think he would ever get.

Chapter 3

Because many of her customers dropped in on their lunch hours, Grace couldn't close up at noon. Instead, she'd gotten in the habit of bringing something from home to eat in what she jokingly called the break room. During her father's reign, it had been a storeroom, but she'd cleaned it out, added a compact refrigerator and microwave, purchased cheap from Reese's nephew, who'd just graduated from college, and a tiny table and chairs picked up at a yard sale. In a few more months, she planned to bring the playpen she'd bought at the same garage sale so the baby would be able to nap there, undisturbed by the activity in the store.

Sometimes on her days off, Ginger joined her, and some days Shay Rafferty brought two daily specials from her café down the street to share. Though she enjoyed their company with all the saved-up pleasure of a woman who'd long been denied the companionship of other women, today she hoped no one dropped in, not even customers. Today she

had company, she thought, as she took her lunch
of the fridge and put it in the microwave to heat up.

But she wasn't sure if she wanted to keep Ethan to herself a bit longer, or if she was afraid that seeing him would
make everyone remember his last visit home and put two
and two together, or if she was…

Stubbornly setting her jaw, she forced the word out.
Ashamed. Just a little. He had such a reputation, and she
didn't want it tarnishing her baby before it was even born.
Grace didn't want people to look at her child and say, Oh,
that's Ethan James's kid. She won't amount to anything,
that's for sure. Grace didn't want people shaking their
heads when they saw her and repeating some version of
what she'd heard plenty of times about Ethan's mother.
*Poor Nadine. All she wanted was a father for her son, and
all she got was a no-good husband who ran out on her and
stuck her with his no-good brat.*

She'd gotten enough *poor Grace*s in her life, thanks to
her father. She didn't want Ethan to supply her with more.

The microwave dinged, demanding her attention. She removed the bowl of stew, spooned a portion into a large
coffee mug for her lunch guest, then carried both to the
table. There was also corn bread, reheated in a damp paper
towel, steaming now as butter melted over it, and a half
dozen of her favorite cookies for dessert. She believed in
eating hearty these days, she thought with a suppressed
smile as she realized how easily her lunch for one could
feed two.

Of course, she was eating for two and carrying more than
enough weight for two.

"So…what are your plans?" Ethan asked as she sat
down across from him. The table was so small that her
knees bumped his as she settled in. She swore she felt a
tingle. He didn't even seem to notice.

"Plans for what?"

"Living. Working. Making ends meet." He pointed toward her midsection with a spoon. "After the baby's born."

"I plan to continue doing what I'm doing now. There won't be many changes."

"A baby changes everything," he said, as if he knew from experience. Maybe he did. Maybe there were little blond-haired, blue-eyed kids with James blood flowing in their veins all over the country. Maybe that was a part of the trouble he was so famous for leaving in his wake.

If that were the case, then he'd be accustomed to notifications of impending fatherhood, wouldn't he? But when he'd come in yesterday morning, that definitely wasn't the impression she'd gotten.

"I can't afford to let it change everything," she said as she seasoned her stew. "I'll still work six days a week. I'll still live on a budget. I'll still take care of myself. The only difference is I'll be taking care of her, too."

"What about a baby-sitter?"

"I can't afford one. I'll bring her to work with me. I've got a playpen that'll fit in that corner. When she's sleepy, she'll stay in it. The rest of the time, she'll be out there with me. It'll be fine—no different from now, except I'll have someone to keep me company when it's slow."

"And, of course, when it's not slow, she'll patiently wait while you take care of customers, order supplies, do the books, straighten the shelves." He sounded skeptical. "You haven't spent much time around babies, have you?"

She was embarrassed to admit that the answer was no. The closest she'd ever been to an infant was passing one with its mother in the aisles of the local grocery store. She'd never held one, never fed one, never changed a bottle, but she could learn. There were how-to books covering every subject under the sun, and Callie, the midwife, would teach her enough to get her started. The rest would come naturally. She had maternal instincts, didn't she? Wouldn't she give her life to protect this baby? Wasn't she ready to devote the next twenty years to loving and caring for her?

"And just how much do you know about babies?" she asked crossly. And had any of those babies he'd learned from been his?

"I know that they cry and require a lot of attention. I know they disrupt everything around them when they're not happy." He scowled. "I know that raising one alone in a hardware store isn't a great idea."

"But I *am* alone," she pointed out quietly, "and I work in a hardware store, and I can't change that."

"You could get married and give her a father."

Her spoon trembled and a chunk of potato slid back into the bowl, splashing broth. She darted a glance at him, but he was staring into his own bowl as if he could stir up a whirlpool that might suck him in and spit him out again someplace far away.

Did he think she hadn't thought about marriage at any time in the last seven months—heavens, in the last thirteen years? Ever since her mother had left her to bear her father's oppression alone, marriage had been her fondest dream, as much for the escape it represented as for the love it promised. After that hot summer night, she'd spun unbearably romantic tales of Ethan: Unable to forget the most incredible one-night stand he'd ever experienced, he tracked her down against impossible odds like Prince Charming searching for his Cinderella. Once her pregnancy had become common knowledge, she'd fantasized a time or two about Reese Barnett discovering a distinctly unbrotherly side to his feelings for her, falling in love with both her and her baby and claiming them for his own. It could happen. It *had* happened in Ethan's own family, with Guthrie and Elly and Emma Miles.

But it wasn't likely to happen again in his family. Ethan

was the only man who'd ever given her a second look, and it wasn't as if he were volunteering—

Was he?

She sneaked another glance at him. No, of course he wasn't. Of all the single men in the state of Oklahoma, Ethan James was probably the least likely to transform into marriage material. He was a drifter, unable to stay in one place long enough to even think about putting down roots. He lived by his wits and did things as a matter of routine that were illegal, unthinkable and unforgivable. He used people until he got what he wanted, and then he disappeared from their lives. He may have had enough conscience to bring him back to Heartbreak, but it was a sure bet he didn't have enough to make him stay. It certainly wasn't enough to turn him into a husband or a devoted daddy.

And a devoted father was the only kind she would accept in her baby's life.

"Well?" he prompted when the silence went on too long.

His insistence on a response roused her temper. He wasn't stupid. He knew she'd been a virgin until that night with him, knew that no man before him had ever paid her any notice. He'd made it clear that even he wouldn't have gone near the *real* her. It was Melissa he'd wanted, Melissa he'd spent the night with. To his great disappointment, it was Grace he'd gotten pregnant, Grace he was now stuck with.

Grace he would like to see married to someone else so he wouldn't feel burdened.

"Oh, I turn down two or three proposals every week," she said, shooting for an airy lack of concern. "There's just no end to the number of men who want to marry me and raise my illegitimate child as their own, but I'm holding out for that one truly special man to come along. Until he does, my child and I will do fine on our own.''

"Too bad you didn't hold out for Mr. Perfect last summer," he said snidely. "Then we wouldn't be having this conversation."

"True," she agreed. "But when your options are limited, you have to be satisfied with what you can get."

He flinched as if her words had the power to hurt. But how could they? She meant nothing to him—less than nothing. She had little doubt he regretted ever laying eyes on her, no doubt at all that he wished he'd never touched her.

It had been the sweetest night in her twenty-five years...and he wished it had never happened.

His expression cleared, cooled, as easily as if he'd pulled a mask over his face. He rested his spoon inside the bowl, then pushed it away and fixed his gaze on her. "Well, it looks as if your options are pretty limited again, so...how about it?"

"How about what?" she asked cautiously, not liking the nervous shiver that crept down her spine.

"Getting married." Ethan's hands were sweaty and unsteady under the table. He clasped them together, then swallowed hard before finishing his answer. "To me."

He'd never proposed marriage before, had never even given it any thought. If he had, he would have supposed the woman's response might be on the pleasantly surprised side. Well, he'd been half right. Grace was surprised.

Moment after moment slipped past while she stared at him. Maybe *surprised* was too mild a word to describe the look in her brown eyes. *Stunned* might be more accurate. Or *shocked*. Maybe just plain *horrified*.

Hell, that was no surprise. He'd never been anyone's first choice—at least, not for anything good. There wasn't a person alive who trusted him, not a soul who could accept him the way he was, without wishing he was better, kinder, more honest, more decent. He'd spent his whole damn life wishing he was better. There was no reason Grace Prescott should be any different.

She looked as if she was torn between hysterical laughter because he couldn't possibly be serious or hysterical shrieks because he was serious. With her hands shaking, she cleared the table, then looked out into the store as if a customer might appear and save her. When the door remained closed, she finally had no choice but to look at him—or at least in his direction. She couldn't bring herself to look him in the eye. "Why-why in the world w-would we g-get married?"

Why in the world would I marry a liar, thief and loser like you? He had little doubt that was the question bouncing around in her head, but she'd had the courtesy to tone it down, to make it sound as ridiculous for him as for her.

"Because you're pregnant," he said flatly as heat flooded his face.

"Marriage isn't a requirement for giving birth," she pointed out cautiously.

"Maybe it should be."

"I admit that in a perfect world everyone would be happily married before having babies, but this is hardly a perfect world. You don't even know me."

"So we do it backward. First we had sex, then we get married, then we get to know each other."

She was shaking her head in dismay. No doubt she'd had a few dreams about some incredibly perfect hero who would sweep her away from the bleak misery of life with her father, who would treasure her in ways no one else ever had and make up for all the boys who'd never noticed her, all the dates she'd never gone on, all the affection she'd never gotten.

Well, he was nobody's hero. There had never been any shortage of women in his life, but not one of them had ever dreamed of falling in love with him and spending the rest of her life with him. He wasn't that kind of guy. Women liked him fine for short-term flings, but when it came to permanence, they always looked to men like Guthrie.

But Guthrie was taken, and no one like him was offering, and nothing changed the fact that Ethan had a claim on the baby, which gave him some small sort of claim on the mother.

"Look, I know this isn't the sort of marriage proposal most women hope for," he said gruffly. He wasn't into gestures—romance, flowers, bended knee. He couldn't offer heartfelt declarations because his heart wasn't involved, couldn't make sweet promises because he'd never kept a promise in his life. He could lie, he supposed. He'd always been good at that—even so, he doubted Grace would believe him. "But most women aren't about to give birth to a stranger's child."

"And most women have a reasonable expectation of marriage. Unlike those few of us who are supposed to feel great gratitude at ever receiving a proposal—any proposal." Her face was pale, her brown eyes magnified by the glasses that were inching down her nose.

"I don't want your gratitude," he said sharply. He knew she must feel cheated—hell, he felt cheated for her, and that made him feel guilty, when he already had enough guilt to deal with.

"And I don't want your name." The instant the words were out, bright spots of color appeared in her cheeks, making her look even paler in contrast, but she didn't back down. "You grew up here as Gordon James's son, and it wasn't easy. I know, because it was just as hard being Jed Prescott's daughter. My baby can't escape being Jed's granddaughter, but she *can* escape the stigma of being Gordon James's granddaughter... or Ethan James's daughter."

The stigma. That was what he'd lived twenty-eight years

to become. There was less shame in his daughter being born illegitimate than in bearing his name. Less embarrassment for Grace to be pregnant and abandoned by some anonymous bastard than pregnant and married to *him*.

She stood utterly still, looking as if she wanted to crawl into the corner and not come out again. When he stood up, she stiffened as if expecting some show of temper, but otherwise she didn't move.

He went to stand in the doorway, gazing out across the empty store. What did you say to a woman you hardly knew who'd just told you that you weren't fit to give your child your name? He could think of only one thing.

Looking over his shoulder, he offered the words he knew she wanted to hear. "Then I won't bother you anymore. Goodbye, Grace." In that instant before turning away, he saw the relief sweep over her, and then he walked out.

On the sidewalk outside, he stood motionless a moment, staring at his old truck. He could head back to Key West, where the days were warm and living was so much easier, or he could try someplace new. There were plenty of towns in the country where people had never heard of Heartbreak, Oklahoma, where the names Gordon and Ethan James meant nothing, where he could learn to pretend that Grace Prescott meant nothing.

But he was tired of new places. He was tired of constantly moving, of never having a place to call home, of never being welcome in his own home. He was tired of being a stranger to the only family he had, tired of being a bad brother, a worse son, a totally unacceptable, unwanted father. He wanted more.

The thought brought a mocking smile to his mouth as he climbed inside the truck. Ethan James, who'd never been able to deal with what he already had, wanted more. Wasn't that a hoot?

He started to drive straight through town, then on impulse stopped at the grocery store to call Guthrie's number. Olivia answered on the second ring. "Hey, it's Ethan," he said grimly. "I'm about to head out that way. Do you need anything from town?"

"Bless your heart, I do. I was planning to drive in and pick the kids up at school so I could stop at the grocery store, but if you'd save me the trip, I'd be grateful. You'll join us for dinner tonight, won't you?" she asked, then went on with her list before he could answer.

At the grocery store he selected Olivia's items first, then added his usual week's shopping to the cart—canned soup, sandwich makings, bacon and eggs, frozen dinners. He debated tossing in a six-pack of beer, a perfectly innocent purchase that half the men in town made on a regular basis. But half the men in town didn't have the stigma of his name or his history. They didn't have teetotaler Guthrie for a brother, and they hadn't gotten the shiest, quietest little mouse in town pregnant.

The beer stayed on the shelf.

Back at Guthrie's place, he parked in front of the cabin, put his own purchases away, then carried Olivia's bags across the broad spread of yard. She opened the door before he'd knocked twice and gave him her usual welcoming smile.

"Hey, Ethan, come on in." She opened the door wide, then closed it behind him before leading the way into the kitchen. The instant he walked through the doorway, he literally felt the welcome disappear, diminished by the force of the disapproval directed his way from the opposite door, where Guthrie stood in the laundry room, tugging off one muddy boot, watching him as if he were some dangerous criminal come to do harm.

Ethan had never been able to win with Guthrie, not since they were kids. Guthrie had never wanted him in his house, but when Ethan had disappeared for weeks at a time, he'd gotten angry about that, too. If he knew that Ethan was the father of Grace's baby, he would be furious that Ethan hadn't stayed hell and gone away from her, but he would also be angry that he'd come back when she obviously didn't want him, and he would be even angrier if Ethan walked away from both Grace and the baby. Where Guthrie was concerned, Ethan was damned if he did and damned if he didn't.

Olivia's tugging on one of the bags he held drew Ethan's attention from his brother. "Have you had lunch?" she asked as she pulled the bag from his arm and set it on the counter. "Can I fix you a sandwich?"

"No. No, thanks. I've eaten."

"How about dinner tonight? Six-thirty?" Her smile was meant to manipulate him into accepting, but it only served to warm him. "We're having roast beef with all the trimmings, freshly baked bread and peach cobbler from our own peaches."

It had been more years than he could count since he'd sat down to a home-cooked meal. The idea held a certain appeal—the family gathered around the table, good food, friendly conversation. Except there hadn't been a friendly conversation between him and Guthrie in at least ten years.

"I appreciate the invitation," he said awkwardly, "but I've got plans."

If Olivia suspected he was lying, she didn't show it. "Okay. Maybe tomorrow. How much do I owe you for the groceries?"

"Don't worry about it." He was temporarily living on their property. Buying a few groceries didn't come close to balancing that. "I—I'll see you later."

As soon as he closed the door behind him, the tightness in his chest eased, allowing him to breathe a little easier. The relief didn't last long, though. Before he'd reached the bottom step, the door opened again and Guthrie came out onto the porch. "Why did you come back?"

Ethan considered ignoring his brother and heading for the cabin, anyway. Guthrie was in his socks. He wouldn't follow, at least not right that moment. But he would eventually, and he would get an answer to his question. He always did.

Slowly he turned, climbed the steps again and faced his brother. Looking Guthrie in the eye knowing he didn't measure up to his brother's expectations had always been one of the hardest things Ethan had to face in his life. That afternoon it was no easier. "Do you want me to leave?"

His question seemed to knock Guthrie off balance. He wanted to say yes, get out and never come back. Ethan was certain of that. But being the all-around nicest guy in the whole damn world, he couldn't be so blunt. "You've always been welcome to stay as long as you want," he said stiffly.

Nice words, Ethan reflected, but not true. From the moment the family had realized how much like his father he was, his welcome had been shaky at best. Once their mother had died, it had crumbled. He'd let Nadine down too many times, disappointed and hurt her too often. Guthrie would have been happy never to see him again.

"I'm just trying to figure some things out," Ethan said at last.

"What kind of things?"

"Personal things." And they'd never been the sort of brothers who shared personal problems. Guthrie had always had plenty of friends and admirers to turn to for help, and Ethan... He'd kept his troubles to himself.

He wished he could talk to someone now, wished there was someone he trusted enough to take into his confidence. But the closest thing he had to a confidante was Olivia, and there was no way he could ask her to keep any more of his secrets from her husband.

"What are your plans this evening?"

Ethan shrugged, unwilling to lie again.

Guthrie hesitated, looked away and grudgingly asked, "Why don't you come to dinner first? The girls would enjoy it. You're the only uncle they've got, and they hardly know you."

"Under the circumstances, I'd think you would want to keep it that way."

Then Guthrie did look at him, wearing that irritated, temper-barely-in-control look he so often wore with Ethan. "You can come or not. It doesn't matter to me."

"So what's new?" Ethan murmured, earning him another sharp look from Guthrie. "I appreciate the invitation, but there are some things I have to do."

With a polite nod he descended the steps, then headed for the cabin. It hadn't been a complete lie. He did have things to do that required all of his attention—plans to make, options to consider. Whatever decision he made would affect not only the rest of his life, but also the rest of his baby's life.

He had to be damn sure it was the right one.

After work, Grace locked up the store, then huddled in her coat for the short walk to Doc Hanson's clinic down the street where she had an appointment with Callie. Regular patient hours ended at five, but the midwife made exceptions whenever necessary.

Callie was in the waiting room, watching the television mounted to one wall. She didn't own a TV, she'd once told Grace. She'd grown up without one—without electricity, too—in a commune in northern California, the place for which she was named. For a time she'd rebelled against her upbringing—had gone to college, become a nurse and discovered her materialistic side.

Then the rebellion had passed, she'd said. She'd gone back to school for her training in midwifery, sold the condo and most of the possessions she'd acquired and returned to the more natural life-style her parents had embraced. That had included a move to Heartbreak, where she lived in a small cabin outside town, grew much of her own food and ignored the folks who treated her like an oddity. After all, she freely admitted she *was* odd. A low-tech midwife in a high-tech world, a vegetarian in cattle country, a dreamer in a land of realists.

Grace liked her a lot.

Callie took her back into the exam room—not one of the cold, drab rooms that lined the hall, but a space that wouldn't be too out of place in most homes. The walls were papered with a floral print, and drapes covered the window. Instead of an exam table, there was a bed. Instead of nervousness-inducing sterility, there was a pleasant, natural feel to the room.

Callie's exam was unhurried but over fairly quickly. After making a few notes in Grace's file, the older woman sat back and studied her. As moment after moment ticked past Grace began to squirm, until finally she demanded, "What?"

"What's going on? You seem distressed."

She'd had customers all afternoon and none of them had noticed. She was chagrined that Callie had. "I'm entitled to be distressed. I'm single, pregnant and have no family, little money and no insurance. Remember?"

Callie's wave was dismissive. She wasn't overly concerned about payment for her services. She knew people would pay when they could, and even bartered for some services. "Being single, pregnant and without insurance has been your life for the last seven months. This is something new. What's happened?''

Grace laced her fingers tightly together as if the action could keep the answer inside her, but she wanted to talk to somebody and there was no one else. Taking a deep breath for courage, she blurted out, ''He's back in town.''

''The baby's father.'' Though it wasn't posed as a question, Callie waited for her nod before she went on. ''You've talked to him?''

Grace nodded again.

''What was his reaction to the news?''

''He—he asked me to marry him.'' The words sounded so strange in her own ears. She'd practically given up hope of any man ever proposing marriage, not when there were other single, more attractive, less needy women around. She'd never imagined that someone as handsome and generally charming as Ethan James could ever possibly want her. She'd certainly never imagined that she could receive a marriage proposal from someone so handsome and turn it down.

Of course, Ethan didn't want *her*. He didn't even want her baby. He just wanted, for once in his life, to do what tradition said was right.

''And you told him no because…?''

''It would be wrong. You don't get married just because you've had the bad luck to get someone pregnant.''

Callie smiled faintly. ''People get married for a lot of reasons, Grace. For love, for money, for companionship, for sex and, yes, for a baby. One reason isn't necessarily better than another.''

''Marriage is hard. If you don't love each other from the start, it'll never last.''

''Arranged marriages rarely involve love from the start, yet they usually last. Marriages between two people who are madly in love often end once the passion fades—and it *does* fade, Grace. In a truly successful marriage, there are other things as important as love, if not more so—things like respect, commitment and trust.''

And she and Ethan certainly didn't share any of them, either. There was nothing respectful about telling a man trying to do the right thing for his child that he was a burden neither she nor the child should be saddled with. And what kind of commitment could she expect from a man who didn't really want to be a part of their lives? As for trust, the only thing she trusted Ethan to do was stir up trouble before moving on again.

''So,'' Grace said, ''if you were in my situation, you would get married just because you're pregnant.''

''It's a reasonable thing to do. And it's not *just* because you're pregnant. There are other advantages. You would have someone to share the responsibilities of raising your child with, someone to contribute financially and emotionally to the child's welfare as well as your own. You'd have an extra pair of hands to give a bottle when it's three in the morning and you're absolutely going to die if you don't get a few hours of uninterrupted sleep, someone to make plans with, to make a future with.''

''And what if he's never accepted responsibility for anything in his life? What if the chances of him being there at three in the morning to give a bottle are somewhere between slim and none? What if he's never stuck around anywhere long enough to even think about a future?''

''What if he's just never had a good-enough reason to stick around?'' Callie countered. ''Being a father is an awesome responsibility. It can totally change a man.''

''And it can be too much for some men to bear. I could end up a single mother, with no family, little money and divorced to boot.''

''But you would have tried.''

"And failed." And any marriage between her and Ethan would be doomed from the start.

Callie shrugged, then returned her attention to the chart once more. "Are you taking your vitamins?"

"Yes."

"I know you're walking every day, and still working too-long hours. But you're disgustingly healthy. Just don't let your emotions drag you down. I'll see you in two weeks, okay?"

Grace agreed and walked as far as the door before turning back. "You never did answer. If you were pregnant by a man you hardly knew and he wanted to get married, would you?"

"I don't know. Maybe. But I do know I wouldn't rule it out simply because we weren't in love. Love's a wonderful thing, Grace, but none of us are guaranteed that we'll find it. Even if we're lucky enough to find it, there's no guarantee that we'll be able to make it last. Sometimes it's better to settle for a commitment based on something solid, like a child, than to hold out for something so elusive as love."

Grace's smile felt unsteady as she said goodbye. *Better to settle.* Was Callie too cynical, or was Grace too much the dreamer? All her life she'd settled for what little she'd been given, accepting that she wasn't getting more. And then she'd gotten pregnant. Having a baby to love was almost as good as having a loving husband, maybe even better. Of course, other women got to have both, but for someone who'd never expected either, one was enough. It was a blessing.

Now Ethan was offering half of the rest of her dream. There was no love involved, but she would have a husband. Her house would no longer be so empty, nor would her life be so lonely. No matter how few months—or maybe even weeks—the marriage lasted, she would always be able to say *my husband.*

And she should be satisfied with that. She should settle, just as she'd settled for twenty-five years.

Well, damn it, she wasn't going to.

She didn't need a husband who had no feelings for her other than a sense of obligation that stretched to include her. She didn't need a father for her child who might devote the next eighteen years of his life to being the best dad in the world or might disappear minutes after she was born, never to be heard from again. Her daughter certainly didn't need a father who drifted in and out of her life the way Ethan's own father had.

She wasn't going to settle for anything less than love, commitment, permanence. Other women held out for it all and got it. She wanted it, too.

And if it meant living the rest of her life alone except for her daughter?

She gazed up at the night-dark sky as she trudged along, and her breath caught in her chest. She'd lived with someone without love for twenty-five years, and she would never do it again. She deserved better than Ethan's guilt-inspired offer, better than marriage to a man who never would have looked at her again if she weren't pregnant, better than to be left behind by a man who knew all there was to know about leaving and nothing about staying.

She deserved better than Ethan James.

Chapter 4

Saturday morning dawned gray and cold. Unable to sleep, Ethan got up and dressed, then put on a pot of coffee. He hadn't left the cabin since delivering Olivia's groceries Thursday afternoon, and the space was beginning to make him feel itchy. Usually when he got that itch, he loaded up the truck and took off down the road, but that wasn't an option this time, at least not yet. Not until he'd decided what he thought was best and saw how that fit with what Grace thought was best.

He didn't expect it to be a very good match.

As soon as the coffee was ready, he poured a cup and stood at the window, gazing toward Guthrie's house and the barn out back. In the thin morning light, he saw his brother come out of the tack room, a saddle braced against one hip. A lot of people Ethan had known wouldn't think much of Guthrie's life. It was all hard work with very little profit, stuck in the same backwater town where he was born, with simple needs and simpler rewards.

But truth was, Guthrie was damn lucky. This place was as much a part of him as his brown hair and his sterling reputation. He spent his days working the land he loved, his evenings with the family he adored and his nights with Olivia. He earned enough to pay his bills, and he had friends, respect and that untarnished reputation.

Ethan had never found anything he truly loved, he had disreputable acquaintances rather than friends, and his reputation had lost its shine when he was little more than a kid.

Grace had certainly heard enough about him to scare her away. She intended to make certain his child heard nothing about him. She was convinced that was in the child's best interests, and he couldn't even argue the point, because he thought it might be, too.

But it still hurt.

Too restless to stand there one moment longer, he put down his coffee, grabbed his jacket and went outside. The northwest wind bit right through the denim and chilled his ears and fingers before he'd gone twenty feet. He didn't turn back, though. Hunching deeper in the coat, he crossed the frozen yard to the corral, where Guthrie was tightening the girth on his gelding's saddle.

His brother gave him an impassive look but didn't speak. Ethan didn't, either, until he was finished with the task. "Is that the horse Easy gave you years ago?"

"Yup. This is Buck."

The Rafferty family had lived down the road a bit, and Easy and Guthrie had been best friends from the cradle. They'd done everything together and had even planned to go into the horse-and-cattle business together after high school—at least, until Easy had run off with Guthrie's fiancée a couple days before the wedding. For the first time in his life, Ethan hadn't borne the brunt of Guthrie's disapproval and hostility by himself. He hadn't been able to enjoy it, though. Losing his fiancée and best friend at the same time had been hard on Guthrie. It would have been easier all around if he'd simply continued hating Ethan, who was used to it, and had gotten over Shay and Easy.

Ethan assumed he was over it now. Shay had been at Guthrie and Olivia's wedding last summer, and according to Grace, she and Easy were married now, too. No doubt all those years of friendship had eventually won out over Guthrie's sense of betrayal and he'd forgiven them both.

Too bad his capacity for forgiving family was more limited than his capacity for forgiving friends.

"What are you doing up so early?"

Ethan's nerves tightened as he looked for some subtly critical undertone to the question. After a moment, he cautioned himself to treat it as exactly what it appeared and nothing else. "I couldn't sleep. I was wondering…I'd kinda like to go for a ride. If it's all right. If I can use one of the…" Trailing off, he shrugged awkwardly.

"How long has it been since you've been on a horse?"

"Ten years." The time was significant to both of them. Their mother had just died, and for some godforsaken reason, Guthrie had offered him one half of the ranch's acreage if he'd stay and work it with him. Ethan had been flabbergasted—and flattered beyond belief—and he'd accepted the offer, fully intending to live up to his end of the bargain.

Of course he hadn't. It wasn't that he was lazy, though that was what everyone had thought. He'd hated the days on horseback, fixing fence, clearing pasture and grading roads. He'd hated digging ponds and cutting hay, had hated the very sight, smell and sound of the cattle. Ranching just wasn't in his blood, and so he'd done the only thing he did really well. He'd sneaked off in the middle of the night.

And a few years down the line, when he'd needed money, he'd used that deed to phony up another, and he'd sold the ranch, lock, stock and barrel, out from under his brother.

But Guthrie said nothing about that now. Instead, he leaned on the board fence and gestured to the horses inside. "Maverick's a little small for you, and Mustang's a little high-spirited. You'd probably be better off with Dusty." He gave a short, sharp whistle, and the mottled gray horse trotted over for a scratch. "Everything you need is in the tack room. But you'd better get a heavier coat and some gloves. It's not going to get much warmer today. You can borrow mine from the laundry room."

Ethan moved beside him to stroke the gray. "Thanks."

After a moment, Guthrie looked at him. "Are you in trouble? Should we be expecting the sheriff to show up out here sometime?"

"You always expect the sheriff when I'm around." Ethan's quiet words brought a flush to his brother's face. He hastily went on. "It's not that kind of trouble."

"Anything you want to talk about?"

He'd give damn near anything to talk to *someone,* but not Guthrie. He'd get the first sentence out—I'm the bastard who seduced Grace Prescott and got her pregnant, then left her—and whatever generosity had prompted Guthrie's question would disappear in anger. "I can't. Not now."

Guthrie accepted his offer with a nod, then untied Buck from the fence. Before he could swing into the saddle, pounding footsteps approached from the house.

"Daddy, Daddy, wait! Can I ride out with you this morning? Mama said it's okay with her if it's okay with you. Is it? Can I?"

Guthrie swung Elly into his arms, settling her on one hip. "Hey, what happened? You got all soft and squishy, like a snowman."

"That's 'cause I've got lots of clothes on like you taught me. Jeans and sweatpants, a T-shirt, a sweatshirt and a jacket, and gloves and a scarf and a hat. Can I go with you?''

"Sure. I'd like the company. Have a seat—'' he settled her onto the top fence rail ''—and I'll get Cherokee's saddle.''

The scene reminded Ethan of similar versions they'd played out themselves years ago. He'd always wanted to tag along with Guthrie and Easy whether they were working or playing, and for a good number of years, Guthrie had let him. Then one day he'd started making excuses to turn him down, and before long that had changed to simple, flat refusals. No excuses, no apologies, just terse, angry nos.

Ethan would bet his life that his brother never got terse or angry with Elly and Emma. He was a good father. Of course.

What kind of father would *he* be? He tried to imagine himself cradling a baby, playing with a toddler, patiently answering the six million questions a kid like Elly could come up with in one breath. What would it be like to teach a daughter of his own how to ride a horse or drive a car? What would it feel like to watch her go out on her first date, to pace and worry the first night she came home late, to see her graduate from high school?

All he could imagine was the awesome responsibility. Not the fun. Not the pleasure. Not the love. Just the incredible obligation to do it right, to not screw up, to not make his child feel the way his father had always made him feel.

Grace was ready for all that. He wasn't.

But he wasn't ready to walk away, either.

Becoming aware of intense scrutiny directed his way, Ethan brought his mind back to the here and now to find Guthrie gone inside the tack room and Elly studying him as if he were some alien creature. He summoned a faint smile for her, which she returned a hundred times brighter.

"You're my uncle Ethan. I'm Elly."

"I remember."

"Really? Me and Emma's almost identical twins, 'cept we're not really very much alike, I don't think. Emma's shy. That's what Mama says I should call her instead of prissy and timid and scaredy cat. We met you when Mama and Daddy got married last summer."

"You were wearing a red cowboy hat. What happened to it? Did you lose it in a thundering stampede, or did some dirty, thieving outlaw shoot it off your head?"

She giggled. "It got too small for my head, so's Daddy given me this one for Christmas." She snatched the kid-size hat from her head with a flourish, then clamped it back on. "Miss Mary says *you're* an outlaw. Is 'at true?"

Mary Stephens was one of their closest neighbors and had been Nadine's best friend for years. It was her daughter Shay who'd jilted Guthrie for Easy, and it was Mary herself who'd heatedly insisted to Nadine that she was better off without that lying, two-timing scoundrel of a husband. Why, he was no good and never had been, which was no surprise. Being no good was the only thing a James did well.

Ethan hadn't known whether to defend his father or to run and hide. When Mary had caught him listening, he'd chosen to hide. It had taken Nadine an hour to find him and another to coax him out. She hadn't known what to say—after all, Mary had told the truth—and so she'd said nothing. She'd pretended the conversation hadn't happened, and to make her happy, so had he.

But he'd never forgotten it.

Elly was waiting for an answer, but this time he didn't know what to say. He'd been arrested more times than he wanted to remember, so he couldn't honestly deny Mary's description. But he was damned if he wanted to stand there and tell his bright-eyed little niece just what kind of man fate had given her for an uncle.

"Well?" she prompted. "*Are* you an outlaw?"

"What kind of question is that to ask a person?" Guthrie balanced a small saddle over the rail, then gave Elly a swat that she couldn't possibly feel through all her layers of clothing.

"Well, Miss Mary said," she replied in her own defense.

"Miss Mary was wrong. Call Cherokee so we can saddle up." After she raced off, Guthrie fixed his attention on Ethan. "The easy answer to that question is no."

"What about the truthful answer?"

"Kids Elly's age don't always require the truth. On some subjects, they don't need it."

"So it's okay to lie to them."

"At times."

"And how do you know when it's one of those times?"

"You learn."

He didn't even know how to talk to a kid. How in hell could he be a father to one? Parents were supposed to guide, teach, love. He wasn't sure he was capable of any of the three, and he wasn't sure he could learn.

Elly returned leading a pinto. "Are you coming with us, Uncle Ethan? I can catch Mustang or Dusty for you if you want."

"No, thanks, Elly." Though riding with them held a certain appeal, it would defeat his purpose. There'd be no time to think, not with Elly's chatter and Guthrie's silences.

They climbed into the saddles and headed off around the barn. Ethan watched until they were out of sight, then started toward the house. The back door was unlocked, and the heavier coat that Guthrie had offered was hanging on a hook just inside. He left his jacket in its place, buttoned up the fleece-lined corduroy, then pulled on the gloves tucked into the pockets as he headed back to the corral.

It took only a few minutes to saddle Dusty, only a few minutes more to leave the ranch buildings behind. Naturally he didn't know the property as well as Guthrie did, but he didn't have a particular destination in mind. He just wanted to get out, to smell the clean air, to feel the cold.

To find some hope or advice or courage.

While hanging around the cabin yesterday, he'd found his old high school yearbooks in a bookcase and had pulled out the one for his senior year. Grace had been a sophomore and had looked very young, very pale and scared. There'd been no activities listed underneath her name, nothing but the fact that she was a permanent fixture on the honor roll. The class photo had been the only one—no candid shots, no club shots, not even one inadvertent shot with her in the background. There was just that one photo, a bad picture of a plain girl who appeared scared of her own shadow.

Ten years hadn't changed her. She still wore no makeup, wore her hair in that severe, unflattering way, dressed in ill-fitting clothes with no color or style. Even her glasses frames appeared to be the same.

And yet, if she chose, she could also look like Melissa. It was an amazing transformation, and he wondered why she didn't make it every day. She could cut, curl or color her hair, trade the glasses for contact lenses, use a bit of makeup, get some clothing advice from the friend who'd dressed her for her big night out and knock the socks off every man in three counties.

Or she could stay the way she was and attract attention from no one but him. Attention she didn't want. *I don't want your name. My baby can't escape being Jed's grand-daughter, but she* can *escape the stigma of being…Ethan James's daughter.*

If he cooperated. If he told no one that he was the father. If he left town before anyone started counting. If Olivia and Shay kept the secret. If the baby bore no resemblance to her uncle Guthrie or her soon-to-be-born cousin.

So was he going to cooperate? To leave town before anyone figured it out? To never come back for a visit—or, if he did, to avoid Grace and the child completely so no one would figure out the connection?

He didn't think so.

Realizing his rider's attention had strayed, Dusty came to a stop at the crest of a hill and lowered his muzzle to the yellowed grass. Ethan gazed across the land, land that had been in Guthrie's family for generations, land that Guthrie had learned with his father, that he was now sharing with his daughters.

The Jameses had never put down roots like the Harrises. The lack of ties had made it easier for them to pick up and leave whenever life got difficult. *Got a problem? Don't bother trying to work it out. Just move on.* That had been his father's philosophy, and his grandfather's, and certainly his own.

Maybe it was time to change.

Moving on wouldn't solve this problem. It wouldn't ease his guilt. It wouldn't erase that night with Grace and the consequences from his memory. It wouldn't stop him from looking at every child he passed and thinking, Does my son look like that? Does my daughter walk and talk like that? It wouldn't stop him from feeling like the most selfish bastard the James family had ever produced.

Moving on wouldn't allow him to think ever again that he was a better man than his father.

So he would stay, and he would try to be a decent father to his kid.

The decision sent something he thought might be relief mixed with satisfaction through him. It didn't last long, though, because right on its heels came the next problem.

How in the world would he persuade Grace to let him near their child?

A few weeks after her father had left town, Grace had made one small change in the operation of the store that she was incredibly grateful for these days—she'd started closing at four-thirty on Saturdays instead of six. After a week's work, she was tired and wanted nothing more on a Saturday afternoon than to get home, put her feet up and watch TV, or read a book or simply daydream about the future.

She didn't want to think anymore about Ethan and whether he'd left town again. She especially didn't want to think about the look in his eyes when she'd said his name was a stigma their child shouldn't have to bear. Yet on her way home she couldn't help but think about him.

She'd never been cruel, intentionally or otherwise, in her life. She couldn't even begin to think what had prompted her to do so on Thursday. His talk of marriage, she supposed. His blunt proposal. His awareness of her disappointment. His own disappointment.

Whatever her reason for saying the words, she'd said them. And regardless of the guilt she felt, they were true. Though that was small-enough comfort.

The sound of an engine worked its way into her thoughts, and she looked up to see a battered green pickup barely moving beside her. She'd seen it parked in front of her store twice before, and she wasn't happy to see it now. She *wasn't*.

Ethan leaned across to roll down the window. "Can I give you a ride?"

"No, thanks."

"If you don't say yes, I'll have no choice but to pull over and park and walk with you. You wouldn't want that, would you? I mean, someone might see us."

She was embarrassed to admit that no, she didn't want that. How could she hope to keep his identity a secret if people kept seeing them together? How long would it take for everyone to wonder what in the world a man like him saw in a woman like her? How long until one nosy person—and Heartbreak had plenty of them—remembered Ethan's last trip home?

"All right. I'll accept your ride." She stepped to the curb, and he brought the truck to a stop so she could climb in.

The heat blasting from the vents felt wonderful. She was chilled from head to toe and all the way through. In fact, her stomach was unsettled enough for her baby to be shivering…or was that merely her nerves at being alone with Ethan again?

She rolled up the window, then peeled her gloves off and held her hands in front of the nearest vent. He responded by turning the other vents her way, too.

"Why do you walk when it's so cold? Don't you have a car?"

"I'm not very comfortable driving."

"Why not? You've been doing it for—what? Nine years?"

"Three months. My father would never let me learn to drive, so Reese Barnett—he's the sheriff—taught me how after he left."

"Why wouldn't he let you learn?"

She gestured to the road ahead. "I live a mile down this road. A yellow house on the left." Looking out the window as he pulled away from the curb, she shrugged. "It was one of the ways he controlled me. I never had any money, I didn't have access to a car, and even if I did, I didn't know how to drive. It pretty much guaranteed that I wasn't going anywhere he didn't want me to go."

"Why was he so strict? It's not like you were a troublemaker who needed firm discipline. I know, because I was. We recognize each other.''

From the corner of her eye, she caught a glimpse of his grin, but resisted the urge to turn toward him and catch the full impact. ''He did it because he could. Because there was no one to stop him. Because he was Jed Prescott, and by God, Jed Prescott's word was law. At least, in his store and his home.''

''He had a reputation for being a first-class bastard.''

''Believe me, he lived up to it.''

When she gestured, he pulled into the driveway angling off to the right, parking between her battered gray car and a great burned area to the left. She hoped he didn't notice the scorched ground or, if he did, that he wouldn't comment on it.

After shutting off the engine, he gave her an earnest look. ''Not all of us do. Live up to—or down to—our reputations, I mean.''

She looked away. Reputation was all she had to judge him by. Years of gossip and talk. The exasperation and frustration his mother had never been able to hide. The resentment his brother made no effort to hide. When the people who were supposed to love him best didn't think too highly of him, that didn't say much for his character, did it?

But that thought was immediately followed by guilt. Using that reasoning, she was no better than Ethan. Her mother hadn't loved her enough to take her with her when she left Heartbreak, and her father's feelings for her had gone way beyond frustration, exasperation and resentment. So, by her own logic, that meant she was lacking in character, too, and she knew that wasn't true. Maybe it wasn't true of Ethan, either.

When she offered no response to his remark, he climbed out of the truck. She was already sliding to the ground when she realized that he'd come around to help her out. She hadn't expected that small courtesy.

After she eased past, he closed the door, then looked from her car to her rounded middle, then back to the car. "When you said you weren't comfortable driving, you meant literally, physically not comfortable, didn't you?"

Grace patted the Bug's fender as she walked past. "It was cheap, and it runs well."

"And after another five pounds, you're not going to be able to squeeze behind the wheel."

"Probably not." She climbed the steps to the porch, then fumbled in her bag for her keys. "Thanks for the ride," she said when she found them. "I appreciate it."

She opened the door, stepped inside, then glanced back. He was standing beside the car, his expression mostly blank, a look of—resignation? acceptance?—in his blue eyes. He wanted to be invited in. She knew it as surely as she knew she didn't want to invite him. It was Saturday evening. She wanted to put on her nightgown, curl up and relax, not be sociable, not think of conversation.

Out of sight behind the door her fingers curled tightly around the knob, itching to slam the door shut and twist the lock. Instead, she used her free hand to push her glasses back up her nose, then, in a tone that was grudging at best, she asked, "Do you want to come in?"

The invitation sounded as foreign as it felt. In all her life, no one had ever set foot inside this house besides her, her mother and her father. Any repairs that had needed doing, Jed had done himself. Deliveries had come no farther than the front door. They'd never had company—no friends to entertain, no relatives who cared to visit. She'd never invited a classmate home from school, had never invited Ginger or Reese inside in the months since Jed had left.

Interesting—fitting—that her first guest was Ethan. After all, he'd been other firsts, too.

He climbed the steps, his boots sounding heavy on the wood, and noticed when the second step shifted dangerously under his weight. He also noticed that the screen door hung crookedly, a souvenir of her father's last enraged trip out. She'd repaired it the best she could, but while she knew her way around the hardware store, she wasn't much for actually putting the hardware to use.

When he walked through the door, she tried to see the house through his eyes. The place was old, and so was everything in it. There'd been no new paint or paper applied to the walls, no new flooring laid in her lifetime. The rugs were ancient, as was the furniture, and the styles, patterns and colors were all sadly out of date. All that had mattered to Jed, and therefore all that had mattered to her, was that the place was clean. It was spotlessly clean. And ugly. And depressing.

She began removing layers of clothing even as she gestured to the living room, opening off the foyer on the left. "Go on in and have a seat. I'll be right in."

He entered the room, probably feeling as if he'd entered a time warp back to his childhood. She stripped down to dress, sweater and socks, then padded down the hall to turn the heat on, and into the kitchen to check the crockpot stew. She debated offering him something to drink, but had nothing to offer but milk or juice. Instead, she returned to the living room empty-handed.

He was standing at one window, the lace curtain gathered in one large, brown palm, looking out. The nearest neighbor's house was well out of sight—by Jed's design, she'd often thought, so no one would hear the shouts and tears coming from this house.

She switched on several lamps before settling in an easy chair covered with a brown, orange and white afghan. He glanced at her, then gestured outside before letting the lace fall again. "Burning leaves?"

''Or something.''

He sat at the end of the sofa nearest her. ''Interesting answer.''

''Not really.'' Jed had set the bonfire the day he'd discovered she was pregnant, and Reese had put it out, but he'd been too late. There'd been nothing left to save. Only her, and on that chilly, overcast November day, she'd thought she might be past saving.

She hadn't counted on the kindhearted people of Heartbreak, or her own resiliency. She certainly hadn't counted on the strength of her newly discovered maternal instincts to care for her child.

''I thought, after our conversation on Thursday, that you might have left town again,'' she said quietly.

He sounded neither bitter nor hurt when he answered. ''That would've made you happy, wouldn't it?''

She wanted to answer affirmatively, as if there were no doubts, but she couldn't. She'd be lying to herself if she said she hadn't felt some small measure of pleasure back there on the street when he'd pulled alongside. As much as she didn't want to marry him, as convinced as she was that she and her baby deserved a better man than Ethan was ever likely to be, there still existed the part of her that had harbored a secret crush on him in school, the part that had spent a long, lovely night with him last summer.

The part that still found him an incredibly handsome, sexy, devilish and, when he chose to be, charming man.

''I thought about leaving, but the simple truth is I have nowhere to go. And the simpler truth is I *can't* go.''

''Because…?''

''Because, like it or not, my choice or not, I'm about to become a father. Because I know how it feels to grow up knowing that your father doesn't give a damn about you. That you aren't important enough to him to stick around,

to remember your birthday, to call sometime. That you
don't exist in his world.''

Such an honest admission would have embarrassed her
if she hadn't been through the same experience with her
mother. She'd never discussed it with anyone, not even her
father, but somehow this seemed the right time. ''I—I was
twelve when my mother left.''

''I was ten the last time I saw my old man.''

''I used to tell myself that she couldn't take me with her.
She had only one chance to get away, and she couldn't risk
dragging a kid along. I was convinced that whenever she
settled someplace else, she would come and steal me
away.'' But that wasn't exactly true. She hadn't been convinced. She'd hoped and prayed, but deep in her heart she'd
known she was never going to escape her father and his
temper. She was never going to have a chance at a normal
life, never going to know peace or acceptance or love.

It was only thanks to Ethan that she had escaped. He was
also responsible for giving her that chance at acceptance
and love—not his, but their daughter's. She owed him a
tremendous debt for that.

''Did you ever hear from her?'' His voice was low, sympathetic.

She shook her head, and her glasses slipped again. ''In
all fairness, she could have tried to contact me, but my
father opened all the mail. He answered the phone. He controlled every hour of my life.'' On days when she wasn't
inclined to be fair, though, she could admit that Betty Jean
Prescott hadn't run away from only Jed and Heartbreak.
She'd run away from Grace, too. She was a *mother*. If she'd
truly wanted her daughter, she could have found a way.
She could have contacted Grace through the school. She
could have been waiting for her outside the building one
day, could have picked her up during class or snatched her
off the street as she walked from school to the store.

But it was easier leaving her behind. Forgetting about her. Letting Grace take her place as Jed's victim. Hoping he would be satisfied enough with tormenting her that he'd let Betty Jean go.

Giving a shake of her head, she asked, "Have you ever heard from your father?"

"Nope. He never was one to waste much time thinking about anybody else. He was no more attached to me than his father was to him. They figured their responsibility ended once they'd 'planted the seed.'" He gave the last words a sardonic twist.

Based on his reputation, Grace had expected him to agree that that was where *his* responsibility ended, too. It was the easy way out. The James way. "So…because you had a bad father, you think you can be a better one."

"I sure as hell can't be worse."

She wasn't so sure about that. But why? What made her so certain that she, who'd had an uncaring mother, could be a better mother while she doubted that Ethan, whose father had been equally uncaring, could be a better father?

Because all her life she'd dreamed of this, hoped for it, prayed for it, even when she thought it was impossible. Because she had the love to give, the commitment to make, the honor to see it through.

And Ethan… He had a reputation as a con artist, a liar, a gambler, unreliable, disreputable, just like his father. But not everyone lived down to their reputations, he'd said. And he'd come back, hadn't he? Had driven halfway across the country as soon as he'd found out that she was pregnant. Had come ready to accept responsibility. Had offered marriage and financial assistance. Would a true con artist, liar and gambler have done that?

Her stomach growled loudly, bringing a blush to her cheeks and drawing her attention to more important matters. "That's her way of reminding me that dinner's late," she said, scooting to the edge of the chair so she could struggle to her feet. "Would you like to stay? It's just stew."

"I'd like that." He followed her into the kitchen, remaining in the doorway while she took bowls from the avocado-green metal cabinets and set places at the chrome dinette pushed against one wall. "Is it definitely a girl, or is that just wishful thinking?"

"Just a feeling." That was her stock answer. Then, for reasons she didn't fully understand, she went ahead with the truth. "I think I can handle a girl better. I have little experience with males, most of it not pleasant."

"Little boys aren't males, at least not the kind you find unpleasant. Those are men, and most men are far different from your father and me."

She gave him a level look. "You're far different from my father."

"Thank you." When she continued to gaze at him, he grinned. "It's not much of a compliment, but it's the only one you've offered. I'll take what I can get."

Feeling a warmth inside that hadn't been there an instant earlier, she turned back to her task. Perhaps she should take his words as a warning, because when the mere sight of his grin sent a heat through her that no furnace could match, she was obviously too vulnerable. What he could take might be no less than everything, and that could leave her with nothing—no hopes, no future, no daughter.

Just a broken heart.

Chapter 5

"This kitchen reminds me of my mom's when I was a kid," Ethan remarked after finishing a second bowl of stew.

"Nothing's been changed, at least since I was born." Grace looked around as if seeing it all for the first time, and her nose wrinkled slightly in distaste. "My father believed in being frugal. You didn't cover over a perfectly good paint job just because you were tired of the color. You didn't stop wearing a perfectly good coat just because it had gone out of style. You never threw anything away as long as it still had some use."

Except her, Ethan thought as he watched her. Prescott had thrown her away because she'd disappointed him. She'd turned out to be human, with needs and desires, and he'd turned his back on her for it.

It was probably the kindest thing the bastard could have done.

She started to push her chair back, but he stood first, taking their dishes to the sink, rinsing and stacking them there. He found a covered storage bowl in the cabinet, transferred the rest of the stew to the dish and put it in the refrigerator before rinsing out the crockpot, too.

"Do you cook?" she asked, watching him from her seat.

"I make soup and a killer egg-and-bacon sandwich, but that's about the extent of my abilities. But I've washed dishes since I was old enough to reach the sink. Even earned a living at it for a time."

"What other kinds of work have you done?"

"Legal or illegal?"

The way her lips pursed gave her a sour look. "Criminal enterprise hardly qualifies as 'work,'" she said primly.

"Oh, darlin', that's not true. Sometimes it can be very difficult work."

"Then why did you do it?"

His smile faded. "Sometimes it was a lot easier to find someone to scam than someone willing to take a chance on me. Sometimes I got hooked up with the wrong people and couldn't seem to get away. Sometimes I was hungry or needed a place to sleep or money so I could move on. And sometimes I just didn't give a damn." Those were usually the times when he'd just left Heartbreak—again— or when he'd wanted to come home but knew he wouldn't be welcome.

The hold this place had on him…when he was here, he'd always been eager to see the last of it. When he was gone, he'd always wanted to see it again—wanted it so much at times that he'd hurt with it. He couldn't belong but couldn't stay away, couldn't fit in with his family but couldn't give them up.

Resolutely he shook his head, clearing his mind. "Legitimate jobs, huh? Let's see…I washed dishes and tended bar. I mowed yards. I did a lot of day-laborer stuff—setting up and breaking down carnivals, working as a loader for a moving company, hauling off trash from construction sites.

I hired on once as a handyman at an apartment complex, but having a master key to all those apartments was too great a temptation. I quit the first day.'' He shrugged. ''Not much to brag about.''

''I worked for my father for thirteen years, after school and on Saturdays until I graduated, then twelve hours a day, six days a week until he fired me last fall. I never had a time card, never got a paycheck and never got so much as a thank you from him. *That's* nothing to brag about.''

She'd said the words so dispassionately, as detached as if she were talking about a complete stranger, that Ethan knew she, in truth, felt great emotion—resentment, anger, a helpless sense of unfairness. Life should have been better for her. She had *deserved* better.

And she still did, but he didn't know how to be better. All he knew how to do was try…and fail.

''Why didn't you follow your mother's example and leave?''

She looked like a solemn baby owl when she looked at him, her brown eyes magnified by the thick glasses. He wished she would take them off so she wouldn't look so young and innocent. Not that it mattered. She could have a hundred years of experience behind her, could live a long and wicked life, and she would still be too young and innocent for the likes of him.

''He never would have let me go,'' she said simply.

''He never would have let you spend the night with me, either—*if* he'd known about it. You could have run away then.''

''I wouldn't even have known how.''

''You could have left with me the next morning.''

Her gaze as it settled on him was troubled with doubts. ''You would have agreed to that?''

To more nights with pretty, sexy, red-haired Melissa? In a heartbeat. To endless miles with plain, shy Grace?

"Sure," he said. "You would have been welcome to go as far as I was going."

She studied him a moment longer, then almost smiled. "Right. You would have taken one look at me and disappeared before I could even get the question out."

"That's not true," he protested. "I would have been—"

"Disappointed."

"*Surprised* by the change, but that wouldn't have stopped me from giving you a ride." Just from harboring any lustful thoughts about her. From sharing her bed when they stopped for the night. From wanting her with even one-hundredth of the desire he'd felt for Melissa.

"You would have been disappointed," she insisted with the confidence of someone who was convinced she was right. "You were disappointed when you walked into the store last week. I don't blame you. When it comes to being attractive, Melissa's got me beat hands down."

"That's ridiculous. You *are* Melissa. You could look like that all the time if you wanted."

She eased to her feet in that awkward, uncentered way of pregnant women, and took her glass to the sink before facing him again. "And would that make all this easier for you? If I looked like Melissa instead of me? If you knew that, once the truth comes out, people weren't going to be saying, 'What in hell was he doing with *her?*'"

"Trust me, no one in Heartbreak's going to be saying that," he said dryly. "It'll be more along the lines of 'What in hell was *she* doing with *him?*'" He drew his fingers through his hair to calm his impatience. "Grace, you can look like anyone you damn well want. The only person you have to please is yourself. If you want to change something, change it. If you don't want to, don't. It's your call."

"Is that the way you've lived your life? Pleasing yourself?"

"No," he said flatly. "I've never pleased anyone. Not even myself."

Without waiting for a response from her, he walked out of the kitchen, down the dark paneled hall and stopped in the broad doorway that led into the living room. It was a dark room, too, and reminded him of his grandmother's house. When he was a kid, Gordon had built the cabin where Ethan was now staying and moved his mother into it, but before then Estella James had lived in town, in a small drab house with faded wallpaper, worn linoleum, old furniture and too little light.

His kid deserved to live someplace brighter, sunnier, cheerier.

So did Grace.

When he heard the soft rustle of her socked feet behind him, he stepped to one side and faced her. "Do you have a room picked out for the nursery?"

Her gaze darted up the stairs before coming back to him. "I thought I'd keep her in my room, at least for a while. I never had the time to fix up the guest room. There's a lot of stuff to move out."

He glanced up there, too. "Maybe I can move it. Mind if I go up to look?"

She shrugged and stepped back as he started up the stairs. She didn't take the first step up until he had reached the top. Was she uncomfortable coming upstairs with him? There was no denying that bedrooms were more intimate in nature than the living room and kitchen downstairs.

There was also no denying that nothing inappropriate was going to happen. She was seven months' pregnant, and he was not that desperate…though he wondered, as he watched the careful way she moved, her gaze on the steps, her right palm sliding slowly over the polished banister. Her hands weren't pampered, her skin neither soft nor silken, but he still remembered the way she'd touched him that summer night—tentatively at first, later greedily, erotically, helplessly. He still remembered the way he'd reacted to her inexperienced caresses, the way she'd made him hard with fumbling touches, the way she'd made him feel. Wanted. Needed.

Swallowing hard, he turned away. Four doors opened off the hallway. The nearest led into a bathroom, as ridiculously outdated as the rest of the house. The next went into what had surely been Jed Prescott's room—large, plain, obviously unused.

The third opened into a small room with a twin-size bed, worn candy-striped wallpaper, a bedspread and ruffly curtains in washed-out pink and very little else. There were places on the wall showing where pictures had once hung, shelves built into the corners that were uncomfortably bare, a white dresser with nothing scattered across its top, a small desk that was empty. Grace's room, obviously, but...
"Where are your things?"

She stood in the doorway and watched as he crossed the bare wood floor to the windows, then turned back. "What things?"

"Pictures, books, souvenirs, mementoes. As much as I move, I carry more personal stuff with me than you have in this room."

She wiped away an imagined speck of dust from the dresser, then folded her arms across her chest. "They—they're gone."

"Gone where?"

Looking decidedly uncomfortable, she shrugged, then freed one hand for a helpless gesture toward him. No, not him. Toward the window behind him. He pushed one pink curtain aside to look out and saw nothing of particular interest. A yellowed yard, her car, his truck, the burned section of grass...

Burning leaves? he'd asked, and she'd given a cryptic reply. *Or something.*

He stared at her. "Your father burned your stuff?"

The incredulity in his voice increased her discomfort level. She came farther into the room and busied herself with smoothing nonexistent wrinkles underneath the spread, then straightening it again. "In his mind they were his things. He'd brought me into this world. He had housed and fed and clothed me for twenty-five years. He had paid for everything I owned, and that made it all his to do with what he would."

"And he *burned* it? Because you were pregnant?"

"Because I had disobeyed him. Because he had warned me for thirteen years about the consequences of behaving like a tramp and I had done it, anyway. Because I had thrown away my virtue, just like my mother had, and he wanted nothing to remind him of me left in his house." Though she sounded composed, her voice trembled. Worse, her body did—not just her hands, but her shoulders, her knees, her entire body. Ethan had never seen a woman who needed holding as much as she did at that moment, and he'd never found it so impossible to offer an embrace.

She took her glasses off as if to clean them, then saw that they betrayed how shaken she was. Clumsily, she slid them back into place, drew a couple of loud breaths, then faced him. "When he realized I was pregnant, he fired me and threw me out of his house. When Reese brought me here to pick up my things, they were burning in the yard. All my clothes. My books. The photographs of my mother. The toys I'd kept since childhood. Stuffed animals that I'd intended to give to my baby. My high school diploma. Everything."

Ethan turned his back on her to hide how shaken *he* was. He could hardly imagine what a blow that must have been to her. She'd had so little in her life, and to be forced to watch it go up in flames, too late to save even a bit of it, all because she'd done something other young women did all the time.

Jed Prescott wasn't just a mean son of a bitch. He was one sick bastard. Ethan was rapidly developing a new admiration for the courage it had taken for her to defy Jed at all. In comparison, he felt like a coward because both Grace and her helpless unborn baby scared the hell out of him.

After a moment, when his breathing had returned to normal, one of her remarks angled for his attention. *When Reese brought me here to pick up my things...* Why had the sheriff brought her home? Neither firing an employee nor kicking your adult daughter out of your home was a criminal offense. Had she merely wanted protection in case Jed's behavior turned uglier than usual? Or had it already turned uglier?

"Why did the sheriff come with you?"

She made an obvious effort to regain control, and succeeded. Her voice low and steady again, she commented, "You ask a lot of difficult questions."

"You have a lot of difficult answers."

She breathed heavily, then laced her fingers together and unemotionally recited the events. "I was standing on a ladder that afternoon, getting something for Miz Walker. I'd been putting on weight and was just starting to show, and my father...*saw*. He stormed across the room, making accusations, calling me names, and he knocked me to the floor. Reese and some other men in the store pulled him away, and Reese took me to see Doc Hanson, to make sure everything was okay." In direct contrast to the flatness of her voice, she laid her hands across her stomach so carefully, so tenderly. "When the doctor said the baby appeared to be fine, Reese brought me here to get some clothes, and we arrived to find the bonfire."

He crossed the room to stand directly in front of her. "I'm sorry."

"It wasn't your fault."

"If I had been here…"

"How could you have been here? I didn't even tell you my real name."

"But—"

"It's *not* your fault. My father was a bastard before I met you. He'll be a bastard until the day he dies."

Which, as far as Ethan was concerned, couldn't come a day too soon.

With a nervous wave, she gestured across the hall. "That's the room I was talking about."

He followed her into the last bedroom, though not very far into it. The space, not much bigger than her own room, was crammed with dark, heavy furniture, boxes and plastic bags. He would need help to move all but the smallest pieces, and she would need more than the two months remaining before the baby's birth to sort through all the junk.

"Why don't you move into your father's room and let the baby have your room? Then you can take your time going through all this."

Her nose wrinkled again, a small, fastidious movement that was either decidedly rabbitlike or charming. He couldn't figure which. "I don't think I could sleep in his room."

"Remake it so you don't recognize it as his. Get rid of the furniture and use some of this. Paint the walls. Put up new curtains."

For one moment she looked as if she were considering it, then she regretfully shook her head. "The fumes…I can't paint now."

"I can," he said quietly, then forced a smile. "Did I mention that I worked construction for a while? I'm pretty handy with a roller and a brush. You pick out the paint, and I'll do the rest. What do you say?'' Though impatience seeped through him, he held himself very still. He didn't coax, didn't try to sweet-talk or persuade her in any way. He simply waited, and wondered why it felt so damn important to him.

After a moment, she smiled, too, at least that was what he chose to call the faint upturn of her mouth. "All right. If you really don't mind."

"I really don't." He switched off the overhead light, then closed the door as they returned to the hallway. There, in the thin light of yet another overhead fixture, he watched her stifle a yawn. It was early, but she'd worked a long week, dealt with the unpleasant surprise of his return and was pregnant besides.

"I'd better head home. When do you want me to start?"

"Whenever you want."

"How about tomorrow?"

After a moment's hesitation, she nodded.

"Do you go to church?"

"Sometimes. I can skip the morning service, though."

"Then I'll see you about ten." Impulsively he touched her shoulder lightly as he passed, then took the stairs two at a time. When he glanced back from the door, she was watching him from the landing, her hands resting lightly on the banister, the curve of her arms framing the swell of her belly. Beautiful, sexy Melissa had tremendous appeal, he admitted before he stepped outside into the cold.

But young and innocent was growing on him.

The house was cold when Grace awakened the next morning, but she was accustomed to it. Her father had never believed in running the heat when you could put on additional layers of clothing, had never let Grace or her mother turn on the air-conditioning until the temperature slipped over the hundred-degree mark. He was frugal, he'd claimed. Cheap, her mother had argued. Just plain mean, Grace knew.

She turned onto her side, straightened her flannel gown around her and gazed out the window. All she could see was a myopic view of blue sky and the winter-barren branches of maples and gums, along with the brown-leaved limbs of scraggly blackjack oaks. At some point in the past, she'd known the reason the blackjack kept its dead leaves until spring brought new ones, but she'd forgotten. Some things, she preferred to believe, couldn't be explained.

Like why Ethan James, who'd never shown a day's responsibility in his life, had decided to turn over a new leaf with her. If she examined his motives too closely, she would see pity, guilt and temporariness, and so, she decided, she wouldn't look too closely. She would accept the help he was offering, and would be careful not to believe he would be around next month or even next week. Then when he left, when wanderlust started calling his name or his infamous irresponsibility got the better of him and he disappeared, she wouldn't be surprised or caught in another desperate situation.

Leaning closer to the night table clock with its extra-large numbers, she saw that it was later than she'd expected. After a few restless nights in the past week, she'd slept twelve hours last night and felt relaxed. Rested. Like a whole new person.

And how much of that had to do with Ethan?

She'd found her glasses and slid them into place before her feet hit the cold floor. Pulling on her robe, she shuffled into the bathroom, turned on the space heater and turned the water in the tub to hot. While waiting for both the air and the water to warm, she brushed her teeth, then studied her face in the mirror. Every time she looked, she saw the same thing—plain, unremarkable, ordinary. Neither pretty nor interesting nor arresting. Just pale skin, brown eyes, brown hair. Straight nose, ordinary mouth, average jaw.

But once… Oh, once she'd looked and seen pretty, daring, sensual Melissa. *Her* pale skin, her brown eyes, her nose, mouth and jaw, transformed into a woman who could make men look twice. Who could attract Ethan James and bring him back halfway across the country. That woman was inside her. She'd come out once. With the right cosmetics and a good hair stylist, Grace could bring her out again, day after day. She could *become* Melissa.

Taking off her glasses and squinting, she envisioned herself going about her daily routine with the wild red hair, the tight, revealing clothes. The thought made her laugh aloud.

But the realization that there was an in-between choked out the laughter and made her slowly slip her glasses back on and stare. She didn't have to be sexy Melissa…but there was no reason why she couldn't be the new-and-improved Grace. No reason why she couldn't enhance what God had given her with makeup, why she couldn't get this mass of hair cut into a flattering, carefree style. There was no reason at all why she couldn't wear a pretty dress from time to time instead of living in these hand-me-down maternity dresses the community had found for her after the bonfire.

You can look like anyone you damn well want, Ethan had told her last night. *The only person you have to please is yourself.*

Being a new-and-improved Grace would please her.

And maybe it would please him, too.

Vanity—another sin her father had preached against—added to her name, she thought as she stripped off her robe and gown, turned on the shower and stepped into the tub under the spray. If it was sinful to want to look better, to make the most of whatever assets she had, then go ahead and damn her, because that was exactly what she wanted.

And if Grace at her best wasn't a match for Melissa, well, she would still be better than poor Grace, the shy little mouse no one noticed.

She was dressed and finished with breakfast when she heard the unfamiliar sound of an engine outside. Cradling her juice in both hands, she watched out a window as Ethan climbed out of the truck and crossed the yard. It seemed almost sinful for him to be here, like a drug dealer in a church or a preacher in a whorehouse. He was too different from the Prescotts—too cheery, too inclined to take his fun, too optimistic by half. Callie would say that his mere presence changed the aura of the property, from bleak and smothering to full of possibilities. Grace would agree.

His knock at the door, even though expected, startled her. She took a deep breath and calmed the faint tremble in her hands before opening the door.

"Good morning," he greeted her, smiling as if it were true. "What do you want to do first? Get the supplies from the store or start moving stuff out of the room?"

"Supplies."

"Then grab your coat, and shoes, and let's go."

She drained the last of her juice and set the glass on the hall table, something she'd never dared do in her life, then slid her feet into a pair of broken-down loafers. They didn't provide much in the way of support, but getting into her other shoes required more effort than she wanted to expend with an audience this morning.

He walked beside her down the steps, opened the truck door for her and took her arm to help her inside. It was rather an awkward procedure, seeing that she'd never been helped before and didn't quite know what to do.

"Do you always open doors for women?" she asked once he was settled across the seat from her.

"Or am I trying to impress you?" His smile was dry. "You obviously never knew my mama or you wouldn't ask. Nadine Harris didn't raise her boys in a barn. We opened doors for women, gave our seats to anyone older than us, said yes, ma'am, and thank you, sir, and please and you're welcome. We took our hats off when we went into the house, left our boots at the back door and never, ever cussed in front of a lady.''

"You swear in front of me," she pointed out.

"Well, hell, Grace, that's because you're an exasperating woman," he said with a boyish grin. "But if it offends you…"

"It doesn't." She well knew the difference between being sworn in front of and being sworn at. Her father had sworn at her loudly and often. His final words to her had been unforgivable curses regarding her character, her failures as a daughter and her suitability to be a mother, and they'd made her blood cold.

But Ethan's curses… She rather liked that a man noticed enough about her to find her exasperating. It was a nice change from the wallflower she'd been all her life.

He parked in the hardware store lot, then came around to help her out. His hand clasping hers felt so much bigger and stronger, and his other hand, resting on her arm, made her feel both steadier and shakier. She knew she wasn't going to fall in a literal sense, but she wondered if she was in danger of falling in a romantic sense.

Heavens, that was *non*sense. The quivery little feelings she felt right now were no different from the quivery little feelings she felt when Reese Barnett was around, or Guthrie Harris, or any of a number of men. She was an incredibly naive twenty-five-year-old woman getting thrills and chills from whatever masculine contact she experienced. Nothing more, nothing less.

The store was quiet and dark, just as it was every morning when she came to open up, but it felt different. It was never open on Sundays, and she'd never felt the freedom to walk down its aisles and pick what she wanted for herself. This morning she did just that, scanning the paint samples, then offering the one she wanted to Ethan.

It was a deep rose, subdued enough to be restful, intense enough to be certain her father never would have allowed it in his house. She could easily envision herself sleeping in a room that color, with curtains at the windows in rose and navy blue, with a bedspread in matching colors, with pillows in every size and shape spilling all over. It would be rich, luxurious and eye-catching—and a world away from the safe, little-girl, pink-and-white decor of her current room.

It would be a room where a man might sleep.

The sly, unbidden thought whispered into her mind, bringing a flush to her cheeks and making it impossible to even look directly at Ethan.

"That room's probably..." He cocked his head to one side while mentally figuring. "Fifteen by fifteen? Two gallons will be plenty, and leave enough for touch-ups. Why don't you mix up the paint, and I'll get the supplies." But he didn't head for the brushes immediately. Instead, he waited until she picked out two gallon cans, then took them from her and carried them to the worktable. Then he went to pick out his brushes.

She had finished mixing one gallon and was measuring tint into the second when the bell over the door jingled. Looking up, she saw Reese Barnett come in and, for one shameful instant, hoped that Ethan would have the good sense to stay out of sight. The sheriff was protective enough. She didn't want Ethan to make him think he had reason to be even more so.

"Reese," she greeted him as she snapped the lid back on the can, then fitted it into the machine.

"Hey, Grace. I was leaving the café and saw the lights

on in here. What are you doing in here on a Sunday morning? Somebody have a paint emergency?''

"No. This is for me."

"You shouldn't be painting in your condition. You know that."

"I'm not. I, uh, I got someone to do it for me."

"Who?"

She chewed her lower lip, fiddled with her glasses, then looked toward aisle eight where Ethan had disappeared. Finally she folded her arms across her chest and flatly answered, "Ethan James."

Reese's laugh was more like a snort. "How'd you manage that? I *know* he didn't come around here asking for work. Ethan wouldn't know how to do an honest day's work if he was starving. Jeez, Grace, haven't you heard the stories about him?"

She shrugged stiffly. "They're just stories."

"Just stories that are ninety-nine percent true. Get rid of him, Grace, and I'll do your damned painting."

"I appreciate the advice and the offer, Reese, but I can handle this." She ignored his second indelicate snort. "I'm a grown woman, and I'm perfectly capable of making decisions for myself." She also ignored the next snort.

"Oh, yeah, darlin', you've shown a tremendous capacity for handling things yourself," he said sarcastically, then relented. "Just don't be naive enough to believe anything James tells you. Don't pay him until the job is finished. And don't leave him alone in your house. The boy's a first-rate liar, con artist and thief. The family would've been better off if his mama had drowned him at birth."

She tried to think of something, anything, to say on Ethan's behalf, but her mind was blank.

"If you change your mind, give me a call. I'll be off Tuesday and Wednesday this week. I'd be happy to help you out." He headed toward the door, turning once he got there to call a farewell.

Miserably she mumbled goodbye, then stared down at her clenched hands.

A long, still moment later, Ethan came to the counter with a can of white paint for the ceiling and an armload of supplies. He set them down, then reached across to shut off the mixing machine. An eerie quiet settled over the room.

She unknotted her fingers and removed the can from the machine, prying the lid off to check the color. She hardly noticed it, though, before pounding the lid back on and slapping the sticker with the tint formula on the side of the can. Finally still, she shifted her gaze a few inches closer to Ethan, but she couldn't look at him. She was too embarrassed. "I'm sorry." She should have said something, should have defended him somehow, but she just couldn't. Couldn't think. Couldn't make her mouth work. Couldn't find any words that would make a difference.

Anything would have helped, Ethan thought numbly. Even a faked show of skepticism, or a bit of emphasis on the *just stories* line. If she'd done anything but stand there and look ashamed of her association with him… And this was nothing. What would she do if anyone ever found out that he was the father of her baby?

She would probably rather die.

"Listen…" His voice was hoarse. He cleared his throat before trying again. "Why don't you take him up on his offer? Let him come over Tuesday and do the painting for you. It would be better for you, and, hell, he'd probably do a better job." That settled, he turned to walk away, but she impulsively caught his wrist.

"No…Ethan, please."

As soon as he stopped, she drew back and fiddled with the extra-long sleeves of her sweater. "I should have said something. I'm sorry. It's just…"

Just that everyone in town knew the stories. They knew all about Ethan, and they shared the sheriff's opinion.

Just that she'd been an outcast herself for all but a few months of her twenty-five years. With the freedom gained from her father's leaving, she'd also gained friends and a place in the community for herself. Defending him could jeopardize that.

Just that she didn't have any defense to offer for him. What did she really know about him? That he was good on the dance floor and decent in bed? That he didn't mind having sex with a total stranger? With the good people of Heartbreak, tidbits like that wouldn't exactly place him in a better light.

Still, irrational as it was, he wished she had said *something*.

"You don't owe me an apology," he said at last. If anyone should be sorry for anything, it was him, starting with the bad luck of his birth into the James family and including every sin, real or imagined, he'd ever been damned for.

"I *am* sorry," she repeated, and finally she managed to look him in the eye. "If you're still willing to help me, I— I would appreciate it."

He smiled, but it was all surface. "Of course I'm willing."

Appearing genuinely relieved, she wrote out a receipt for the supplies, left it next to the cash register and bagged everything but the paint.

They returned to her house and went upstairs. After setting the paint down, Ethan's first thought was to take his jacket off. When he realized how cold it was inside, he checked it. "I bet your old man didn't believe in frittering away money on luxuries like heat, did he?"

She shook her head. "I'll turn the thermostat up. I'm so used to it that I don't even notice. And I *am* carrying a little extra padding these days."

His gaze slid automatically to her belly. He knew the changes in her body weren't comfortable for her. He'd watched her maneuver to her feet, had seen her rub the small of her back as if it ached. But there was something oddly appealing about the way she looked. Something womanly. Something damn near sensual.

Scowling at such a sappy thought, he turned his attention to the room. Jed Prescott had apparently taken all his personal belongings with him. Every drawer he removed from the dresser was empty, the walls were bare, and the closet held a spiderweb and nothing else.

The bed was full-size, plenty of room for one, cozy for two. It was made with plain white sheets and a quilt so worn that its fabrics had faded to the same pale shade. While Grace was downstairs, he unmade it, carelessly folding everything together. That done, he grabbed the fabric loops on the mattress sides and carried, dragged and manhandled it into the hallway, where he left it leaning against one wall. The springs followed, then the bed, broken down into headboard, footboard, rails and slats.

He was preparing to slide the dresser away from the wall when Grace returned. "I can help you with that," she said, going to the opposite end, ready to lift as soon as he did.

Ethan settled his hands on his hips and simply looked at her.

"I'm stronger than I look." When he made no move, she tried again. "I lift and carry things all the time. It's not that heavy."

"If it's not that heavy, then I don't need your help, do I?" he asked dryly.

If she'd been anyone but Grace, he would have described the position her mouth settled into as a pout. Hell, no matter who she was, that was exactly what it was. She backed away, hands folded above her stomach, and watched as he half-dragged, half-scooted the dresser into the hallway.

When he came back, she was bent over, working a stubborn drawer out of the nightstand. He caught her around the waist, ignoring the tension that streaked through her, and guided her toward the glider near one window. "Sit."

"I was just—"

"Sit. Relax. Be lazy."

The sound that came from her as she sank onto the cushioned seat might have been a snort or a laugh. Never having heard her do either, he wasn't sure. "Being lazy is a mortal sin in Jed Prescott's house."

"But this isn't Jed Prescott's house anymore. It's Grace Prescott's, and she's smart enough to realize that even God rested on the Sabbath."

With a reluctant smile, she settled in and drew the two halves of the cardigan front together over her own front. She'd said she didn't notice the cold, but that wasn't true. He hadn't yet seen her without long sleeves and a sweater, often with a blanket nearby. It *was* true that she'd grown accustomed to being cold, but she still felt it.

She had become accustomed to a lot of things, it appeared. He wondered if she could adapt to a few more. Like having him around all the time. Not caring what her new friends thought. Not being ashamed of him, his name and his role in her pregnancy.

Maybe, if he had unlimited time. With only two months to prove his worth, probably the best he could hope for was resignation.

Shaking off the grimness of his thoughts, he moved the nightstand from the room, then began taking drawers from the tall bureau.

"It feels weird, sitting here doing nothing and watching you work," she commented.

He flashed her a grin. "Enjoy it. I know people who would pay for the opportunity. Most of this town, including my brother, thinks I wouldn't know how to do an honest day's work if I was starving, remember?''

The instant the blush darkened her cheeks, he regretted the comment. ''Reese never would have said that if he'd known you were there.''

The defense she couldn't come up with for *him* in the store came easily when it was for Barnett. Obviously, after the incident when Jed had struck her, the sheriff had taken some sort of interest in her, maybe purely professional, maybe completely personal. What kind of interest had *she* taken in *him?* Did she see him as some sort of white knight who'd rescued her from one bad situation and might, if she was lucky, save her from the rest? Were they friends? Did she harbor hopes of more?

It would have been damn near perfect for her if Barnett had fallen in love with her after saving her from her father. His name alone was enough to earn her respect from the entire county. It was enough to save her child. No one would snicker about the baby's questionable parentage. No one would dare call the kid names, or automatically expect trouble from him, or judge him on nothing more than the blood that flowed in his veins.

By marrying Barnett, she could gain instant approval and acceptance for herself and Ethan's child.

And by marrying Ethan, she could ensure that such approval and acceptance would never be theirs.

And he had no one to blame but himself.

''Barnett would have said exactly the same things if I'd been standing right there beside you,'' he disagreed. ''Which is fine. I have more respect for a man who'll say to my face what others only whisper behind my back. And he was right. I'm the best liar and con artist to ever come out of Heartbreak. And I'm sure there were times when my mama wished I had disappeared along with my father. She had Guthrie, the perfect son, who'd never disappointed a soul in his life. She didn't need a second son who was more trouble than he was worth.''

''She never told you that,'' Grace scolded him. ''If they'd given an award for mother of the year, your mother would have won it every single time. Everyone says she was a wonderful mother, a wonderful friend and a better—''

When she abruptly stopped, Ethan finished for her. ''A better wife than Gordon James deserved. You'll get no argument from me. She was a saint. Guthrie was a saint. They were great fun to live with. They could do no wrong, and I couldn't do anything right. They were saints, and I was a sinner. They were honest, decent and good friends, and I was…''

Realizing that he'd said too much, he broke off and looked around. While talking, he'd taken down the curtains and rolled up the rug, leaving them all in a pile in the hallway. There was nothing left to do but a little cleaning and then work.

''You were what?'' Grace's soft, hesitant question came from behind him. Maybe because she'd had so little gentleness in her life, she could put more of it into her voice than any woman he'd known. Not even Nadine, mother extraordinaire, had ever sounded quite so tender with him. Of course, more often than not, she'd been exasperated with him.

''Nothing,'' he muttered. ''Do you have a ladder and a vacuum cleaner?''

''In the laundry room downstairs. I'll help you—''

He held out one hand to stay her. ''I can manage. Do you want anything while I'm down there?''

''Just an answer.''

He started to walk out without a response. At least, that

was his plan. But at the door he turned back against his will and flatly gave her what she wanted. ''They were so damned perfect, so damned *good*. And I...I was just like my father.''

Chapter 6

As Ethan stirred the paint, Grace left the bedroom, feeling even worse about the way she'd kept her mouth shut with Reese. It wouldn't have hurt her to simply disagree, to point out that sometimes people changed. It wouldn't have changed his mind one bit, but she thought it might have made a lot of difference to Ethan.

If anyone had suggested before this past week that things that had happened when he was growing up still affected him, she wouldn't have believed it. He hadn't had a sober thought in his life. He'd skated his way through school, never buckling down, never taking anything seriously, including himself. In the bar last summer, he'd been funny, charming and thoroughly insincere, but even that had been part of the charm. She'd never met anyone with so few regrets, so little emotional baggage, with such a casual attitude. It had been refreshing, appealing. Exactly what she wanted.

But he had regrets and baggage, more than most people. He just hid them well.

The hallway was filled at the near end with furniture. She had to suck in a deep breath and turn sideways to squeeze through the narrow space left by the dresser, but she was only going as far as the next room. She eased as far inside as the clutter would allow, took a long look around and considered going to her own room to take a nap. Instead she stiffened her spine and went to work.

Her father hadn't believed in throwing things away, she'd told Ethan, and this spare bedroom was testament to the truth in that statement. She started with the nearest box and began building two piles near the stairs—to give away and to throw away. She couldn't imagine that she might conceivably need a third pile for things to keep. She wanted nothing of Jed's for herself, certainly not for her baby.

She was seated on the bed and making serious headway on the mess when she lifted out an old mixer from the box in front of her. The plastic housing was badly melted, the cord neatly cut off, the warranty and instruction manual taped to the side.

"It's amazing what a person thinks is worth saving."

She glanced at Ethan, standing in the doorway with a glass of ice water. She'd been so lost in the junk that she hadn't heard him pass, hadn't heard his footsteps on the stairs that always creaked. "My mother was making a cake one day—devil's food. That was his favorite." She smiled thinly at the appropriateness of that. "She mixed the batter, then set the mixer aside while she got the cake in the oven and took care of some other things. Somehow the mixer fell onto the stove, near a burner that was on. Before long, she smelled the melting plastic. She didn't even try to hide it from him. When he came home from work, it was sitting at his place at the table. He took one look at it, then took a knife from his pocket, cut off the cord and beat her with it. It couldn't have cost ten or twelve dollars new—hell, he sold them in the store—but he beat her for damaging it."

"Where were you?"

"I ran to my room and hid in the closet. I used to hold my fingers in my ears and sing really loud to drown out their voices. The first time he got angry with me after she left, I hid there, and when he found me, we came to an understanding that I wouldn't do that again."

"What kind of understanding?" Ethan's voice sounded dark, threatening, but she didn't feel threatened. She felt...safe, in a way she'd never been before. Maybe it was because she knew she would never have to hide in fear from another man again.

Or maybe it had something to do with *him*.

"He didn't hit me. He'd never needed to. I'd learned enough watching and listening to him beat my mother that I never gave him cause to hit me—at least, not until that day in the store. We just had a talk. He told me how I would act, what I would think, what I would do, what I would say and what would happen if I didn't. And I agreed."

"That's a hell of a way to grow up."

"Yes, it is," she murmured, and for a moment, her fingers tightened around the mixer. She wanted to throw it, to hear it smack hard against something. But when Ethan took hold of it and pulled, she let him slide it from her grip. She wasn't the throwing, smacking-hard type. She didn't want to be.

He tossed it into the trash pile in the hall, then came back to crouch in front of her. "I've never hit a woman in my life, Grace. I don't have much of a temper, and when I do get angry, I usually go off by myself until I cool down."

She had never considered herself a terrific judge of character, mostly because she'd never been allowed much contact with people, but she believed him—and not just because Nadine Harris had raised her boys right. Some men were violent. Most weren't. She would bet everything she'd learned in the last seven months that Ethan was in the latter group.

"If I'd thought you were like him, I never would have gone near you," she said awkwardly. Looking away from him, she glanced at the rest of the contents of the box—all junk—then folded the flaps and lifted it onto her lap. She couldn't stand up, though, because he remained where he was.

"Why did you?"

Her fingers tightened around the box. "I told you…"

"You told me why you were in the bar. It was the first time you'd been free of Jed's control and you wanted to experience everything you could. But why me? You knew who I was. You knew my reputation. There were plenty of other guys in the bar who would have been more than happy to buy you a drink, dance with you and make love with you. Why me?"

She scooted around, preparing to ease onto her feet and into the small space left open to her, then past him and out of the room. He stopped her, though, by taking a secure hold on the box, blocking her exit.

With nothing but the smallish box between them, she looked up at him. She'd never seen him look bad a day in his life, and that day was no exception. His blond hair was a little shaggy, but a little shaggy was as flattering to him as any style could be. She supposed most people would consider his eyes to be an average blue, but to her they were exactly the shade of her favorite blue. She liked the stubborn line of his jaw, the shape of his mouth, the cockiness of his grin, the straight perfection of his nose, the golden-brown hue of his skin.

He was handsome. Incredibly, perfectly so.

And she was so imperfectly plain.

Why me? he wanted to know. She gave a soft sigh. "Because I knew who you were. I remembered you from grade school, middle school, high school. You didn't remember me at all, not as Melissa, not as Grace, but you were coming on to me, anyway. After sixteen years of not even registering in your consciousness, I liked that you had not only noticed me, but you…'' She moistened her lips, but couldn't bring herself to finish.

''Wanted you,'' he supplied, his voice huskier than it had been a moment ago. Raising his hand, he touched her hair so lightly she wasn't sure she felt it, then let the tips of his fingers skim along her jaw. ''I wanted you.''

The desire to close her eyes and turn her cheek against his hand, to rub back and forth and purr like a besotted cat, was almost too great to resist. But she managed, and managed to shake her head, too, dislodging his fingers. ''You wanted Melissa, and she—she doesn't exist.''

His mouth quirked in a grin that was gently teasing. ''*Someone* was there, darlin', kissing me and rubbing against me and making me hot everywhere she touched. If Melissa doesn't exist, then it must have been you.''

The furnace had been running too long. Suddenly, in one instant, the temperature in the bedroom had become almost unbearable. Grace couldn't remember ever getting so warm so fast.

At least, not since last summer.

''Grace, it doesn't matter what name you called yourself, or that you fixed your hair differently or wore someone else's clothes. It was still you in that motel room with me. It was you in that bed. We have proof of that.'' He rested his hand gently on her stomach, then pulled away. It wasn't long enough to get more than a vague sensation of pressure, of warmth, but it felt like so much more. It felt momentous. Significant. Incredible.

''The woman in bed with me that night… That's who I wanted. And that was you. You can't deny it—'' His expression shifted, became grimmer. "Well, you can, but not to me. Everyone else would believe you, but I know better."

For a moment, he held her gaze, and though she wanted very much to look away, she couldn't. Finally, though, he broke the contact, then tugged the box away from her. "Trash?"

All she could do was bob her head in response.

He didn't settle for taking it into the hall, but instead carried it downstairs and outside. A moment later he returned, but he didn't head back to work. Once again he stopped in the doorway, looking decidedly uncomfortable. "If that's what you want to do…it's okay."

"If what…?"

His discomfort level increased a degree. "Deny it. If you want to tell people that we know each other from school or that you hired me to do some work around here. If you want to tell them…" He breathed deeply, then continued in a rushed, taut voice. "If you want to tell them they're wrong when they ask if I'm the baby's father. If you want to deny it for her sake, for your sake. It's—it's all right. I understand."

Before she could respond, he disappeared from the doorway, returning to the other room to work again.

Grace sank down on the mattress once more, feeling ashamed and relieved and grateful and—and so damn ashamed. He'd lied. He would understand, but it wouldn't be all right. It would hurt him to know that she thought so little of him, but he would let her do it, would even support her in her lies.

And he would never forget it. Whether he stayed forever or left next week, he would never forget that she'd been so ashamed of who he was that she'd denied her child a father rather than acknowledge him. He would be entirely justified in never forgiving her.

But was she ready to tell everyone the truth? Could she look them in the eye and admit that her daughter, her precious, innocent daughter who'd never done anyone a moment's harm, was also Ethan James's daughter? Could she face the reactions such news was bound to bring?

Aw, hell, this one won't be any better than its daddy, and he wasn't any better than his *daddy. None of those Jameses ever amounted to anything. They've got trouble in their blood. Bunch of no-good liars and cheats, and she won't be any different.*

Did you hear about Grace and that James boy? He must've been drunk out of his head. Why, no sober man would've gone to bed with her…though they all kinda look alike with the lights out, you know.

She didn't want to be the subject of gossip. Didn't want people to look at her and wonder what Ethan had seen in her, what game he'd been playing, just how desperate he'd been to choose her. Didn't want people whispering behind her back, feeling so sorry for poor Grace who'd been desperate for a man's attention—*any* man, obviously, since she'd settled for that disreputable James boy.

But who was she kidding? She'd been the subject of gossip, whispers and *poor Grace*s all her life. Poor Grace, abandoned by her mother and mistreated by her father. Poor Grace, without a friend in the world, treated like a slave and afraid of her own shadow. Poor Grace, used and cast off by the father of her baby, then thrown out on the streets by her own father. She could live with gossip, snickering, pity, disbelief and skepticism.

But she could not let her baby grow up with them.

Even if it meant lying about the baby's father.

Maybe someday he would forgive her. More likely he wouldn't. But either way, she couldn't worry about it. All she could do was the right thing for her baby.

And acknowledging Ethan James as the father didn't come close.

When Ethan turned onto the overgrown lane that led to the cabin late Sunday afternoon, the first thing he noticed was Guthrie standing on the porch. In a better world, he wouldn't feel the tightening in his gut, wouldn't feel that he had to prepare himself for battle. He would invite his brother inside, offer him a beer, kick back and talk about nothing. He wouldn't worry that Guthrie had come for one of only two reasons—to make accusations or to throw him off the property.

If he'd found out that Ethan was involved with Grace, this time it could be both.

He parked out front and climbed the steps to the porch. Guthrie stepped back to allow him room to open the screen door. "You've been out all day," he said as a greeting.

Who was keeping tabs on him? Ethan wondered. Guthrie or Olivia? Had Guthrie's curiosity gotten the better of him today? Had he come over to check the cabin, to go through Ethan's things, searching for…hell, for anything that could justify asking him to leave?

But the door was locked until he turned his key, and the only thing in Guthrie's hand was a folded piece of paper. And it didn't matter if he did want to search Ethan's belongings, because the only thing he had of any interest was the photograph of Grace, and it was tucked in his wallet in his hip pocket.

"I had some things to do," he said at last. He hoped Guthrie wouldn't ask what things, because he didn't want to lie to him, but he also didn't want to listen to a lecture about how he needed to stay hell and gone away from Grace.

For a moment it looked as if Guthrie would ask. Then

he gave a shake of his head and, instead, offered the note. "This is from Elly."

As Ethan unfolded the paper, he went inside. "Come on in," he said casually, as if it weren't difficult to ask Guthrie into his temporarily private space where he more likely than not would find reason to criticize. Without waiting to see if he would accept, Ethan switched on a lamp, then went on into the kitchen. "Want a Coke?" he called.

"Sure."

It wasn't the friendliest response, either in tone or brevity, but it wasn't hostile. In fact, Guthrie sounded the way Ethan felt—wary. Unsure.

He returned to the living room with two cans of pop, handed one to Guthrie, then sat on the arm of the easy chair to study Elly's handiwork. The note wasn't written at all, but rather was drawings that combined to spell out a message. The stick figure standing outside a brown house he recognized as himself from the yellow hair and blue eyes. The white house on the opposite side of the picture, with two adult sticks, one obviously pregnant, and two small ones, was easy, too. Shapes, unrecognizable but uniform, stretched from the cabin to the house, and forming a border across the bottom were a number of smaller drawings. There was a circle of blue flowers with a fork at one side, a small black-and-white creature with a red *X* over it, what appeared to be an apple surrounded by small white mountains outlined in black, a rectangle holding five circles, and a bird as tall as the house wearing a watch on one wing with two arrows pointed straight down.

"She's eating flowers with a giant bird?" he asked skeptically.

Guthrie's chuckle wasn't at all strained. It had been years—at least thirteen—since Ethan had heard his brother laugh, and a whole lot longer since he'd been the one to make him laugh. "You're not much good at this kid stuff, are you?"

No, but he was going to learn. It was a good thing he was a quick study when he wanted to be, since he had only two months to get the basics down perfectly.

Guthrie came to stand beside him and gestured with the pop can. "That's you and the cabin. This is us and our house. These—" he pointed to the flowers "—are Mom's dishes. Remember? They're white with blue flowers? This rectangle is the dining table, set for five. This is apple pie with whipped cream—Liv's latest craving. The big bird is the chicken she's frying, and his watch says six-thirty, which is when we eat."

"What about this animal with the *X?*"

"I'm not sure. Either it means Skip, their dog, won't be joining us for dinner, which would please their mother immensely, or…" He grinned suddenly. "It means 'no beef.' I'm raising mostly black baldies now. See? His face is white, and he's got long ears. Damn, Elly's gonna be a hell of a rancher someday."

As a teenager, Ethan had learned more about cattle than he'd ever wanted to know, and as an adult, he'd managed to forget most of it. Obviously it was significant that Elly's baldy had long ears, but not to him. If ranching was ever going to get into his blood, it would have happened by now. He'd rather keep his acquaintance with beef on the same footing it was now—through restaurants and grocery stores.

"Okay, hotshot, so what're these?" Ethan pointed to the shapes that crossed the lawn, then recognized them half a second before Guthrie replied.

"Footsteps. They match the shape of the stick's feet, see."

He did, now that he knew.

"So? Will you come?"

Ethan's first impulse was to make excuses. He was tired.

He wanted to consider everything that had happened with Grace that day, from the conversation with Barnett in the store to the way he'd caught himself watching her move, to the instant dislike he'd felt for whatever was between her and the sheriff. Jealousy, some might call it, and though he'd rather not, considering some of the feelings he'd been feeling—remembering how easily she'd aroused him last summer, the unaccustomed protectiveness, the need there in the guest room to touch her, even just for an instant— he might have to give in and admit it.

But he would have plenty of time for all that. It wouldn't hurt him to have dinner with Guthrie's family, and it *could* hurt if he didn't.

He glanced at his watch and saw that it was a quarter after six. "Tell Elly I'll be over as soon as I clean up."

That made Guthrie give him a closer look, his eyes narrowing. "What have you been doing today? Painting?"

Ethan swallowed hard, feeling as guilty as if Guthrie had caught him sneaking back from a wild night of drinking and partying. "Why would you think—"

"Because you've got pink paint in your hair." He peeled a glob of latex out, taking a few hairs with it, and dropped it on Elly's note. "What are you up to, Ethan?"

Ethan searched his voice for some hint of suspicion or distrust. He wasn't sure if he didn't find it, or he didn't *want* to find it. "N-nothing. Honest."

As recently as a year ago, such a response would have earned him a dry, mocking retort. *You've never been honest a day in your life.* Or *What do* you *know about honesty?* This time Guthrie just looked at him, then walked to the door to gaze out. In a voice that he probably used with Elly and Emma, he asked, "If it's nothing, then why can't you tell me?"

Swallowing hard again, Ethan laid Elly's note aside and stood up, then wiped his hands on his jeans to dry his palms. "It's no big deal. I—I was doing some work for—for someone."

Guthrie turned to give him a surprised look. "Work? You mean, like a real job?"

He was completely justified in being surprised, Ethan admitted. Still, it hurt. "I've held a few real jobs," he said quietly. "I worked at the same place from the time I left here last summer until I came back. I didn't get into trouble, didn't get arrested—just worked, paid my bills and saved what I could." Just like you, he wanted to add, but he didn't. The last thing Guthrie deserved was to be compared as equals with *him*.

Guthrie looked as if there were about a dozen questions he wanted to ask. Instead, he simply said, "That's good." He opened the door, then turned back. "By the way, Elly's going to ask if you figured out her message. Do me a favor and lie about it. After all—"

"That's one of the few things I do well."

His brother stiffened, then relaxed. "I was going to say you came close, and it'll give her a kick. We'll see you when you're ready."

For a time after he left, Ethan merely stood there. Guthrie had passed up more than one chance to point out Ethan's shortcomings. Ethan couldn't remember him ever having done that before, not since they were kids. Maybe there was hope for them yet.

But even gaining some measure of acceptance from Guthrie wasn't going to help him with the rest of the town, or with Grace.

Half encouraged, half discouraged, he showered, then dressed in clean clothes. He knocked at Guthrie's door two minutes past the appointed time and received a relatively warm greeting from Elly and Emma as soon as he'd hung up his jacket.

"Hey, Uncle Ethan, did you unnerstand my message?" Elly asked, grabbing his hand to pull him down the hall.

"Of course I did. You're a good artist."

"And clever. My teacher says so. But Emma doesn't think I'm clever, so *there!*" She stuck her tongue out at her sister, then dragged Ethan into the formal dining room. "You sit here beside me, Uncle Ethan, 'cause Emma usually gets me in trouble."

Emma circled to the chair on the opposite side and gripped its back with both hands as she fixed a suspicious look on him. "Are you sure you figured it out, or did Daddy help you?"

Elly slapped her palm to her forehead. "He *said* he got it, Em. Boy! What was there to need help with, anyway?"

"Your chicken that didn't look like a chicken. Your cow that didn't look like a cow. Your silly people that were nothin' but lines and circles and squiggly hair."

"He's here, isn't he? And it's six-thirty, isn't it? And he's come to eat, hasn't he? You're just jealous 'cause I'm cleverer than you."

"Elly!" Olivia called from the kitchen. "Come wash your hands."

She'd started to climb onto her chair but huffed heartily and headed for the kitchen. "Why only me? Why doesn't Emma have to wash her hands? She gets dirty, too."

Ethan turned back from listening to Elly to find Emma watching him. "I already washed my hands," she announced.

He smiled awkwardly and nodded.

"Elly's not so clever. She's mostly just loud. And I draw better 'n her. And I'm *not* jealous."

"No, of course not," he murmured, not knowing what else to say. He didn't believe he'd ever faced a female besides his mother when he hadn't known what to say. Elly was easy. A person didn't have to talk to Elly, just react.

But Emma was so quiet, so watchful. He felt dim-witted and tongue-tied with her.

That was how he would feel with his own daughter if he didn't stick around so he could know her from the start. He could all too easily imagine painful visits where she watched with suspicion while he fumbled for something to talk to her about.

He didn't want that with his daughter, or his niece, either. A man should know the important people in his life, should be able to carry on a conversation with them. If he didn't, he wasn't much of a man.

He pulled out the chair Elly had assigned him and sat down. "What kind of pictures do you like to draw, Emma?"

Never taking her eyes off him, she slid into her own seat. "I draw horses. I have a horse all my own. He's a pinto named Angel. When you lived here, did you have a horse?"

He nodded. "I had a pinto, too, named Ranger. Later, when I got too big for him, I had a paint."

"Uncle Easy raises the best paints in the state. He and Aunt Shay live down the road that way." Without looking, she pointed in what Ethan would bet was the exact direction of the Rafferty ranch. "Do you know them?"

Ethan nodded. He'd spent more than half his life jealous of Easy's relationship with Guthrie. They'd shared a friendship stronger than any Ethan had ever known, but when it ended, it had ended hard. Of all the people who'd disappeared from Guthrie's life in those few years so long ago—Easy, Shay, Nadine and Ethan himself—there was no doubt it was Easy he'd missed most. Ethan couldn't even find it in him to envy that Easy and Guthrie were friends again.

"Uncle Easy's not our real uncle," Emma said. "A real uncle has to be Daddy's brother, and Uncle Easy's not."

"No, but he's as good as."

"As good as what?"

"It's a saying you use when something's almost true. Easy's as good as your dad's brother."

"Mama says Daddy loves him better 'n a brother."

Ethan's smile was thin. "I always thought so, too."

Fortunately, he was saved from any further conversation on the subject when Elly returned, followed closely by Guthrie and Olivia. He got to his feet, took the serving platter Olivia carried and set it on the table, then waited until she was seated on Elly's right. Guthrie moved the last setting from the other end of the table to sit across from Ethan and next to Emma.

Ethan didn't miss Emma's satisfied smile as Guthrie sat down. He wondered what it would be like to be on the receiving end of smiles like that. To be able to make a little girl happy by doing nothing more than sitting beside her. To be part of a family, with family routines and rituals.

He wanted to find out...and was afraid to know. Afraid of being a lousy father. Of not fitting in. Of disappointing and letting down. Of earning fear instead of adoration, scorn instead of love.

He was afraid of finding out that life could be as perfect as it was for Guthrie and Olivia, and yet still not be able to satisfy him. Still not be enough to shake the James curse.

The meal had just ended when a knock sounded at the door. Elly was about to jump from her chair when Olivia restrained her with one hand. "Remember the rules—you don't answer the door at night."

"But, Mom, this is Heartbreak, not Atlanta. We know *everybody*."

"Don't argue with your mother," Olivia said gently but firmly as Guthrie left the table.

A moment later he returned, his expression grim. "It's Reese Barnett. He wants to talk to you, Ethan."

Ethan's gaze skimmed around the room. Emma looked disinterested, Olivia concerned. Elly's eyes were opened wide, and so was her mouth. "Is Sheriff Barnett gonna arrest you, Uncle Ethan?"

"Of course not," Olivia answered before Ethan could even think about it. "Why would he do that?"

"Because Uncle Ethan's an outlaw." Immediately she darted a look at Guthrie. "Miss Mary said so."

"I'm going to have a talk with Miss Mary," Olivia said pleasantly as she stacked her dinner plate on top of Elly's. "Take those to the kitchen for me, sweetie, then come back for the rest. Emma, why don't you help me with the serving dishes?"

Ethan slid his chair back, the legs scraping across the floor, then turned toward the door. He caught only a glimpse of the grim set of Guthrie's features, but that was enough.

Barnett was waiting just inside the front door. He'd changed clothes since this morning, but the absence of the uniform, the handcuffs and the gun didn't make him appear any friendlier.

Ethan stopped in front of him and shoved his hands into his hip pockets. "You wanted to see me?"

Barnett's gaze flickered past him, then back. "Is there someplace private we can talk?"

If he were feeling accommodating, he would invite him to the cabin. He wasn't. "Outside." He waited for Barnett's agreeing nod, then took his jacket from the coat tree and led the way onto the front porch.

The night was quiet, the air still. Not even a whisper of a breeze disturbed the trees. Ethan walked to the top step, then turned and leaned against the railing. Barnett chose his own section of railing about halfway between him and the door.

"I saw Grace Prescott today. She told me you were doing some work for her."

Ethan's stomach knotted. "Yeah." He forced the word out. "What of it?"

"Why?"

Because it was the least he could do. Because he owed her for all the problems he'd helped cause her. Because he wanted her to think he was a better man than everyone else knew he was. Because he wanted her to make a place in her family for him, if he could prove to them both that he deserved it. Because he wanted to spend time with her.

He had a dozen reasons—and only one he could give the sheriff. Only one that wouldn't give their secret away, and he couldn't give that away. Just this morning he'd told her he would support whatever lies she wanted to tell, for her sake as well as the baby's.

"I needed work," he said flatly, hating the lie with a passion, "and she had work that needed doing."

"And that's the only reason?"

Ethan's jaw tightened. "What other reason could there be?"

"It occurred to me today that you were back last summer. What was it? Six months ago?"

"Something like that."

"Actually, it was seven months, wasn't it? Funny. That's how far along Grace is. Seven months. That means you were in town about when it happened."

Knotting his fingers tightly around the rail cap, Ethan glanced the sheriff's way. "Are you suggesting that I might be the father of Grace's baby?"

"I'm asking, because the timing seems mighty coincidental."

"Don't you think, Sheriff, that if I'd gotten Grace Prescott pregnant, Heartbreak is the *last* place I'd come to?

Accepting responsibility doesn't come high on my rules to live by. Ask anyone. They'll tell you."

In the dim light Barnett didn't look completely convinced. "Do you know who the father is?"

"Haven't a clue. I was only here for one evening. I left early the next morning."

"So she really did hire you to do some painting."

"That, and some heavy lifting."

After a long, still moment, the floorboards creaked as Barnett moved to the top of the steps. "Then let me give you a bit of advice. Don't lie to her. Don't cheat her. Don't take advantage of her in any way, or you'll answer to me. Do the work she hired you for, take the money she owes you, and get the hell away from her. Don't mess with her, Ethan, or you'll be sorry. I promise you that."

Barnett descended the steps, and Ethan turned to watch him go. Long after his truck was out of sight, his warning still hung in the air. So did Ethan's lies. He hadn't come right out and said, No, that's not my baby, but he'd sure as hell given that impression. No matter how he accomplished it, a lie was a lie, and this one stung. He'd denied any connection to his own child, and he felt like a bastard for it.

Behind him, the door opened, followed by the squeak of the screen door. Guthrie come to make sure Barnett hadn't slapped handcuffs on him?

It was Olivia, with a quilt wrapped around her in place of a coat. She came to stand beside him, gazing out in the same direction he was. After a moment, she quietly asked, "What are we looking at?"

He glanced at her and smiled. "Just making sure the law's gone before this outlaw sneaks over to the cabin."

She turned to lean against the rail. "Everything okay?"

"About as good as can be expected."

"How's Grace?"

"She's having trouble reconciling her desire to protect her baby and herself with her need to not hurt anyone's feelings."

Olivia tsked. "That nasty reputation of yours is getting in the way, isn't it?"

"Yes, ma'am. My mama used to tell me to be careful about what I did, because harm done to a good name was awfully hard to undo. Of course, my name wasn't good to start with, but I did my best to make it worse."

"But that harm *can* eventually be undone, if you're willing to work at it. If you're patient. If you stick around and don't let them scare you away."

"I'd like to be able to swear on my life that I'm going to stay, Olivia, but…I don't know. In ten years I've never been in one place longer than seven months. I don't know if I'll still be here next month. I don't even know if I'll stick it out for another week. I don't have any experience at that."

"You can learn. You can change anything if you have a good reason—and I'd say you have the two best reasons in the world." She rearranged her quilt so her fingers were tucked inside the fabric. "When I first brought the girls here, I wanted more than anything in the world to go back to Atlanta. I promised Emma we would return the very instant I got enough money together. Even after I fell in love with Guthrie, I simply couldn't imagine myself staying here in Heartbreak. I was a Southerner, and I was determined to go back to where I belonged." Her voice took on a note of wonder. "And Guthrie was willing to go with me. He was willing to sell the ranch, move to Atlanta and get a regular job, just so he could be with us. Can you imagine it?"

Ethan shook his head. Guthrie was a born rancher if ever there was one. He'd never lived anywhere but Heartbreak, rarely traveled anywhere outside the state. He loved this land and this life more than anything in the world...except Olivia and her girls.

"You've done a lot of traveling. You stay in a place until you get tired or bored, and then you move on. Maybe it's been fun, but you've cheated yourself, Ethan. You've never stayed anywhere long enough to get involved, fall in love, settle down, make friends, make a home. You don't have any roots, and no matter how footloose and fancy-free a person is, he always needs roots." She paused before quietly adding, "Now you've got a woman who needs you and a baby who's going to love you, if you stay long enough to give them the chance. You've got those roots started. You just have to stay and nurture them."

"Maybe Grace needs someone...but she's pretty convinced it's not me. She doesn't want anyone to know that I'm the baby's father. She thinks a connection to me is more than any child should have to bear."

"Do you want to prove her wrong?"

He wanted to be responsible. Respectable. A better father than his own father had been. He wanted a family of his own, wanted someone who cared about, understood and depended on him. He wanted, just once in his life, to do something he could be proud of, to be someone Guthrie could be proud of.

"Yes," he said quietly. "I do."

Olivia's smile came quickly and was light and teasing. "Then keep those last two words in mind. And keep trying. Don't get discouraged. Don't give in when it gets to be too much and take off again. Make a commitment, if not to Grace, then to your baby, and do everything in your power to honor it."

He scoffed to disguise the bleakness he felt. "Anyone who knows me will tell you that I have no honor."

Olivia wriggled one hand free and laid it against his cheek. "I'm beginning to think that nobody really knows you. You only let them see what they want to see. You keep everything else locked up deep inside you. Let Grace see. Let her know you.''

He didn't tell her that he'd already been more honest with Grace than anyone else, that he'd told her things he'd never told anyone else. ''What if I do, and she's still ashamed?''

''Then she's not the woman I thought she was.''

''Maybe I'm not the man you think I am.''

She smiled confidently. ''You're a good man, Ethan. I have no doubt about that.''

You're a good man. No one had ever said that to him. That Olivia, whose life he'd helped turn upside down, could say it as if she believed it meant more to him than he could put into words. So he didn't try. He simply wrapped his arms around her in a tight embrace.

When he released her, he murmured, ''Guthrie's a lucky man.''

She laughed. ''Oh, darlin', I tell him so every day. Now, you get things worked out with Grace, so she can tell you the same thing.''

''I'll do my best.''

But could his best ever be good enough?

Chapter 7

Closing time arrived not a minute too soon on Tuesday. Grace had spent most of the afternoon fighting the overwhelming need for a nap with few customers to help her stay awake. She was counting on the walk home to revitalize her so she could work once again on the piles of stuff in the guest room. If she didn't, she thought as she flipped the Open sign to Closed, then she would just be lazy and watch TV, because Ethan had been right Sunday. She was smart enough to realize that even God had rested.

It wasn't until she'd locked up and stepped away from the building that she noticed Ethan's truck at the curb, the motor idling. Her first thought was that she would rather walk home. Her second was that she was awfully tired, and it'd been a long day, and she had spent too much of it wondering where he was and what he was doing and when he would return to finish his work at the house. She hadn't seen him since Sunday evening and, frankly, she'd missed him. She shouldn't, of course, not if she had good sense, but what could she say?

Crossing the sidewalk, she opened the door and gave him a level look. "I don't suppose you're waiting here to offer me a ride home."

"Only if you don't tell your sheriff friend. I think he plans to rearrange my face if he catches me hanging around you."

"I'm good at keeping secrets," she said as she eased onto the seat.

Immediately his expression shifted from amused to somber. "Yeah, I understand that." As soon as she was settled, he pulled away from the curb. "Have a busy day?"

"No, just a long one." Striving for a casual tone, as if she were only asking to be polite and not because she cared, she asked, "What about you?"

"I went to Tulsa to pick up some parts for Guthrie."

"I've never been to Tulsa. Sometime I'm going to go," she remarked wistfully. Feeling his incredulous gaze on her, she flushed and darted a look at him. "I know it probably sounds stupid to you, but... My father saw no reason why my mother and I couldn't find everything we possibly needed right here. I've never been anywhere but Heartbreak, except for that one trip to Buffalo Plains." The county seat was twenty miles north of town, wasn't much more substantial than Heartbreak and would always hold a place in her heart, because that was where she'd met Ethan, where her daughter had been conceived. But it wasn't Tulsa.

"Let's go Sunday," he suggested. "We'll spend the day."

"And do what?"

"Everything. Go shopping. Catch a movie. Have dinner in a restaurant. Look at baby things."

"Really? You don't mind?"

"If I minded, Grace, I wouldn't offer."

Slowly she smiled. "Thank you. I'd like that."

"Then it's a date."

A date, she repeated silently to herself. She'd never had one of those before, either. Of course, this wouldn't be a *real* date, but dinner and a movie, regardless of what came before or after, regardless of the reason behind it, was about as datelike as she could imagine. It would do.

He turned into her driveway and parked beside her Bug. Before shutting off the engine, he turned to face her, but his gaze didn't quite reach her face. "After I picked up Guthrie's stuff today, I did a little shopping of my own. I, uh, bought some things for the baby, if it's okay with you. It's not new stuff, but it's—it's well made, and I didn't know if you'd rather have new, but...I can always return it or—or something."

Grace was touched. Other than the clothing the Ladies Auxiliary had gathered to replace what her father had burned, no one had ever given her a gift before, and his hesitancy made this extra special. It was nice to know that she wasn't the only one stricken by uncertainty, that someone as handsome and charming as Ethan could find words hard to come by, too.

She glanced at the back of the truck, where a tarp made a large hump, then at him. "Can I see it?"

"Go on inside. I'll get it."

She was halfway out of the truck by the time he came around to help her. She had turned on the porch light and the heater and was taking off her coat when he came through the door with two pieces of wood that he braced against the wall.

A headboard and a footboard for a crib, made from solid oak that gleamed under the hall light. She moved forward to rub one hand over the wood, cold enough to form a sheen of condensation in the warmer temperatures of the house. The pieces were solid, intricately carved, old and elegant.

"Ethan, it's beautiful." Her throat was tight, her voice husky. She was about to cry, because her very first gift ever was also the very best gift ever. She'd been prepared to look for a cheap, hand-me-down crib at garage sales or in one of Buffalo Plains's antique-junk stores because she'd known she couldn't afford anything better. Now she wouldn't have to, because she wouldn't be able to find anything better.

"You don't mind that it's old?"

"It's old and beautiful. Think of all the babies who have probably slept in it over the years—all the sweet dreams and peace and love it's witnessed." She smiled at him. "No, I don't mind at all that it's old. Thank you."

"I'll get the rest of it," he said with obvious relief.

She eased down onto a step and watched as he made several more trips, bringing side rails, their spindles delicately curved, and the metal frame that supported the mattress, as well as the mattress, brand new and still in its plastic wrapping.

He made one last trip, coming through the door backward, pushed the door shut, then turned and set a cradle on the floor between them. It was old, too, the workmanship not as expert, the wood not as fine. It looked like something a loving father or grandfather might put together in a garage workshop, and she adored it.

"Oh, Ethan." She awkwardly slipped to her knees to touch it, setting it rocking, then stopping it gently.

"I thought you could use it downstairs for naps and—and things, or maybe at the store if you don't need it here."

"Of course I need it. It's perfect." When she started to get to her feet, he quickly moved to help her. Finding herself closer to him than she'd been in seven months, she impulsively rose onto her toes and pressed a hesitant, chaste kiss to his cheek. "Thank you, Ethan."

They stood there a moment, Ethan looking as awkward

and unsure as she felt. Finally he made a move toward the door. "I didn't bring my work clothes, so I—I guess I'd better head home."

"Would you like to stay for dinner?" The instant she blurted out the invitation, she wanted to call it back. Wasn't it enough that he'd given her a ride home, a beautiful crib and an adorable cradle? Did she have to have his time, too? He had a life of his own that didn't include her, one that had taken his Sunday evening, all of Monday and most of that day. He probably hadn't even remembered she existed except when the baby was on his mind.

But after a moment, he smiled, and it was almost a normal smile. "Sure. I'd like that. Can I help you with anything?"

She forced herself to smile, too. "I thought your talents in the kitchen extended only to egg-and-bacon sandwiches. My midwife doesn't let me have eggs or bacon."

"I may not cook much, but I follow directions pretty well."

"All right." She led the way down the hall, giving the crib headboard a furtive pat as she passed.

She assembled the makings for meat loaf, mashed potatoes and salad on the counter, and they went to work. Ethan followed directions to the letter, chopping and peeling as efficiently as she ever had. He even volunteered for the messy job of mixing and forming the meat loaf while she sat at the table, her feet propped on the other chair.

"Have you picked out names yet?" he asked idly as he shaped two small loaves on the rack of her broiler pan.

"I can't decide. I want something pretty, classic, not at all trendy, a name that will suit her as well at six and sixteen as it does at sixty."

"Something like Grace."

She wrinkled her nose and made her glasses slip. "Grace

is *my* kind of name, not at all what I'd choose for my daughter."

After washing up, he placed the pan in the oven, set the timer, then faced her. "Grace is pretty and classic, and it suits you very well."

"It's plain, drab and old ladyish." And it suited her very well, she admitted, the corners of her mouth turning down.

He lifted her feet and sat down on the other chair. When she would have lowered her feet to the floor, he held them on his lap and began matter-of-factly unlacing her left shoe. "Plain and drab. Is that what you see when you look at yourself?"

"That's what everyone sees when they look at me."

He shook his head.

"Please don't tell me you don't think I'm plain. If you do, I'll believe you need these glasses worse than I do." She'd intended the words to be playful, teasing. She was embarrassed to find her voice a bit quavery.

He pulled one shoe loose and dropped it to the floor, then turned his attention to the other. "You're not plain, Grace. You just dress and act like it."

"I dress plain, act plain and look plain. Gee, where did I get the idea that I *am* plain?" she asked sarcastically.

He dropped the other shoe on the floor, then claimed one socked foot in both hands and rubbed. She gave a start, thinking for an instant that she should stop him; what he was doing was too intimate. Then logic stepped in, reminding her that they'd been far more intimate than this when they were perfect strangers. They were fully dressed, sitting at the kitchen table, and it felt so incredibly good. What could it hurt to let him continue?

"What do you want?" he asked, his fingers working magic on her tired foot. "To be some great natural beauty?"

"Yes. That would be nice."

"And how do you define that?"

"Shay Rafferty. Your sister-in-law Olivia."

He shrugged. "They're pretty enough. They're not beautiful."

"I bet Easy and Guthrie would disagree with you."

"They're allowed to do that. And I'm allowed to disagree with you. Ask me what I see when I look at you."

"No."

"Ask me," he repeated. When she stubbornly shook her head, he gentled his touch on her foot until it was no more than a tickle that made her squirm. "Coward. I'll tell you, anyway."

Before going on, he sobered. "I see skin as creamy and smooth as I imagine the finest china must be. Good cheekbones, delicate features, great eyes behind those glasses." His mouth slowly curved up into a smile. "Nice blush. You have a mouth made for kissing and smiling that doesn't do enough of either and a jaw that really ought to be shaped more stubbornly to be in keeping with your personality.

"I see a woman who gave me one of the best nights of my life, a woman with the potential to change the entire rest of my life. A woman who is stronger and braver than I've ever had to be. A woman with an incredible capacity for giving, for loving and, I hope, for trusting." His voice softened. "I see the best mother any child of mine could ever be lucky enough to have."

For a long time after he fell silent, Grace stared at him. He was a charmer, she reminded herself. A sweet talker who'd always found it much too easy to talk his way into and out of any situation. He'd easily talked her into his bed, and could just as easily talk his way right into her heart. Heavens, hadn't he made a start before that pretty speech?

He was a liar, a thief, a con artist. He manipulated people to his own advantage, played games with their feelings and their lives. And he was a drifter, liable to pack up in the middle of the night and disappear down the road.

And knowing all those things did nothing to diminish the warmth and wonder that had seeped through her. It couldn't steal her pleasure in his words. Maybe they were lies, she admitted, but even so, they were sweet lies, and she wanted, needed, to believe them.

She gave a soft, satisfied sigh, then said, "You are good."

He concentrated for a time on the tightness in her right heel, rubbing, twisting, then quietly said, "That wasn't a line, Grace. It was the honest truth. Believe it or not, I do recognize the difference."

"So do I." And to some extent, she believed she did. At the bar last summer, he'd told her she was beautiful, had complimented her in flowery, effusive, insincere tones. She recognized the difference between those compliments and these. She *felt* the difference.

Abruptly, he lowered her feet to the floor. "Let's go into the living room. You'll be more comfortable."

Once they were settled again down the hall, he returned to their earlier subject. "Do you have any names at all in mind?"

"Just one. If it's a boy, I—I might call him Seth." She watched from beneath her lashes to see if he attached any particular significance to the name. He didn't.

"Seth." He said it without inflection, no sign of like or dislike. "You're partial to that name, huh?"

"I like it. It's a nice, strong name, neither trendy nor too unique. A Seth could be anyone, could do anything." And it had meaning to her, if no one else. Back in the early hoping-for-a-white-knight days of her pregnancy, she'd gone to the trouble of finding out Ethan's full name—not hard to do, since the library had issues of the Buffalo Plains newspaper dating back over seventy years. Each May the graduating senior class received their own insert, with photographs and full names. She'd looked up her own—plain, drab Grace Lynn Prescott—before finding Ethan's two years earlier. Looking much the same as he did today—though younger, cockier, more brash—Stuart Ethan James had smiled up at her in glorious black and white.

It wasn't a name to love, not one that rolled off the tongue. But by combining his first and middle names, she'd found a name she could love, and no one would ever guess how she'd chosen it.

"What are your favorite girls' names?"

"Elizabeth. Rachel. Sarah. Anne."

The last one made him smile. "Annie. Annie Grace."

"Annie's nice," she agreed. "But not Annie Grace."

"I like it."

"And you say *my* jaw should be stubborn," she muttered. "What other names do you like?"

He shrugged. "I never gave it any thought. I never intended to have kids. I was always really careful about that, I thought. I realize now that I was just lucky."

The all-over pleasure she'd been feeling began to shrink like a balloon with a tiny leak. "Until your luck ran out with me."

"That's not what I meant, Grace."

"You said you were lucky to never get a woman pregnant. Now I'm pregnant. Your luck ran out. That's *all* you could have meant." Scooting and sliding to the edge of the cushion, she struggled to her feet, then went to the door. "I think you should go now."

He got up so agilely, so easily, coming to block the doorway so she couldn't leave the room. "Damn it, Grace, listen to me, would you?" When she neither spoke nor tried to push past him, he lowered his voice. "It's true. I never wanted to be a father. My old man was so bad at it, and I figured I wouldn't be any better. I never wanted to do to a kid what he did to me, to make some kid feel the way he made me feel. So I *always* used a condom. I did with you. And you got pregnant, anyway. Maybe it was a mistake. Maybe it was just bad workmanship. But maybe…it was meant to happen. Maybe it was fate's way, or God's or whatever's, of giving us both what we wanted.''

She wanted to ignore him, to remain unswayed by his words, but couldn't, and so she deliberately made her tone grudging. ''And what would that be?''

''A family. A reason for being here. Someone to love who will love us back.'' He dragged his fingers through his hair. ''Since I left here last summer, I've been trying to get my life straightened out. It hasn't been easy, but I kept trying because…I wanted to be someone a person could be proud of. I thought I was doing it for Guthrie. He was the only family I had. But maybe, without knowing it, I was doing it for you, and our baby. Maybe I was working at becoming a better person so you wouldn't be ashamed. So *she* wouldn't be ashamed.''

She wanted to deny that she was ashamed of him. She liked him, and she liked spending time with him. But the simple fact was that she wanted to spend time with him in private. She didn't want to walk down the street with him, didn't want to sit down across from him at the Heartbreak Café in full view of all her friends and neighbors. She didn't want to admit to those friends and neighbors that he was the father of her baby.

And that, no matter how she looked at it, translated to being ashamed.

''You put a lot of burdens on a baby not even born yet,'' she said quietly. ''She's supposed to make us both happy, turn us into a family, give us both reasons for becoming the best people we can be…. What if her being here is simply a mistake? What if I'm pregnant for no reason other than a defective condom, and this baby was never meant to save either of us?''

He shook his head. ''I'm a gambler. I have to believe in fate, luck and God.''

''But you don't believe in yourself.'' And the sad truth was, *she* didn't believe in him, either. She wasn't sure whether he felt an obligation to her baby—Annie, she thought with a surge of maternal warmth—or if he was simply trying to do the right thing. Having no experience with either honoring obligations or doing the right thing, he was more likely to give up and disappear again than stick it out through the good and the bad.

And then where would she be? Alone except for their daughter. Lonely. And quite possibly brokenhearted.

Ethan wished he could argue with her, but he couldn't without lying. Hell, he couldn't even look at her without seeing the truth—that she had no more faith in him than he did in himself. ''What would it take to make you trust me?''

Grace shrugged. ''I don't know. Time, I guess.''

It was a perfectly reasonable answer. Before she put her faith in a man who'd never stayed in one place longer than seven months, who'd never gone longer than that without getting into trouble, who'd never committed to anything or anyone for more than twenty-eight lousy weeks, she wanted him to prove he could stay, out of trouble and committed, for longer than that.

But how long would he have to stay before she trusted him? Twenty-nine weeks? Eight months? Fourteen? Would any amount of time ever be long enough, or would she forever be watching and waiting for the day when he took off again?

And what exactly did she want him to commit to? Keeping her secret? Hiding his relationship to her daughter? Being a part of their lives only in the out-of-sight confines of this house while pretending to be strangers in public? That seemed a little one-sided.

But he could live with one-sided, at least for a while. Sooner or later she would have to trust him, would have to publicly acknowledge him as the baby's father. He *would* be here to see that happen.

He hoped.

"Okay," he said, forcing a grin. "I'll give you all the time in the world."

"And what do you want in return?"

"A chance, Grace. Just a chance."

She looked as if that was too much to ask for, too much to give. But after a moment, she smiled a tight, stressed little smile. "All right."

In the kitchen, the timer beeped. She used it as an excuse to step around him, then leave him alone to deal with the emotion—damn near elation—her answer had caused. It wasn't much, he sternly reminded himself. Just a chance. One chance. Guthrie had given him a hundred, his mother a thousand more, and he'd screwed up every single one of them. Odds were better than even that he'd screw up this one, too, and then he'd be in pretty sorry shape, because this wasn't just another chance.

It was his last chance.

That thought chased away the last of his elation.

Turning away from the door, he found himself facing the crib, filling half the hallway. "I'm going to move the crib into the dining room," he called, "unless you want it some-place else."

"That'll be fine."

He carried the pieces into the next room down the hall, a room as old-fashioned and drab as the rest of the house. The furniture was good—a matching table, chairs and side-board of oak—but between its size and the heavy drapes that blocked every ray of light at the windows, the room appeared cramped and overwhelmed even though, in reality, it wasn't. It was easy to imagine the countless unpleasant meals the Prescotts had shared in this room, with Grace hoping to go unnoticed in her chair, her mother dreaming of escape at her place, and her father ruling with an iron fist from the head of the table. Old Jed seemed the sort who wouldn't tolerate idle conversation at the dinner table. Life with him must have been unbearably oppressive for Grace.

Could anyone blame her for wanting an easier life now for herself and her baby? For not wanting to take on a man with a reputation every bit as widely known and unaccepted as her father's? For requiring time and proof that he deserved his place in their lives?

Ethan certainly didn't. Placing blame squarely where it belonged was a lesson he'd learned early in life, and where it usually belonged was on him. This situation was no exception.

Once he'd moved all the baby furniture, he joined Grace in the kitchen. She'd moved the meat loaves onto a serving plate, taken the salad from the refrigerator and was mashing potatoes with cream and real butter. Already more familiar with her kitchen than any other he'd been in, he set the table, then filled two glasses with milk. While he had the refrigerator open, he studied the bottles secured in the door racks. "What's your favorite salad dressing? We have ranch and...ranch."

"Hmm. I think I'll have ranch."

He took both bottles from the shelf. "Your refrigerator's getting a bit bare. Want to go shopping this evening?" When a cautious look crossed her face, he had to struggle to hide the tightening of his jaw. "I'd wait outside. No one would have to know I was with you."

"That's usually the only time I take the Bug anywhere," she said, almost succeeding in her attempt to sound casual. "It keeps the battery charged. But thanks, anyway."

Yeah. Thanks for nothing.

Neither of them broke the silence again until they were halfway through the meal. Grace heavily peppered her mashed potatoes, then scooped a forkful but didn't lift it from her plate. "Where have you lived all these years?"

Assuming that she was merely making conversation, he shrugged. "Everywhere. Mostly the South and the Southwest. Mostly small towns, but with the occasional city thrown in."

"What did you like most about being someplace different all the time?"

"None of the towns were Heartbreak."

"What did you like least about it?" She watched as his expression shifted—he couldn't help it, try as he might—then softly answered for him. "None of the towns were Heartbreak?"

He shrugged again. "I used to think I was running away from home, from Mom and Guthrie, from being Gordon James's kid. And I wasn't very good at it, because no matter how far I ran, all that stayed with me. It took me a long time to realize that I was running away from *me,* from who I was, who I wanted to be, who I thought I could never be."

After a brief silence, she continued the questions. "What was your favorite place?"

"New Orleans. Or maybe Miami. New Orleans is a great city, and there's not much finer than winter in Miami."

That made her smile a bit. "Usually Oklahoma winters don't bother me. We always have plenty of mild days to offset the really cold ones, and I can't even remember the last time we had a lot of snow. But sometimes, usually in February when I know spring is coming, but it isn't here yet, I get so tired of cold days and bare trees and yellowed grass. Sometimes I think I'd sell my soul to look out the window and see green, to have bright sunshine and warm breezes and leaves on the trees.''

"You wouldn't have to sell your soul. Just your hardware store."

"And do what?"

"Move south. Go to New Orleans or Miami or Key West. Head for the tropics. Have an adventure."

She laughed and for that instant looked younger, softer, prettier. Incredibly pretty. "I'm not the adventurous type."

"Hey, you let that James boy pick you up in a bar and take you for a wild ride. By anyone's definition, that's adventurous."

"By most people's definition, it was foolish."

His lighter mood began slipping away. "Because of who I am."

"Most people don't know who you are," she reminded him. "It's just that these days it's not safe to go off with a stranger. Things happen."

"Yeah, you might get pregnant."

"Or raped, beaten or murdered."

"But you knew you were safe with me. You never would have left the bar with me if you hadn't."

"True, but—"

"You trusted me."

"I hardly knew you."

"But you trusted me to not do anything more than seduce you. You got naked with me. You shared a bed with me. You turned your back on me and slept beside me. Admit it, Grace," he said with a cocky grin. "For that one night you trusted me."

Her smile was rueful. "So what if I did?"

"It's a start, darlin'." He fiddled with his fork for a moment, then pushed it and the plate away. "When I woke up the next morning and you were gone... All my life I'd been the one to skip out in the middle of the night. I always figured it didn't matter. We'd done what we'd set out to do, so why bother with goodbyes? But I woke up that morning, and I could smell you on the sheets, on my skin, and I could still taste you and feel you, and I was hard as stone with wanting you…and you were gone. The room was still. The sheets were cold. And I felt cheated. Sorry. I thought I would never see you again, and I *really* wanted to see you again.'' His voice dropped to little more than a hoarse whisper. ''I still do.''

He could see that Grace was flustered. She didn't know where to look, what to do with her hands or what to say. She settled on gathering their dishes, pretending to focus her attention on them. ''Bet you never counted on seeing me like this.'' She made a scornful head-to-toe gesture, taking in her swollen belly, then reached for their dishes.

He caught her hand, holding her close to his side. ''You seem to think that being pregnant makes you—''

''Fat? Awkward? Ungainly?''

''Less than attractive. But you're wrong, Grace.'' He ignored her disdainful snort. ''There's something oddly appealing about a pregnant woman. Something…I don't know. Natural. Womanly. Something lovely.''

''Oh, yes,'' she said, her voice equal parts sarcasm and wistful uncertainty. ''I've gained a ton of weight. I waddle like a duck. I can't even get up from the sofa without a lot of effort or help from someone, and forget about getting down on the floor for any reason. Of course I feel incredibly lovely these days.''

''Oh, come on.'' He gave her fingers a gentle squeeze. ''Don't tell me you aren't awed by all the changes taking place in your body. Don't kid me that you don't marvel over the fact every single day that you're carrying a *baby*. Don't tell me that you've ever felt more womanly than you do right now.''

Still holding a plate in her free hand, she gazed down at

him. Behind those damn thick glasses, she looked so serious, so baby-owl intense. "You're right. I am in awe. I like being pregnant. I like knowing that in a few more weeks, I'm going to have a baby. It means the world to me to know that I'll have someone to share my life with, someone to love and nurture and teach. And, frankly, it's a constant reminder that, once upon a time, the handsome, charming, popular jock who dated all the pretty, popular cheerleaders just for one night chose *me*. I like that, too. But you know what the big difference is, Ethan? I *want* this baby. I have from the beginning. I see her as a gift to be thankful for, while you see her as an obligation you have no choice but to accept."

When she tugged her hand free, he let her. She took his plate and turned toward the sink. He picked up the serving dishes and joined her at the counter. "You're not being fair, Grace," he said quietly. "You didn't give me the chance to want her from the beginning. You found out you were pregnant—when? August? September?—and you never made any effort to tell me."

"How could I tell you? I didn't know where you were!"

"But you knew where Guthrie was."

She rinsed the dishes as if she might scrub the pattern right off. "And what was I supposed to do? Go out to his house and tell him that I was pregnant with his irresponsible brother's child? You think he would have even believed me?"

"Of course he would have. He can believe damn near anything about me."

"And what would he have done? In all the years you've been disappearing, he never knew where you were. Everybody said that this time, after what you did to him and Olivia, you probably wouldn't come back, at least not for years."

"Guthrie and Olivia have known where I was since early

December, which is beside the point. The point is, Grace, you never told them about the baby. You never asked them if they had a way to contact me. You didn't *want* me to know. You didn't want me to surprise you and want this baby. You wanted to keep her all to yourself.''

''That's ridiculous.''

''No, it's not.'' He reached past her to take the aluminum foil from the cabinet in front of her, then began wrapping the leftover meat loaf. ''And it's understandable. Because of your background, this baby is even more important to you than it would be under normal circumstances. You want everything to be perfect for her. You would have been better off without your father, and because of *my* background, you thought she would be better off without hers. As an added benefit, you would get all her love for yourself. You wouldn't have to share her with anyone.''

''That's not true,'' she protested, but weakly, because they both knew it was.

''What if Olivia hadn't guessed? You would have raised our daughter completely alone. Just minutes away she would have had an aunt, an uncle and cousins who would have adored her, but you would have denied her that. You know how important the love and support of a family are, but you would have kept them from her.''

''I couldn't tell them,'' Grace murmured stiffly. ''I couldn't tell anyone.''

''Why not?''

She filled the sink with hot, sudsy water, then began washing dishes. His first impulse was the offer to do them for her, but he suspected she needed something to do to make the conversation easier. Instead, he leaned against the counter and watched her.

''When it first became common knowledge that I was pregnant, the question of who the father was became common gossip. Everyone had their ideas. Some people rightly assumed it must be a stranger I met in a bar, since no one local could possibly be interested and, obviously, a sober man wouldn't waste his time with me. Some wondered if the unlucky guy had been the loser in some sort of hazing or bet. Some people even wondered if—if it could be…if it was possible…'' She drew a deep breath and blurted it out. ''Some people wondered if my father was the father.''

Ethan's jaw tightened. ''I'm sorry.''

''Nobody thought for a minute that any normal man could look at me and think, 'Hey, I'd like to have sex with her.' Not plain, shy, mousy little Grace. If I'd told them it was you, they never would have believed me. Even your brother, who can believe damn near anything about you, wouldn't have believed that you'd slept with me.''

''You're wrong, Grace. People think more highly of you than that. As for people who gossip about you where you can overhear, they don't have any opinions worth voicing in the first place.'' Judging by the sad look on her face, his words had done nothing to sway her. He tried again. ''Olivia and Shay had no problem believing that you and I had been together. As for everyone else, if you'd give me half a chance… Oh, hell.''

Closing the distance between them, he slid one arm around her waist, pulled her up snug against him and kissed her full on the mouth. Unlike her earlier kiss, there was nothing hesitant or innocent about his. He coaxed her lips apart, then her teeth, and slid his tongue inside her mouth, and the memories from last summer came flooding back. Of heat, hunger, fevered passion, greed. Her body so soft and pliant beneath his. His husky encouragement. Her desperate pleas. Their incredible connection.

He drew her closer and realized with a jolt that he was aroused. Holding her tighter, he lifted her against him and wished he had the right to take her upstairs and make love to her just one more time. But once more would only make him want a dozen more, and it would do nothing to convince her that, though he had some ambivalence, he wanted to be a father to her baby. He wasn't even sure it would convince her that he wanted *her*. She had so many doubts, so many insecurities. It might take years to convince her that she was a woman worth wanting.

Lucky for him, he thought as he ended the kiss in a half-dozen smaller, sweeter kisses, he had all the time she could need.

In fact, he had a lifetime.

Chapter 8

That kiss stayed with Grace through the rest of the week. It got her through the long hours at the store and kept her warm through the long dark hours of the nights. It made her feel incredulous. Stunned. Even the littlest bit desirable.

Right, her practical nature scoffed. She was seven months' pregnant, twenty-five pounds heavier. If no man had ever found her desirable before she got pregnant, what were the odds any man would now?

But one man had, a tiny voice reminded her. As he'd pointed out, she and Melissa were one and the same. Maybe her hair, makeup and clothing had been different, but it was her he'd danced with, made love with. It was very definitely her he'd kissed.

She was alone in the store on Saturday afternoon while Ethan was at her house. Now that the paint job in her father's room—in her new room—was done, he'd gotten an old friend of his, a cowboy they'd both gone to school with, to help him move some of the years' accumulation of furniture and junk from her house. The junk was going to the landfill outside of town, the furniture to an antique store-flea market in Buffalo Plains.

She had already arranged a trade with the owner for a new bedroom set, a simple Shaker set that was in good shape and was old enough to appeal to her, but not so fine or so antique to make it valuable. On their trip to Tulsa the next day, she planned to splurge on new bedding and to move into her new room that night.

Then Ethan would start the job of converting her childhood room into a nursery for Annie. She could hardly wait to see the finished product.

And then what would she do to keep him coming around?

The arrival of customers saved her from having to consider the question at length. She eased to her feet and went to the counter to greet—oh, wonderful—the Harrises. Not just Olivia who knew her secret, or Guthrie who didn't, but the whole family.

One of the twins skipped right up to the counter and offered a broad grin. "Hey."

"Hello."

"I seen you at church sometimes. I'm Elly Harris, and I've got an almost identical twin sister named Emma. Who're you?"

"I'm Grace Prescott."

"When's your baby due?"

"At the end of March."

"My mom's gonna have a baby brother for us at the end of this month, and we're gonna name him after our daddy's daddy, but we're not gonna call 'im that, on account of Mama says no baby boy should have to answer to Vernon. What're you gonna name yours?"

"Seth, if it's a boy."

"What if it's a girl?"

"Annie." Grace's smile was private and sweet. That was the first time she'd said the name out loud since she'd decided to use it, but already in her heart and mind it was too familiar to consider anything else. Maybe just Annie or maybe, as Ethan had suggested, Annie Grace, but definitely Annie.

"I guess them's pretty good names," Elly announced as her mother and sister joined her.

"Oh, gee, lucky you, you've got Elly Harris's vote of approval. We're still struggling with names around our house." Olivia ruffled her daughter's hair. "You girls go help your daddy find whatever it is he's looking for, will you?"

Grace watched them go, then became aware of Olivia's steady gaze. Her face growing warm, she finally looked at her.

"How's it going?" Olivia asked softly.

"O-okay."

"I realize I should have talked to you before getting in touch with Ethan, but… My first husband wasn't much of a father. He thought if he provided the kids a place to live and food to eat, then he'd lived up to his end of the bargain. But with this pregnancy, I've seen how different things can be—how much a man can want a baby, how important it can be to him. I just…I thought Ethan deserved to know. If he cared, he would come back, and if he didn't…" She shrugged.

"I—I should have tried to tell him myself. I was just afraid."

"Afraid he wouldn't come back? Or afraid he would?"

"Both," Grace said with a regretful smile. "Can you tell me something? When you figured it out…were you surprised?"

"That Ethan had finally gotten a girl pregnant?"

Wishing she hadn't said anything, Grace shook her head.

Unable to find a graceful way out of it, she barreled on. "That he'd gotten *me* pregnant. That he'd even noticed I was alive."

Bless her heart, Olivia looked puzzled. "Why wouldn't he notice you? You're about his age. You're single. You're—" Understanding slowly dawned. "What? You think you're not his type? Not pretty enough, sexy enough, vivacious enough?"

Grace let her awkward shrug be her response.

"I have to admit, I don't know Ethan very well. His relationship with Guthrie hasn't been an easy one, which I think is as much Guthrie's fault as Ethan's. But I believe he's a better man than most people give him credit for. I think family is very important to him. I *know* love and acceptance are very important." Olivia reached across the counter to lay her hand over Grace's. "I also know you and your baby are important to him."

"And how do you know that?"

"He told me so."

Grace searched her face and saw that she was telling the truth. It sent a shivery, pleasing warmth through her. It gave her hope and quieted a few of her doubts, at least temporarily.

"Truthfully, Grace, the only surprise when I first thought Ethan might be the father was that *he* wasn't *your* type. You're so quiet and serious, and he's such a…"

"Charmer. And a scoundrel," Grace supplied.

Olivia's smile beamed. "Yes. But every scoundrel needs a little steadiness in his life, and every woman, quiet and serious or not, needs a charmer in her life. I think each of you could be exactly what the other needs."

"Provided he stays."

Grace's flat remark dimmed the light in Olivia's eyes. "Yes," she agreed gravely. "Provided he stays. He's trying. He really is. But it might not hurt for you to give him a little incentive.''

''What kind of incentive?''

Olivia laughed again, then patted Grace's stomach. The easy, casual touch was strangely foreign, and curiously comforting. ''You're not *that* far along yet. You can think of something.''

Grace remembered Tuesday night's kiss, with its sweet heat, the need that had curled around her stomach and made her legs weak, the solid feel of his arousal pressing against her. She had instantly recalled every incredible sensation, every new and amazing emotion he'd taught her last summer, and she'd wanted more than she could put into words to experience it all again.

But last summer neither her heart nor her baby's future had been involved. As far as that went, neither had her modesty, not once he'd undressed her, touched her, made her shudder. But now, the idea of standing naked in front of him in all her seven-months-pregnant glory sent a shudder of a different kind down her spine and a totally different heat into her face.

It made Olivia laugh. ''Oh, Grace…it's easy to see why Ethan's trying so hard to make this work. You are so sweet.'' After a moment, she looked over her shoulder to make sure her husband and the kids were nowhere around, then turned back. ''It would be easier if he didn't have to be secretive. He says you're ashamed of him.''

Grace's cheeks flamed hotter. ''He has a reputation…''

''You're right. He does. You have one, too, and Guthrie and me and everyone else in the county. And you know what a reputation is? It's just talk.''

''But everyone admires and respects Guthrie. His reputation is good. Ethan's isn't. And maybe it is just talk, but a lot of the talk about Ethan is true.''

''Maybe, at one time. But people change, Grace. Did you

ever dream a year ago that this year your life would be like
this? That you would have the freedom to do what you
want? To have friends, go to church, run this store and your
own life? That you would have a baby with Ethan James,
itinerant scoundrel?''

"Of course not," Grace murmured. A year ago, she
never would have looked at her future because she'd known
it would hold nothing but more of the same. More oppression. More of her father's anger. More of her own quiet
desperation.

"But here you are—and, in part, thanks to Ethan. He's
trying to do the right thing by you and the baby, Grace.
For his sake, for all our sakes, I wish you would consider
doing the right thing by him." She smiled gently. "Between the three of us, we don't have much of an extended
family. I'd love to have a sister-in-law to come to Sunday
dinner and a cousin for my kids to play with."

Did Olivia have any idea, Grace wondered, how much
she wanted those things, too? To have someone to share
birthdays and holidays with, to trade off baby-sitting
chores, to ask for advice and offer support. She couldn't
imagine anything more wonderful—more *familial*—than
Sunday dinners with eight or ten or more gathered around
the table.

And she could have it, not just for herself, but for Annie.
All she had to do was let go of the secret she'd guarded so
long and trust Ethan. Even if he let her down, Olivia and
Guthrie never would. They would always be there for her
and Annie because they were forever sort of people.

Even if Ethan was a temporary sort of man.

Before she could form a response to Olivia's last comment, Guthrie and the twins joined them at the counter. He
greeted her politely, and Emma offered a shy smile as
Grace rung up their purchases.

After Guthrie had pocketed his change and picked up his

bag, Olivia issued an invitation. "We have dinner at home every Sunday after church with Shay and Easy. We'd be happy to have you join us sometime."

Grace didn't miss the curious look Guthrie gave his wife. He was wondering why in the world she was inviting that odd little Prescott girl to dinner and assuming it was charity. Grace was sure of it. "Thanks," she said quietly. "I'll remember that."

When they were gone and silence had settled over the old store once more, she reached for the phone. When her friend answered, she cleared her throat, took a breath for courage and said, "Ginger? I need a favor."

By the time Grace got home from work, Ethan had put in a full day of lifting, carrying and running up and down the stairs, and was feeling it in his bones. But the enormous pile of junk that had grown on the porch over the last week was gone, and the new bedroom furniture was upstairs, set up, arranged and awaiting Grace's approval. He had accomplished a lot, and he felt...proud. Satisfied. Damn near smug.

In spite of the cold, he was resting on the porch, a glass of water in hand, when Grace got home. He'd offered to pick her up, but she'd insisted she needed the exercise. She stopped at the bottom of the steps, facing him. Her cheeks were pink, her eyes watery from the stiff north wind. The coat she wore practically dragged on the ground and was about three sizes too big, but it barely buttoned across her stomach. She looked chilly, young, amazingly cute. "Hi."

"Hey. You've got good timing. Leroy left about ten minutes ago. Everything's ready for your inspection." He hesitated, then went on as if his next words weren't totally out of line, under the circumstances. "After you see what you want changed in the bedroom, why don't we drive over to Buffalo Plains for dinner? I know a couple of places there where we won't run into anyone you know.''

Guilt flashed across her face, and she ducked her chin to hide it. ''I—I can't. I'm sorry.''

He'd convinced himself before he'd asked that it wasn't important. He really wouldn't care if she refused. But he'd lied. It hurt, even though he tried to hide it behind a shrug and a grin. ''No problem. I can pick up a couple of to-go dinners at Shay's place or run by the grocery store—''

''I've already got plans for tonight,'' she blurted out.

Ethan's gut tightened. ''Plans?''

''With—with Ginger. She—she's the one who took me to that bar in Buffalo Plains.''

''I know who she is.'' He remembered her vaguely—young, not particularly pretty but so overwhelmingly confident that it took a while to realize it. Provocative clothes and the body to wear them, great hair, heavy on the makeup, the cologne and the sexuality. He'd spent his share of anonymous nights with women like her all across the country. He'd thought she and Grace seemed an odd pair when he'd watched them walk into the bar together last summer. Now that he'd gotten to know Grace better, he was even more convinced of it. ''I didn't realize you saw much of her.''

''I—I don't. But we're still friends, and I'm supposed to be at her house in—'' she pushed back her sleeve to check her watch ''—fifteen minutes.''

He jumped edgily to his feet. ''Oh, hey, sorry to keep you standing here. I'm leaving now. Have a good time.''

When he passed her, she caught his sleeve with such timidity that he hardly noticed. ''Ethan… What about the bedroom?''

''No big deal. You can see it later tonight or tomorrow or whenever you can find time.'' He gently removed his sleeve from her fingers and started toward the truck.

"*Ethan*... You hadn't said anything about going out to dinner, and this is the only chance I've had to see Ginger in a while, and—and—I'm sorry."

The plaintive tone of her apology stopped him in his tracks. He stared at the frozen ground for a moment, then slowly turned to face her. "Don't be," he said quietly. "You haven't done anything to apologize for. I just thought that, since we'd had dinner together every night since Tuesday, we would...I was disappointed."

She pushed her glasses up on her nose and peered at him. His admission pleased her, if the blush on her cheeks and her shy smile were anything to judge by. "I disappointed my father all the time," she said. "But this is a good kind of disappointment, isn't it?"

He couldn't help but smile at her. "Better for you than for me, sweetheart, since I'm going to be spending my evening all by myself while you and Ginger have all the fun." Returning to her, he pressed a kiss to her forehead, then eased her glasses up another half inch. "Have a good time. I'll see you in the morning around ten, right? We're still on for that?"

She nodded as he headed for his truck. As he backed out of the driveway, she gave a wave, just a flutter of her fingertips. It wasn't much of a gesture, but somehow it created a corresponding flutter in his chest. He tried to remember the last time he'd felt something remotely similar and couldn't, and he wondered what, if anything, that meant.

He didn't have the vaguest idea. Life couldn't be that easy, could it?

Now that he had his evening unexpectedly open, he didn't have a clue what he wanted to do. Sitting home alone at the cabin wouldn't be much fun, with no television or radio. He could probably finagle an invitation to Guthrie's for dinner, but he wasn't really up for that. Leroy had invited him for a drink at the County Seat, a cowboy bar in

Buffalo Plains where some of their old buddies from high school hung out weekends, and most weeknights, too, but even that idea held no appeal.

Truth was, he wanted to spend the evening with Grace, and if he couldn't do that, then it didn't much matter what he did do.

He settled for driving around a while—past the high school where he'd been a frequent guest in detention hall, but had managed to graduate, anyway, the baseball field where he'd been a star pitcher, the park where he'd once gotten arrested for vandalism and public drunkenness. He couldn't remember how many times first his mother, and later Guthrie, had driven twenty miles to Buffalo Plains to get him out of jail. Five? Ten? Probably more.

He *could* remember the look in Guthrie's eyes every time. The disappointment. The sense of failure.

After a time, he returned to Main Street and, on impulse, pulled into a parking space in front of the Heartbreak Café. There were only a few customers inside, and none that he felt a particular need to avoid, so he went in and headed for the farthest booth.

He was halfway there when the swinging door between the dining room and the kitchen opened and Shay Rafferty—neighbor, almost a sister-in-law, pesky-older-sister type—came through and spotted him. "Ethan James! I can't believe you've been home all this time and haven't come to see us!" She smacked his upper arm, the way she'd done when he was a kid, then hugged him tightly.

He was surprised by the warmth of her greeting. "I, uh, wasn't aware that you wanted to see me."

At that, she looked equally surprised. "Why wouldn't I? Just because you were the biggest pest in the whole world when you were a kid—which is exactly what little brothers are supposed to be." She held him at arm's length. "Well, you look good. The scoundrel's life has treated you well. Are you here to stay?''

"I think so."

"Are you keeping busy?"

"Yeah, I am. I heard you and Easy finally got married."

She raised her left hand and wiggled her fingers to show off the gold band there. "Last October. He's incredibly happy."

"And you are…?"

Her smile softened and her features became about ten times more serene, more beautiful. "Blessed," she said simply. "Listen, have a seat and look at the menu. I'll get you a Coke—you do still drink that?—and be right with you."

As she briskly moved away, Ethan sat down and opened the menu. He'd never thought Shay would be happy to see him. She'd barely tolerated him when they were kids. Whatever slack she had cut him had been out of respect for Nadine or love for Guthrie. But now…she seemed truly happy that he was back. Imagine that.

After a few minutes, she brought him a soft drink and sat down on the opposite bench. "I can't get over how good you look. The scrawny little pest has finally turned into a real, full-grown man."

"Life has a way of doing that to you," he said dryly.

"Especially when it's not as kind as it should be. But it has a way of making it all up to you in the end. Look at us. Guthrie's got Magnolia—I mean, Olivia—and the kids. I've got Easy. And you—" She lowered her voice. "You're going to be a daddy. Can you believe it?"

He shook his head. "Logically, I know it's true. I can look at her and understand that in another six weeks or so, she's going to deliver this child that I helped cause—"

"Create," she interrupted, giving his hand a pat. "It sounds less like an accident that way."

Even though it *was* purely an accident, he nodded in agreement and went on. "That I helped create. But realistically, I have no clue what to expect. Guthrie's kids are the only ones I've been around in…hell, since I was a kid myself. I don't know anything about babies, or what they need, or what you do."

"What you do is simple. You love 'em. You're there for 'em."

"When have you ever known me to be there for someone?" he asked scornfully.

"Right now. You found out Grace was pregnant, and you immediately came home."

"And everyone expects me to up and take off again. Including Grace."

"You've proved them wrong before, Ethan. Do it again."

"When did I…?"

"When you came back last summer. When you signed the deed back over to Guthrie and gave Olivia her husband's money. Everyone thought that money was lost forever and that as soon as you got in a bind and needed cash, you'd run the same scam on someone else." She gestured expansively. "When you came back this time, nobody knew why but Olivia and me, but if they had, a lot of people would have bet that you'd never come back."

Ethan knew she was right. They would have gossiped about it, would have laughed that *this* would keep him out of town for good. Why, nothing set a James to running quicker than responsibility. He'd be so afraid of getting stuck with a squalling baby that he'd never set foot in the county again.

Shay smiled smugly. "And they would have been wrong. You would have surprised the hell out of them all when you not only came back, but came back prepared to accept responsibility for your child and its mother. They never would have believed it.''

But even he wasn't sure he believed it. He *wanted* to stay, but he couldn't swear he would.

But he wasn't the one he had to convince. Grace was.

Feeling weary, he glanced down at the menu. ''What's good?''

''All of it. I have a particular fondness for our specials. Today's is roasted chicken with mashed potatoes and gravy.''

''I'll have that.''

Shay looked up, caught the waitress's eye and signaled something that, apparently, translated to one special.

''As I recall, you were the first girl in the history of Heartbreak High School to fail Home Ec because you couldn't cook worth a damn. So how'd you wind up in the restaurant business?''

''The café needed an owner who could work fourteen-hour days, seven days a week, and I needed to feel needed,'' she said airily, then sobered. ''It was right after Easy left me. I had no place to go, nothing to do and no hopes that life would get better. If it hadn't been for this place, I probably would have crawled into a hole and never come out.''

''Is he still on the rodeo circuit?''

''No. He gave it up last spring. He's raising and training paints out at his folks' place. He and I are neighbors with the Harrises once again, so if you're ever in need of a baby-sitter…''

He waited for her to offer her services, an offer she never would have made fifteen years ago, one which seemed perfectly reasonable now.

With a grin and a wink, she finished. ''I can probably tell you where to find Guthrie or Olivia.''

The waitress delivered a plate and silverware to Ethan,

commanded Shay to see the cook in the kitchen, then left again. Shay slid to the edge of the bench, then paused. "When are you going to tell Guthrie the real reason you're back?"

"Whenever Grace says it's all right…and I find the courage." He felt pretty damn sure his brother wouldn't understand how Ethan could have let such a thing happen or why it had taken him so long to find out or why he hadn't already sweet-talked Grace into the church and marriage. Of course, Saint Guthrie had probably never had a one-night stand. No condom would ever dare fail him, and if by chance it did, he would intuitively know before the deed was finished and would have his marriage license and his happily-in-love bride both in hand before the next sundown. He wouldn't have any patience with his careless, luckless brother who couldn't do the same.

"He'll understand…eventually. Sometimes I think it would be easier for the rest of us if he'd ever had one moment of irresponsibility or recklessness himself. But he's always been so *good,* which can make us look bad instead of just normal." She gave a heavy sigh. "But we love him, anyway, don't we?"

While she went to see what the cook wanted, Ethan turned his attention to his dinner. He was thinking about Guthrie and Shay, about the futures that had seemed so certain when they were all younger, and how differently everyone's lives had turned out, when Grace eased into his mind. What was she doing with Ginger this evening? Wasn't there even some small part of her that would have preferred to spend a cold Saturday night at home with him? What did it really matter that she'd chosen to visit with Ginger instead? He'd been in too many relationships where he would have been grateful if the woman had had some other interests, if she'd left him one night a week to do whatever he wanted.

But that wasn't exactly true. He'd been in a lot of *affairs*. He'd never stayed around long enough to call it a relationship. He'd never been involved enough to care where she spent the time when she wasn't with him. He'd never felt that odd little tightness in his chest.

If asked to place his bets, he'd say odds were better than even that he was falling for Grace. In a perfect world—where she would welcome him into her life, where shame and embarrassment and disreputable backgrounds played no part—that would be fine. In his all-too-*im*perfect world, it could be good…or bad. It could mean the difference between living honestly and happily for the next fifty years and spending the rest of his life feeling like the worst failure the James family ever produced.

It could also mean a lifetime of heartache. He'd already had more heartache than any one man should have to bear. He didn't think he could take much more.

He'd risen from the booth and pulled his wallet from his pocket when the bell over the door rang. He would have recognized the man who walked in anywhere, even if Shay hadn't greeted him with the sort of blatantly sensual kiss she reserved for her husband, Easy. He was fifteen years older than the last time Ethan had seen him, and he moved with a lot more care than he had back then. His limp was pronounced, and the scars that marred the right side of his face were eye-catching. He gave up the rodeo last spring, Shay had said. It looked more as if the rodeo had given him up and kicked him, head over heels, right out of the arena.

Shay turned him toward Ethan, and Easy gave him a speculative look. "Ethan."

Ethan closed the distance between them and offered his hand. "Easy."

For a moment, Easy just looked at his hand. As the seconds mounted, so did the heat, creeping up Ethan's neck.

Even with all the ill will he'd inspired, he'd never before encountered anyone who'd refused to shake his hand. Of course, this was the first time in fifteen years that he'd faced Guthrie's best friend.

Slowly Easy stretched out his gloved hand, and Ethan's fingers closed around empty leather. Startled, he stopped himself from snatching his hand away, but he couldn't keep the dismay from flashing across his face.

Easy didn't appear to notice. "I don't shake hands too often these days. Not since I left three fingers in the wreckage of my truck in New Mexico last year."

"I—I'm sorry. I didn't—didn't know."

"If you came home more often, you would have," Easy said dryly. "It's okay. I can get around without my cane now, and I can still ride my horses."

"As long as you can do what's important," Ethan said, feeling awkward and hearing it in his voice.

Easy and Shay exchanged the sort of look that Guthrie and Olivia were always sharing—intimate, eloquent, silently communicating. It made Ethan feel left out, made him wonder if Grace could ever be persuaded to look at him that way. It would be his loss, he knew instinctively, if she couldn't.

"I haven't had any complaints yet," Easy replied with a grin that actually made Shay blush. "Be neighborly. Stop by the house sometime."

"Sure," Ethan replied, hiding his surprise at the invitation. Like Shay, Easy had merely tolerated him when they were growing up. He'd never expected anything more from him.

He tried to pay his tab, but Shay waved his money away. "Consider it a welcome-home dinner. Put your money to better use." Her smile was nothing but friendly innocence, but he knew from the gleam in her eyes what better use she was referring to. He would gladly spend every dime he had, and every one he might ever get, on Grace and the baby if it would make her trust him, but money wasn't the way to Grace's heart. Decency was. Honor. Respectability. Reliability.

Trust couldn't be given freely, not to someone like him, who'd betrayed everyone who'd ever had a bit of faith in him. He was lucky Grace was willing to give him the time of day. Asking for a place in her life just might be out of the question.

After saying his goodbyes, he left the café for the truck and headed in the direction of home. He hadn't gone far, though, when, on impulse, he turned off the gravel road onto a narrower dirt lane. There was only one destination ahead—the cemetery, where generations of Harrises and a James or two were buried. He drove through the arched gate, then stopped in the middle and simply sat there.

It was nearly eight o'clock at night, dark, cold, with a stiff breeze blowing out of the northwest, a poor time for visiting graves that he hadn't seen in ten years or more. But he climbed out of the truck, anyway, and followed a cracked sidewalk to a familiar headstone. It stood upright, a slab of granite with the surname carved on one side, the full names and dates on the other. Crouching, he drew his fingertips over the cold, smooth letters of his mother's name.

The day of her funeral was one of the clearest in his memory. The entire county had turned out, gathering around Guthrie, offering their support, while watching Ethan as if he were an unwelcome interloper. They'd whispered about what a disappointment he'd been to Nadine, how marrying Gordon James had been the biggest mistake she'd ever made, how fortunate she was to have had Guthrie, as if one good son offset the bad one. They'd commented on the fact that Guthrie had been there through Nadine's slow, lingering death, while Ethan had been sitting in jail down around San Antonio. They'd been scandalized that he'd waited until an hour before the funeral to show up at Guthrie's house, and had snidely remarked on the fact that he'd had no more respect for his mother than to come to her funeral hungover.

No one had ever known that he'd spent the day and a half before the funeral in a motel in Buffalo Plains, trying to work up the courage to face his brother. They'd never guessed that his bloodshot eyes and unsteadiness had had everything to do with grief and nothing to do with booze. They had assumed the worst, and he'd let them.

He'd stood three feet from Guthrie that day and listened to the pastor's words, empty of comfort, and the prayers, and he'd wondered what in the world was left for him now that his mother was gone. The answer had been painfully clear that day—nothing. No relationship with his brother that was worthy of the name. No place to call home anymore. No one to give a damn what happened to him.

For the first time in ten years, he'd gotten a different answer to the question. He had a baby to be responsible for, and maybe the baby's mother. Maybe a place to call home, and someone to give a damn. Maybe even a family all his own. If only he didn't ruin it the way he'd always ruined everything.

Please, he thought as he got to his feet, unsure whether he was pleading with his mother, God or whatever other powers there might be. *Please don't let me screw it up.*

Chapter 9

Sunday's forecast called for snow, but when Grace got up that morning, the sun was shining brightly and there wasn't a cloud in the sky. She managed to shower, dress and brush her teeth without looking at herself in the mirror, then ate a bowl of oatmeal on the stairs while keeping one eye on the clock, the other on the door.

Ethan had said he would pick her up at ten. Ginger had said she would come over at nine. Grace had wanted her there earlier, but Ginger had laughed and said there was no way she was getting out of bed that early on a Sunday for anyone less than Brad Pitt. Besides, she'd promised, she needed only thirty minutes to work her magic.

Grace really wanted some magic.

She was tapping her spoon against the empty bowl when footsteps sounded on the porch. With the doorbell echoing into silence, she crossed the few feet to open the door. "Thank heavens you're here. I was starting to worry."

Ginger popped her gum as she walked inside. "Great

place. This house has fabulous bones. You should let me redecorate it for you.'' She grinned slyly. ''I'd make it a wedding gift.''

Not long ago, mention of a wedding for her would have struck Grace as an unkind reminder of one more thing she, unlike normal women her age, couldn't have. This morning, it sent a spasm of pain through her, because she knew she *could* have it, if she could learn to trust Ethan. If she could have faith in him. If she could find a little faith in herself.

Turning her attention from the house to Grace, Ginger gave her a measuring look. ''Even without makeup, this is a major improvement. How do you like the hair?''

Grace automatically reached to her shoulder and found only air. Self-consciously she smiled. ''I don't know. I've never had short hair before. I'm trying to get used to it.''

''It looks great. Take my word for it. Where shall we get started?''

Grace led the way upstairs to her soon-to-be-old room, where Ginger dumped her oversize straw bag on the bed. Out tumbled a hair dryer, curling iron, not one but three cosmetics cases and a half dozen brushes and combs, as well an assortment of perfumes, sprays and gels. ''Let's change your clothes first,'' Ginger suggested.

Grace looked down at her dress. It was, like all her clothes, a hand-me-down, fairly shapeless, large enough to cover her expanding stomach. That particular shade of green wasn't her color, but the dress with its fine cotton weave was the nicest piece in her wardrobe. ''I—I was planning to wear this.''

''I was afraid of that. The dress is fine for working in the hardware store, but, girl, you're going out with a handsome man for a day's shopping and dining. You want something a little less—'' Ginger gave the dress an offended once-over ''—well, a little *less*.''

''But I don't have—''

"Ah, but Fairy Godmother Ginger suspected you would say that. That's why I brought an alternative." From the bottom of her straw bag, she whipped out a plastic grocery bag, removed the items inside and held them against her own impossibly slender body for Grace's perusal.

Grace took the pants from her, held them up and burst out laughing. "You've got to be kidding. I'm pregnant, remember? There's no way these will fit me."

"They will. Trust me. It's the miracle of modern fibers. My sister wore these through her whole pregnancy, and at the end she was a whole lot bigger than you are."

Indigo-blue leggings, white T-shirt, blue chambray men's shirt. Grace could see the potential for a darling outfit—but *she* didn't wear darling outfits. Put one on her, and Lord knows what she might do.

The last time, she'd gotten pregnant.

It was on the tip of her tongue to refuse the outfit. She wasn't the cute type. Frumpy and shapeless wasn't just a description of her clothing, it was a description of *her,* and changing clothes couldn't change that. Cutting her hair and asking Ginger to once again do her makeup was about as far as she had the courage to go. Making herself look like someone she wasn't was not the way to make Ethan appreciate the person she was.

But she wanted to look cute. She wanted to wear clothes that any normal twenty-five-year-old pregnant woman might wear. On her first trip to the city, her closest-she'd-ever-come-to-a-date, she wanted to give up frumpy and shapeless. She wanted people to see her with Ethan without wondering what in hell he saw in her.

Miracle fibers or not, it took her a few minutes to maneuver into the leggings, then discard her dress for the loosely cut T-shirt and the chambray shirt. Ginger adjusted the collar, folded back the cuffs a time or two, then fastened the bottom few buttons.

"There. That's much better. Now sit down over here at the desk and take your glasses off."

Grace sat quietly, eyes closed, while Ginger worked her makeover magic. She used an astounding array of products and applicators, deftly applying, swabbing and blending, humming softly to herself. She gave an occasional command—"Pucker up, quit frowning, don't squint"—then stepped back and fell silent for a moment. Finally, she spoke. "You can open your eyes now. You have good bones, too, Grace. You ever consider contacts?"

"No." Grace put her glasses on, felt them slip, then pushed them up again. "But I have considered glasses that fit."

"They have those one-hour eyeglasses places all over Tulsa. You could get a new pair today. Where's a mirror?"

"In my fath—my new room." The new bedroom set had come with a cheval mirror that Ethan had placed in one corner. She had looked at it last night, had thought that maybe she would take it out again.

Or maybe not, she thought as she faced her reflection.

When she'd asked for Ginger's help, she'd feared her friend might go overboard and turn her into Melissa again. She hadn't. She was still Grace, only better. Softer, prettier. Not beautiful—she would never be beautiful—but prettier. Less plain. Less forgettable.

Her hair was short, the style not too sleek but rather tousled. The rinse Ginger had put in it last night brightened the color, gave it shine. The clothing fit well and made her look less rounded, reminding her that all her weight gain had been in her stomach and her breasts. Everywhere else, she was still relatively slender and not the ungainly beached whale she felt like.

She was a new-and-improved Grace, and she liked it a lot.

"Thank you, Ginger—"

The doorbell interrupted her. Ginger patted her arm. "My pleasure. Let me grab my stuff, then I'll let your date in. Take your time about coming down. Let him anticipate the moment. And have fun in Tulsa."

Grace watched her leave, then let her gaze slide back to the mirror. She felt silly, admiring her own reflection, and yet she couldn't help it. The face there was so familiar, and yet different.

What would Ethan think? Would he like the new Grace better than the old? Or, since she was going to the trouble to change, would he prefer Melissa?

She heard the murmur of voices as Ginger told him Grace would be right down, then the closing of the front door. Taking a deep breath, she started down the hall and the stairs. She was halfway down when a step creaked and he turned to look at her.

His smile came slowly. "You cut your hair. I like it."

Self-consciously she tugged at a wisp of hair. "I—I'd had enough of ponytails and and braids."

"I like the clothes, too."

Her hand dropped to the shirt, her fingers plucking as if they could stretch the chambray a few inches longer. "I don't— Do I look foolish?"

"Of course not. Why would you think that?"

"Because I'm trying to look like someone I'm not."

"You look like Grace Prescott, and unless I'm mistaken, that's exactly who you are." He met her at the foot of the stairs, touched her hair, let his hand slide down to her shoulder. "You look lovely, Grace."

She shook her head. "Not me. It's the makeup...."

"Sweetheart, makeup only enhances what's already there. It doesn't create beauty out of nothing. Now, let's try this again. I'll give you a compliment, and you'll smile sweetly and say, 'Thank you, Ethan.' You look lovely, Grace."

She couldn't help but obey him and smile. "Thank you, Ethan."

"Are you ready to go?"

When she nodded, he took her coat from the coat tree and held it for her, then wrapped her scarf around her neck. He opened the door for her, and a minute later opened the truck door, helping her inside. She'd never seen her father hold a door for a woman in her life, had never seen him offer her mother any sort of assistance whatsoever. It gave her a warm, gee-this-is-special sort of feeling.

Didn't take much to impress her, did it?

"I bought this truck while I was living in Louisiana," Ethan said as he backed out of the driveway, "and the heater doesn't take its job seriously. It'll keep us from freezing, but you're not going to have to worry about getting too warm."

"I'm fine," she replied, and she was. She was dressed warmly enough. Besides, today it was the destination—and the company—that mattered.

Once they crossed into the next county, Grace's gaze kept moving from side to side. They weren't far from Heartbreak, and the landscape looked the same, but somehow it *felt* different. Each passing minute put more miles between her and the home that had been more of a prison. She felt so free that she was giddy. She wanted to laugh out loud, but she settled for a deeply satisfied smile.

"When is your slowest time at the store?"

She glanced at Ethan before shifting to watch a herd of cattle disappear from view. "We don't really have one. There's always work to be done."

"Then let's make one. Sometime next winter. We'll take a vacation in Florida, where the sun is always shining and the air is always warm."

"Vacation…that's a magic word to a woman who's never been anywhere."

"Why not?"

"Why not what?"

"Why didn't you run away ten years ago?"

"I was only fifteen."

"I was fifteen the first time I left home."

"Yes, but you were so much…*more* than me." More mature, bolder, brasher, braver. He hadn't been afraid of anything, while she had been afraid of everything. "I thought about running away. I used to lie in bed at night and make these elaborate plans about where I would go, what I would do and how I would live."

"But you never tried to carry them through."

She smiled faintly. "Oh, they weren't real plans. They were dreams. Fantasies."

"Tell me your fantasies, and I'll tell you mine," he said with a sly grin.

She would have brushed him off and gone back to staring wide-eyed at the countryside that wasn't Heartbreak if she hadn't wanted to hear *his* fantasies. Since she did want to, she sighed and shrugged. "Sometimes I dreamed that I would magically find my mother, and she would be so happy to see me and would want me to live with her. Mostly I dreamed that I would run away and make it to the next town or the next state or maybe even California, and I would meet somebody—the perfect mother and father who would want me for their own or, as I got older, Prince Charming. It would be love at first sight, and he would take me away to live happily ever after in a nice little house with nice little kids and a dog and a cat, and we'd do the scouting thing and the PTA and soccer. We'd have friends over for a barbecue on weekends and we'd take a vacation every summer and go to Disneyland or Six Flags or maybe just to the lake." She made an apologetic gesture. "I never dreamed that I could leave and survive on my own. It just seemed impossible."

Ethan didn't argue the point with her because he suspected that she was right. He'd been fine on his own, but he'd never been painfully shy or afraid to open his mouth. He'd never met a stranger or found himself in a situation he couldn't talk his way out of. He'd been a lot like his father in that respect.

All his life he'd believed he was exactly like his father in every aspect, but it wasn't true. He knew it. One of these days, maybe everyone else would know it, too.

Unless he was lying to himself. Gordon had been pretty good at that, too.

"Your turn."

He glanced at Grace, struck again by the changes in her. Judging by her question at the house—*Do I look foolish?*— she'd been the last female in Heartbreak over the age of fifteen to learn what makeup and a good haircut could do for her. And they did a lot. She could catch the eye of any man who happened to pass by, could walk into any gathering of single men and have her pick of the lot.

She could make a better choice than him now.

"My turn for what?" he asked, absently rubbing his chest as if he could make the dull ache that had just settled there go away.

"Fantasies. I told you mine. What about yours?"

He could give her any number of answers. He could tell her what he'd like to do with her and make her cheeks flush and her blood hot. He could conjure up a few teenage dreams and make her laugh. He could dig up another old fantasy or two and bring tears to her eyes. Or he could be honest and tell her the one dream he'd always had, the one that had driven him away from Heartbreak and brought him back, the one that he sometimes feared would never come true and sometimes feared would come true just so he could screw it up, the way he screwed up everything.

"My dream was about belonging," he said at last, gazing

at the road ahead as if it required every bit of his attention. "All those times I left home, all the times I came back…I was looking for a place to belong. For people who weren't happier without me. For people who could forgive what I was. For family."

"But you had family," Grace gently pointed out.

"I did. And I had no doubt that my mother loved me. I also had no doubt that she loved Guthrie more. That she was disappointed in me more often than not. That she agreed with everyone else that marrying my father was her biggest mistake, which made me her second-biggest mistake."

"You're wrong, Ethan. She could regret marrying your father without feeling one second's regret over having you."

"And you know this from personal experience," he said quietly. "You can honestly say that your regret over sleeping with me has no effect at all on your feelings for this baby?"

She pushed her glasses up, lifted her chin and gave him a level look. "I've never regretted spending that night with you."

"But you do regret that I'm her father."

This time her answer came neither as quickly nor as firmly, and that fact sent a stab of pain through Ethan. "I don't— I regret that your reputation could make life more difficult for her."

"So do I." As much as he regretted the fact that Grace remained ashamed of him. All the time they'd spent together had done nothing to alter her opinion of him. In her eyes, he was still a stigma she didn't want their daughter bearing.

They fell silent after that, neither of them speaking until they'd reached Tulsa. They ate lunch first—her first McDonald's meal, she announced—then hit the stores.

Though she was wide-eyed with wonder at everything available, there wasn't an impulse indulgence in any of the bags. She'd bought bedding for her new room and for the crib, along with a handful of impossibly small blankets, sleepers and gowns. She let him add a few purchases of his own for the baby—stuffed animals, a brightly colored mobile, a teddy bear night-light that glowed faint yellow— but when he maneuvered her and the shopping cart to the maternity clothes section, she balked.

"I don't need any clothes," she said, then her face flushed. "I can't afford any right now."

"I can."

She shook her head. "You can't buy me clothes."

"Why not?"

"It's—it's not proper."

"Not proper?" he echoed. "Grace, I've kissed you. I've seen you naked. I've made love to you. Hell, I'm responsible for you needing new clothes. What could possibly be improper about my buying you a pretty dress or a pair of jeans?"

She looked at the racks of clothing, wistfulness in her eyes. For more than three months, she'd lived in ill-fitted, unflattering hand-me-downs, and the prepregnancy wardrobe her father had destroyed, he would wager, hadn't been any better. Like other women, she wanted pretty clothes. Unlike other women, she didn't seem to feel she deserved them.

While she stood there looking torn, he lifted a sweater from a display. It was emerald green and knitted from amazingly soft yarn. He held it to him, then lifted her hand, stroking her palm across the garment, rubbing it back and forth over his chest. "Do you like that?"

Against her will, her expression softened. "Yes," she admitted softly, freeing her hand, touching the sweater— and him—voluntarily.

"Me, too." As the heat spread from her fingertips outward across his skin, he closed his eyes and caught his breath. "And the sweater's not bad, either," he murmured in a strangled voice.

Abruptly Grace snatched her hand away. He opened his eyes and gave her a rueful smile. "Aw, well, it felt good while it lasted."

Giving him a chastising look, she reached for the sweater. "You're sure you don't mind?"

"I'm positive."

"Because I really don't need—"

He interrupted her. "Let me buy this for you, Grace. Just once, forget about what you need and let me give you something you want. Please."

After a moment, he released the sweater and she pulled it away. She added a pair of jeans from a nearby rack, then headed for the dressing room.

Ten minutes later she returned, her face flushed, her hair mussed. Without a word, she added the clothes to the cart, then started toward the cash registers at the front of the store. Ethan lingered long enough to grab another sweater, this one rich royal purple, and a pair of black jeans, and slid them in with the rest of his purchases.

From the store they went to the theater. He got more of a kick out of watching Grace watch the movie in the giant-screen, surround-sound theater than he did from watching the film. He couldn't get over how many things she'd never done that most people took for granted—or how lucky he was to be the one to introduce her to all these firsts.

He was planning another first—a leisurely dinner at a nice restaurant—after the movie, but when they left the theater, his plans changed. The sun that wouldn't set for another hour or so was completely blocked by ominously dark clouds, and snow was falling in heavy flakes that stuck where they landed.

Concern drew Grace's brows together in a frown. "Do you think we can make it home?"

"I don't know." Heartbreak was west and north of Tulsa, and if this storm was like most Oklahoma winter storms, it had come from the northwest. The last thing he wanted was to get Grace stuck somewhere in the middle of a snowstorm. "Let me find a pay phone and see what I can find out."

It took two calls to track down Leroy, watching a basketball game at a buddy's house. It was snowing in Heartbreak, he said, but it had just started and the streets were clear. No accumulation, none expected, no problem.

No problem, Ethan thought derisively two hours later, as the truck crept along a road that at times disappeared in the snow. They should have found a motel in Tulsa. He should have checked with the highway patrol. As soon as the snow began getting heavier, he should have turned back.

"I should have called Guthrie," he muttered aloud.

From the other side of the frigid cab, with all their bags around her, Grace looked at him. Her face was pale, her eyes worried. She hadn't said a word for the last twenty miles, not when he'd nearly lost control on an icy bridge, not even when an oncoming car, driven by another complete fool, had fishtailed into their lane before sliding back into its own. Now she asked one simple question. "Why?"

"Because he would have told me not to try it."

"You called Leroy. It wasn't bad and wasn't expected to get bad. Guthrie would have told you the same thing."

Ethan shook his head, feeling the pull in the taut muscles in his neck. "Guthrie doesn't make mistakes. He would have known."

"The forecasters didn't know. They predicted a sixty percent chance of *light* snow."

"Guthrie would have known."

In spite of her nerves, she smiled a bit. "Haven't quite gotten over that big-brother hero worship, have you?"

Heat flushed his face, providing welcome warmth. "It's not hero worship. Just the facts. He knows everything. He's always right."

"He's not perfect."

"Yes, he is. Ask anyone." Loosening one hand from the steering wheel, he flexed his fingers, shrugged, then rotated his head. He was stiff from head to damn-near-frozen toe. When he got home—*if* he got home—he was going to soak the rest of the night in a long, hot bath. "I should have turned back as soon as it started getting bad."

"We were already much closer to home. We'll be there long before we could have reached the nearest motel back the other way."

"I should have—"

"Ethan." Plastic crinkled as she reached across the shopping bags to lay her hand on his forearm. "It's not your fault. You can't control the weather. You're not responsible for the snow."

"No, but I'm responsible for us being out in it."

She sighed heavily, patted his arm, then drew back, falling silent once again.

His eyes gritty and dry, Ethan focused hard on the road. At one point he thought they might have passed the Heartbreak town limits sign, though the snowfall was so heavy it was impossible to say for sure. If they had, they were safe. It was still a half mile to the town itself, and another mile and a half beyond that to Grace's house, but there would be houses along the way where they could find shelter if necessary.

Fortunately, it wasn't necessary. About the time his fingers went numb from clutching the steering wheel so tightly, he caught a glimpse of Grace's yellow house on the left. With her help, he found the driveway, pulled in and shut off the engine, then sat back with a loud sigh.

She gave him a pleased, I-was-never-worried smile. "See? There was no reason for us to turn back. We're home safe and sound."

We're home. He liked the sound of that, though he knew she didn't mean it the way he wanted to hear it. "You're home," he pointed out. "I've still got about ten miles to go."

Her smile transformed into worry. "Don't be ridiculous. That'll take you another hour, if you make it at all."

"Is that an invitation to stay here?"

Her gaze darted away, came back, then left again. "I guess it is."

"Gee, thanks for the enthusiasm," he said with a wry chuckle. "Let's get inside."

He would have left the bags for later. She insisted on filling her arms with them. Leaving one arm free to wrap around her waist, he grabbed the rest, then they struggled to the porch through drifts that reached his knees.

After stamping off the snow, they went inside. She headed for the kitchen to see about dinner while he carried the bags upstairs. On impulse, he took the linens into Grace's new room and began making the bed. He was smoothing the flat sheet when she joined him.

"You did a great job in here," she remarked as she stuffed new pillows into new cases.

"Thank you, ma'am."

"You could make a business out of this."

"Painting pregnant women's bedrooms?"

"Utilizing your varied skills."

"And be what? A handyman for hire?"

"Basically, yes. A lot of people have neither the time nor the desire to do small jobs around the house. People like me don't have the ability or anyone to ask for help."

"You can ask me."

"Right now, I can. But..." Suddenly the second pillow and case required all her attention, at least until he circled the bed and yanked them from her hands.

"But you can't ask if I'm not here, and maybe tomorrow I won't be, or maybe the week after, or the week after that." He shoved the pillow into the case, then tossed it on the bed, clamped his hands on his hips and glared at her. "And maybe I will be. Maybe I'll be here next month and next year and ten years from now. Maybe I've run away for the last time."

"Maybe," she murmured, but she wouldn't look at him. Because she didn't want him to see that she doubted him?

"Damn it, Grace—" Gritting his teeth, he broke off. She had a right to doubt him. He'd never lived up to a responsibility in his life. She had no reason to believe that this one was any different.

For a moment, she simply stood there, eyes downcast, hands clasped tightly over her stomach. Finally she said in a subdued voice, "I'm heating the chili I froze last week. It should be ready soon. Come on down when you're finished."

She was at the door before he spoke. "I'm sorry, Grace."

"For what?"

For getting angry. Expecting too much. Having a reputation. For not being the sort of man she deserved. For wanting her, anyway. "For everything."

"You can't be sorry for everything. Everything isn't your fault." She hesitated in the doorway, then came back and stretched up to hug his neck. "Thank you for today," she whispered before brushing a kiss to his jaw, then leaving.

He touched his fingertips lightly to his jaw, then sank

down on the bed, his head bowed, and though it was much too late for her to hear, he whispered, "You're welcome."

Grace dished up the chili, filled two glasses with milk, then cut fresh-baked corn bread into squares before sitting down at the kitchen table.

She'd hurt Ethan up there in the bedroom and hadn't even had the decency to apologize for it. She wanted to trust him. She wanted to believe in him with every fiber of the desperate girl who'd once dreamed of a charming prince who would rescue her. But better people than she had tried to change him, with no success. He'd loved his mother, but had still let her down. He loved Guthrie fiercely, but still let him down. He *didn't* love her. How could she believe he would always be there for her?

Down the hall, a stair creaked beneath his weight, then she heard his footsteps. He came into the kitchen, but he didn't sit down. Instead he reached for the phone mounted on the wall near the door. "I'd better call Guthrie and let him know I won't be home," he said quietly.

She made no effort to pretend that she wasn't listening to his end of the conversation. He kept the call short—told his brother that he'd just gotten back from Tulsa and wasn't going to risk the last ten miles home. When Guthrie asked where he was staying, Ethan hesitated, then hedged. "I'm at a buddy's," he said, then went on without a pause. "I'll be home as soon as the roads are clear."

As he sat down, she bit back the urge to tartly point out that she most certainly was *not* his "buddy." But what right did she have to point out anything? *She* was the one who'd insisted on secrecy. What other answer could he have given without outright lying?

They ate without conversation, beyond a couple of half-hearted compliments on the food from Ethan. They did the dishes in silence, too, and were facing an evening of TV-watching the same way, she thought, until the storm once again changed their plans.

They were halfway out of the kitchen when the lights went out. The refrigerator stopped mid-hum, and the electric blower on the heating system cut off mid-blow. Ethan bumped into her, steadied her, then rested his hand on her shoulder. "The power lines are probably down. This sort of wet snow is heavy. You'll probably lose some branches, too."

As if to punctuate his words, into the stillness came the sharp crack of a breaking limb. The peach tree out back, she thought. Fortunately, none of the trees close to the house were tall enough to do any damage, and the trees big enough to send a branch crashing through the roof were too far away.

"Do you have any candles?"

"I have oil lamps. Let me get them." She felt her way into the dining room, grateful for once for her father's rigid habits. All her life two lamps, their bases filled with oil, their wicks neatly trimmed, had sat on the sideboard, with a box of matches in the top drawer. She lit one and handed it to Ethan, then lit the second.

Back in the hallway, he paused at the bottom of the stairs. "If you don't mind, I think I'm going to bed."

"It was a long day, with a long drive back. You must be tired."

He nodded once. "I'll take your old room—"

"No. That twin bed's too small for you. Take the new one."

"I don't mind—"

"Please. I'll get you some extra blankets." She led the way upstairs, gave him two of the three extra blankets, then turned to leave. His quiet words stopped her in her tracks.

"This bed's big enough for two."

She'd noticed that every time she'd looked at it. She'd

thought about it when she'd picked out the sheets, when she'd matched the comforter. She'd wondered if she would ever share it with anyone else. Now he'd just offered her the chance. Damned if she wasn't afraid to take it.

She risked a quick, apologetic look, said, "Good night," and went to her own room, closing the door firmly behind her as if the solid wood could stop her from changing her mind.

When he'd brought the shopping bags upstairs, he'd left them on her bed. By lamplight, she unpacked each one, stacking the baby things on the desk, hanging her new green sweater and jeans in the closet. They looked so pretty and stylish among her secondhand clothes. After the baby was born, she would expand her wardrobe one pretty outfit at a time, she decided, until no one remembered her lifetime of shapeless, colorless, lifeless dresses.

She was sweeping up empty plastic bags when she picked up one with some weight to it. Looking inside, she found another amazingly soft sweater and another pair of jeans. In the store, she remembered, Ethan had gathered his purchases and taken them to the next checkout stand. She'd thought he was just saving time. Now she knew he'd been hiding these additional purchases.

Cradling the sweater to her chest, she sank down on the bed and buried her face in it. They were simple gifts, practical, relatively inexpensive, but they meant the world to her. In thirteen years no one had ever bought something pretty and new just for her. No one had ever bothered to consider what she wanted as opposed to what she needed. She was touched beyond words.

Rising from the bed, she quickly stripped down to her panties and socks. She carefully tore the tags from the sweater, then, shivering in the cold, she pulled it over her head and smoothed it down to mid-thigh. Next she pulled her covers off the bed, leaving only the sheet behind, then picked up the lamp. Shadows flickered around her as she carried both blankets and lamp in trembling hands down the hall to her new room.

Ethan's lamp was extinguished on one night table. Hers showed his jeans and shirt folded over the arm of the glider, his boots and socks on the floor below. It also showed him in bed, nothing more than a long, narrow lump under a stack of covers.

"Ethan?" Her voice was husky, quivery. "Are you awake?"

"Yeah." He rolled over, rose onto one arm. The covers slipped to reveal his shoulder, a smooth expanse of back and lightly furred chest. The sight made her mouth go dry. "What do you need?"

"I—I thought…" She cleared her throat. "We—we could probably stay warmer if we com-combine our, uh, c-covers and, uh…uh…"

For one long moment he simply looked at her. Then, with the faintest of smiles, he lifted the covers and repeated his earlier invitation. "This bed's big enough for two."

She set her lamp on the other nightstand, then laid her glasses beside it. After draping the extra blankets over the foot of the bed, she slid underneath the covers. Part of her wanted to slide right up close to him, to absorb his heat, to snuggle against him and feel safe. Part of her found such behavior much too forward.

Forward. Heavens, in another six weeks she was going to have his baby. With that in mind, how could she possibly be too forward with the man?

She lay on her side, her knees brought up as much as her stomach allowed, her back to him, and tried not to breathe too fast or too loud. It was silly to feel so nervous. They were simply sharing body heat in a winter emergency. That had been the motivation behind his invitation. It had

been the reason for her acceptance. After all, in her condition, what else *could* they share?

"Grace? Sharing body heat is a little tough when my
body's over here and yours is way over there on the edge."
He sounded wide awake now, and amused. Tender. "Scoot
back here and let me hold you. I won't bite, I promise.
Unless you want me to."

His hand on her arm encouraged her to slide back across
brand-new sheets warmed by the heat of his body. When
she was near the middle of the bed, he moved to meet her,
fitting his body to hers, sliding his arm over her middle.
His fingers brushed hers, then curled around them. "You
really are cold," he remarked as if surprised. "And here I
thought it was just a ruse to get into my bed."

"A ruse? There's nothing wrong with your ego, is
there?"

"Sweetheart, there's nothing wrong with any part of me
that you can't make right."

Within seconds his warmth began seeping into her,
bringing with it an incredible sense of lazy security. Her
eyes grew heavy and her breathing slowed. They could
wake up in the morning with snow up to the eaves and no
chance of regaining power before the spring thaw, but even
that knowledge couldn't cause her a moment's concern tonight. She felt too safe. Too protected. Too convinced that
right there in his arms was where she belonged. Where she
wanted to be.

And even that knowledge couldn't worry her tonight.
Without a doubt, tomorrow she would consider the foolish-
ness of getting any closer to Ethan than she already was.
She would remove her own needs from the picture and look
at it solely as it involved Annie, and she would worry
whether she was making a mistake.

But tonight she was simply going to enjoy it.

Chapter 10

Awakening in the middle of the night in an unfamiliar place was nothing new to Ethan. While he'd be willing to bet that his brother had never slept in a bed other than his own, there had been entire months when Ethan had spent every night in a different bed—or, if his resources had failed him, in no bed at all.

Awakening in the middle of the night with a warm, soft feminine body pressed against him wasn't unusual, either, or with a lust so powerful that it was damn near painful. But a warm, soft, seven-months-pregnant feminine body, and a lust that wasn't the slightest bit diminished by the thought of that pregnancy, that was maybe even intensified by it...that was new. Intriguing.

Apparently, the power was still off. The oil lamp Grace had left lit was still burning, casting its soft uncertain light on her face, and the air in the room was cold enough to fog when they breathed. Underneath the pile of covers, though, he couldn't be warmer. He was just checking to make sure Grace was warm enough, he told himself when he ran his hand along her thigh. He wasn't copping a feel, wasn't noticing how soft her skin was, or how nicely rounded her muscles were. He certainly wasn't remembering last summer when her hips had cradled him and her long, lean legs had wrapped around him.

But her skin *was* soft and warm, and her muscles were nicely rounded, and she had clung to him last summer, helpless, innocent, a virgin, getting taken for the ride of her life.

Last July he hadn't appreciated the fact that he was her first. Oh, he'd enjoyed it. He'd had fun with the initiation. But he'd thought it odd that a woman as beautiful and sexy as Melissa was, in fact, more innocent than he'd ever been.

Now, though, he found something macho—some primitive male pride, some elemental satisfaction—in knowing that he'd been her first, and so far her only, lover. He *liked* knowing, with a bone-deep certainty, that no other man had ever seen her naked, kissed her breasts or stroked between her thighs. No other man had ever buried himself inside her, or sent shivers through her, or made her cry out in that incredibly erotic way. No other man had ever known the pleasures of her body.

And if he had any say in the matter, no other man ever would.

With only the tips of his fingers touching her, he inched his hand along her thigh, to the hem of the sweater and underneath. The panties he encountered were cotton—no surprise there—and bikinis. Big surprise there. In spite of the torment-inducing lingerie she'd worn last summer, he'd figured her for plain white cotton with no frills like lace or a tiny bow centered over her abdomen.

Now he *was* copping a feel, he admitted, and from a sleeping woman, no less. Regretfully, he withdrew his hand from the enticing warmth of her sweater and instead cupped his hand over the curve of her belly.

If anyone had told him two months ago that the time would come when he was sexually attracted to a pregnant woman, he would have laughed. But right now he'd never felt less like laughing. He was so aroused that he might explode right here, without any stimulation beyond the soft heat of her bottom pressed against him. All he'd have to do was thrust against her...slowly...just hard enough to create a little friction....

Choking back a groan as desperate need shot through him, he moved until he wasn't touching her, at least not where he needed it. But with a soft little whimper of protest, she moved, too, seeking the same position, pushing intimately against him. He tried to swallow, but his throat was dry; tried to breathe, but his lungs were paralyzed.

''Grace?'' he whispered in a strangled voice. ''Scoot over, darlin'. Give me a little room.''

She moved, all right, snuggling even closer, settling with a great, soft sigh. Instead of her stomach, now his hand rested beneath her breast, the tips of his fingers just touching the beginning swell.

He wondered if he could wake her and seduce her. Wondered how much of a bastard he would be if he seduced her, then woke her. If she had come to this bed with sex on her mind, he wouldn't hesitate, but she hadn't. She'd trusted him enough to sleep with him for warmth, trusted him not to take advantage of her, trusted that she would be safe—

With a helpless whimper, she moved again, twisting, arching her back until her breast was beneath his palm, pressing against soft fabric and callused skin. He gave in to one, two gentle caresses, then withdrew his hand, but she caught it, pulled it back, shaped his thumb and finger to fit her nipple. He pinched it, and it swelled in immediate response, drawing another tiny whimper from her.

"Gracie?" he whispered again. "You've gotta wake up, darlin'. You've got to tell me this is all right, that you want this, or I've got to get out of this bed."

For a moment she lay utterly still, barely breathing, then she murmured, "I'm awake."

He waited for more—"This is all right" or "Stop it now." When she remained silent, he hesitantly rubbed his palm across her nipple. He brushed her hair away from her ear, brought his mouth only a breath away and said, "It's not that easy, Gracie. You've got to tell me. What do you want me to do?"

She wanted it easy, he suspected—wanted him to make the decision for her. Then, afterward, she wouldn't be responsible. She wouldn't have to admit, even to herself, that she'd wanted him.

And he wanted it plain, simple, with no room for misunderstanding. He wanted to hear her say the words, wanted to know that she wanted *him*. Not just sex, but sex with him.

His breath tickled and raised goose bumps on her neck. His tongue, tracing the shape of her ear, sent shivers through her. "Tell me, darlin'. What do you want?"

She remained silent so long that he thought she was going to refuse to answer, which meant he was going to have to stop, and the rest of the night would be damned uncomfortable. But finally, as he was about to move away, she answered more bluntly, more honestly, than he'd ever expected. "I want you to touch my breasts. I want you to kiss me. I want—I want you inside me."

Now it was his turn to be utterly still. After a moment, though, he burst into laughter. "Oh, babe," he murmured between kisses to her jaw. "So shy...and so bold. You're amazing."

He slid his hand underneath her sweater, gliding over soft, impossibly warm skin to her breast, gently rubbing, squeezing. She tried to turn to face him, but he didn't let her. Instead he pressed close to her, thrusting his arousal against her, achingly aware of how easy it would be to slide inside her from behind, to fill her again and again, to bring her the most incredible satisfaction and find his own incredible pleasure in doing so.

Twisting her head, she sought his mouth, and he gave it to her, kissing her hungrily, sliding his tongue into her mouth, probing, tasting. The noises she made—soft little cries, breathless gasps, heavy, throaty moans—were incredibly erotic. They sensitized his skin and made it ache everywhere they touched and everywhere they didn't. They made him tremble.

"Please," she whispered, pulling at him, pushing at her clothing, and he was happy to help cast aside her panties. She tried to turn onto her back once more, and once more he stopped her.

"Like this, Gracie," he said, positioning her on her side, lifting her leg. "It'll be easier..."

"I've never..."

"It'll be good." Sliding inside her was as easy as he'd imagined, filling her as satisfying as he'd remembered. Her body was hot, and it gloved him in a perfect fit. If he were one millimeter bigger, if she were one whisper of a breath tighter, it would be too much. But they weren't. They were so damned perfect.

He thrust into her, setting an easy rhythm, all the while kissing her, tasting her, caressing her breasts. When he was close to completion, he slid one hand between her thighs, parting damp curls, seeking swollen, sensitive flesh. When she gasped and sucked in a frantic breath, he knew he'd found what he was looking for. With his hands and his body, with kisses and words of encouragement murmured in her ear, he brought her to climax only an instant before reaching his own. Barely aware of her ragged cries, he filled her, his body straining against hers, throbbing inside hers, and even before he was finished, he knew he wanted her again. This one time could never be enough. He wasn't sure a thousand times could come close to satisfying his need for her, but he'd bet it would take ten times that.

If he were a betting man.

Grace felt weak. From the tips of her toes all the way to the hair standing on end on her head, she felt quivery and trembly, as if she'd barely survived some great madness. Her breathing was slowly returning to normal, her heartbeat had finally stopped echoing in her ears, and her body temperature was gradually cooling down to normal from the spontaneous-combustion range.

And all she'd done was lie there and feel while Ethan had done all the work. Amazing.

He was pretty damn amazing.

Behind her, he drew a breath, then let it out, cooling her sweat-dampened skin.

"Are you okay?" he asked, his voice ragged.

"I'm fine." *Fine?* She was incredible. She felt as if she could dance around the room, lighter than air…and as if she couldn't move a muscle if her life depended on it. She was wide awake and in awe, and could doze off in a heartbeat for the most restful sleep of her life. She felt fabulous, frightened, wondrous, smug, feminine, delicate, womanly. And, best of all, normal.

But rather than try to put all that into words, she pressed a kiss to his palm and repeated with heartfelt emphasis, "I'm fine."

He nuzzled her neck, then settled his big hand on her stomach, his fingers spread wide. Almost immediately she felt the increased warmth, bringing with it a sense of increased security. "You're an incredible woman, Grace Prescott," he murmured.

It was the nicest compliment anyone had ever given her. With a lump filling her throat and tears threatening to fill her eyes, she squeezed them shut, forced a smile and said, "I didn't do anything. You get all the credit."

He brushed her hair back from her ear, then brought his mouth close as he slid his hand to just beneath her breast. "Marry me, Grace. This week. Tomorrow. As soon as we can get to the courthouse in Buffalo Plains. Marry me. Be my wife. Let me be Annie Grace's father. Please."

She couldn't breathe, couldn't twitch a muscle. She stared wide-eyed at a muddle of shadows and listened to the stillness that had wrapped itself around them, broken only by the rapid beat of her heart.

For one sweet moment, she pretended that it was a legitimate proposal of marriage—that he loved her and she loved him, that they were destined to be together, that they would marry and, just like in all her dreams, live happily ever after.

But the moment didn't last long. That was the extent of his proposal. There was no declaration of love, no promise of forever, no hint of happily ever after. Just impulse, obligation, duty.

Was she wanting too much? Wasn't she lucky that he'd ever given her his attention, that he was willing to accept responsibility, that he'd stuck around these last few weeks instead of taking one look at the real her and running away again? Shouldn't she be grateful for what he was offering instead of mourning what she might never have?

"Come on, Gracie," he murmured, his voice teasing. "Don't get all stiff on me. We don't have to do it this week. We can do it anytime before the baby's born. Disreputable though I might be, to the best of my knowledge,

I've never fathered an illegitimate child. You don't want to
spoil my record and tarnish my reputation, do you?''

Maybe Callie was right. Maybe it was better to base a
marriage on something solid and tangible—like the baby—
than on something as elusive as love. Maybe settling for
Ethan's poor substitute was better than having nothing at
all.

"I won't ask you to answer now," he said carelessly.
"We've got six weeks. Just think about it."

She hated that he could be so casual about it—hated the
proof that neither she nor marriage were of any particular
importance to him. He only wanted to do what was right,
meaning what Guthrie would expect. If not for his brother,
she doubted that he would have come back in the first
place. She doubted he ever would have proposed marriage.

She doubted everything about him.

Except that he really did want to do what was right. And
that he'd certainly taken the disappointment of surprise fatherhood in stride. And that he'd treated her well in the
time he'd been back. He'd made her laugh and feel less
lonely, had shown her kindness, had treated her as if she
mattered.

And had told her with that proposal that she didn't. She
was just part of the deal he had to accept to live up to his
brother's standards.

"Grace?"

She wanted to pretend that she'd fallen asleep, to plug
her fingers in her ears and block out his voice. She wanted
to weep.

"Gracie?" He sounded more serious now. He'd stopped
rubbing her middle and moved away so his voice wasn't a
tickle in her ear.

When she didn't answer or turn to look at him, he easily
lifted himself over her, settling into the narrow space between her body and the edge of the bed. He cupped her

chin in his long, strong fingers and ducked his head so he could look into her eyes. Realizing she couldn't see much, he claimed her glasses from the night table and slid them into place on her nose, then fixed his solemn gaze on her. "I'm sorry I'm not the man you deserve. I'm sorry it wasn't love at first sight. I'm sorry I'm no prince, no prize, no Guthrie. But if you would give me a chance, I swear I would do my best by you and the baby. I'd do my damnedest to never let you down, to never make you sorry and to never make her ashamed. If you'll just give me a chance."

Even with her glasses, Grace couldn't see for the tears that flooded her eyes. How could he follow that careless, teasing proposal with a speech like that? How could he make her feel that marrying her was no more important to him than the movie they'd seen, and then bring her to tears with his next words?

Maybe because he relied on his careless, teasing manner for protection when something was important to him. Because then, if he got the wrong response, he could shrug it off as if it were no big deal. All his life he'd been charming, flippant, careless or cocky about things that mattered so no one would guess exactly how much they mattered. She would bet Guthrie didn't have a clue how much of the adoring kid brother remained in Ethan, that he couldn't begin to guess how much influence he had in Ethan's life. Even his mother had probably never guessed how much he loved her and needed her love and acceptance in return.

So maybe the baby really did matter to him.

Maybe *she* really did matter.

If you'll just give me a chance. There were people in town who said he'd been given too many chances and had messed up every one. They said he was just like his worthless father, that he would never grow up and never settle down, that he would never be half the man his brother was.

Well, Guthrie was so perfect that half the man he was

was more than she would ever need. Half of Guthrie's honor, half his responsibility, half his decency, added up to one hell of a man.

"Gracie?" With more tenderness than she'd ever known, he dried a tear from her cheek.

"Just one chance?" she whispered.

"That's all I'm asking for."

Good, because one chance was all she had to give. One disappointment, one letdown, one broken heart, and she would have nothing left. But that one chance...

She put tremendous effort into a smile that was almost as cocky as some of his and whispered, "I'll think about it."

After removing her glasses, Ethan gave her a kiss that was sweet, hot, hungry, greedy, then whispered his own response. "I hope you won't be sorry."

God help them, so did she.

By Monday morning, the storm that had dumped nearly four feet of snow on Heartbreak had moved on, and in one of the quirks that made Oklahoma weather so interesting, the sun had warmed the temperature to fifty degrees by eleven o'clock. Ethan awakened to the steady sound of water dripping from the eaves and to a room warm enough to make any cover heavier than a sheet unnecessary.

Before moving so much as a muscle, he knew Grace was no longer beside him. How far had she found it necessary to go this morning? Last time she'd run out of his life completely. But this time, he thought with a humorless smile, he knew where to find her.

But it wasn't necessary. When he finally opened his eyes to throw back the heavy layer of blankets that had gotten them through the unheated night, he saw her sitting in the glider in front of the west window. That was his first surprise. The second was that she hadn't gotten dressed yet.

She still wore the deep purple sweater and nothing else. Her feet were drawn onto the chair cushion, her left hand curled loosely around an oversize coffee mug, and her gaze was directed outside. She looked... Not beautiful. She would never be beautiful except to someone whose love blinded him to reality. But she wasn't plain, either, not anymore. Lovely. Yes, that was a good word. She looked incredibly lovely and maybe, maybe, just the littlest bit beautiful.

He plumped the pillows behind his back and waited for her to notice him. What was she thinking about that kept her so still, her expression so serious? Was she considering whether to give him that one chance he'd asked for last night? Guthrie would scoff that he'd had a hundred one-more-chances followed by a thousand last-chances; what made him think that this one would be any different?

But it would be, because the odds were different. The stakes were higher. Screwing up all those other chances had hurt only him for the most part, but screwing up this one chance would hurt Grace, who had already been hurt enough. He'd be damned for hurting her once. He'd be doubly damned if he'd do it twice.

One chance. No mistakes, no foul-ups—and he was the king of mistakes and foul-ups. Maybe he should save them all the heartache and leave now. He'd faced much better odds and still lost—and this time he had so damn much to lose. If he left now...

Grace would be alone again, believing that no man would ever want her. He would never know his child. And he would have indisputable proof that he was no better than his father—worse, even. Gordon had left Nadine to raise Guthrie and Ethan alone, but Nadine had never needed Gordon. Grace did need *him*. She needed him to help take care of this old house, to introduce her to all the other firsts missing from her life, to make her smile.

She needed him to love her.

And he needed to try, he admitted, his throat growing tight as he watched her. But even loving her couldn't guarantee that he wouldn't hurt her.

God, he'd never been so scared in his life! He didn't have the courage to make all this work...but he *couldn't* not try. He couldn't run far enough or fast enough to be free of her, and if he failed this one chance, there would be no place to run to where he could forget her.

So he couldn't fail. Whatever it took, however long, he had to make this work.

Something caught her attention. Looking his way, she smiled shyly. ''The heat's back on,'' she said unnecessarily.

''And here I thought that was just me looking at you.''

Her smiled deepened. ''The snow's melting. The roads will be clear by midafternoon.''

''Too bad. But until then, why don't you come over here and seduce me?''

Color flooded into her cheeks—embarrassment, he thought, though he wouldn't rule out arousal. Just the idea was enough to make him start getting hard. ''I wouldn't know where to begin.''

The innocence of her reply made him laugh. ''You've already begun, sweetheart. Just sitting where I can see you makes for a damn fine start. Come here.''

He extended his hand, and after one long moment, she set her cup aside, carefully stood up and started toward the bed. The sweater clung to the curves of her breasts and her belly, then skimmed over to her hips to mid-thigh, leaving the rest of her long, lean legs exposed. It was an erotic combination—the long-sleeved, high-necked sweater, about as concealing as a garment could get, and the lush, responsive naked body it covered.

She stopped beside him, clasped her hands together,

dropped them to her sides, then protectively hugged her arms to her chest. "I don't know what to do," she confessed.

"I'll show you." He held his hand out for hers. When she hesitantly took it, he drew her onto the bed. He was lying at the near edge, so she had no choice but to move over him—no choice at all once he stopped her in mid-slide so that she straddled him.

Through the sheet that was all that separated them, he could feel her heat. Combined with the shifting of her body as she sought a comfortable—and, he suspected, less intimate—position, the sensations made him harder, hotter, than ever.

"Let me lie down."

"Just sit here. I'm enjoying this," he teased, making her blush.

"But I'm too heavy."

"Oh, yeah, babe. Why, you must weigh… What? A hundred and forty pounds?" He placed his hands on her hips to subtly reposition her, then let one slide across her stomach, where the movement beneath his palm startled him. His first response was to snatch his hand away as if it burned. The second was to touch Grace again, seeking it out again. When it came, it was a solid kick, directly beneath his fingers. "Oh, my God… I didn't think… It didn't occur to me… She's *moving*. Like a real baby."

Grace's smile was sweet. "I'm surprised this is the first time you've felt it. She can be pretty active."

On cue the baby kicked again, bringing a big, goofy grin to Ethan's face. It was amazing. He knew, of course, that babies kicked, but she'd never mentioned it and he'd never realized that *his* baby was kicking. It was incredible—and frightening. It made the whole prospect of becoming a father so much more real. Up until now, the baby had been a symbol, more or less, of something that didn't yet exist, that wouldn't actually exist for six more weeks.

But she *did* exist. She was as real now as she would ever be. He had proof. He could *feel* her.

"Are you ever afraid?" he asked, cradling both hands to her stomach, feeling a few settling-in sort of tremors, then nothing.

"Of what?"

"All this. Being pregnant. Giving birth. Being responsible for another human being. Do you ever worry that you won't be a good mother, or that you won't know what to do? Does the responsibility ever intimidate you?"

"Everything intimidates me," she said with a faint smile. Then she shrugged, and he felt it in the most sensitive part of his anatomy. "I admit, I'm a little afraid about giving birth, but Callie says there's nothing to worry about, that it's as natural as breathing. Of course, she's just a midwife. She's never given birth herself." She said the last with another little smile before turning serious. "I don't worry about being a good mother. I want this baby. I love her, and I'll do anything for her."

"But you didn't have a good mother yourself. You have no role model." He knew what he was actually saying and suspected she did, too. *He* had no role model. How could he ever be a good father when the only father he'd ever had was lousy?

"You're right. My mother was a bad mother. I'll get no help from her. But I remember the things I needed from her. I know what I thought, as a child, a good mother was." She fell silent for a moment, and an uneasy look came into her eyes. "You have Guthrie. He can be your role model."

Ethan stared at her. That was the first time she'd acknowledged that he would have a place in the baby's life. He was more touched than he could say...and it made him want her more than words could express.

Pulling her to him, he kissed her, lifted her, yanked the sheet out from beneath her. ''You're going to be on top this time, babe,'' he murmured as he grasped the hem of her sweater. ''And this time I get to see you naked.''

She started to protest, but he got the sweater halfway up and got distracted by her breasts, and for a time, talking was the last thing on her mind.

When he finally managed to discard the sweater, when, with her clumsy help, he pushed inside her, filled her and felt her tightly gloving him, when she let her head fall back as her eyes glazed over with sensation, he took a good long look at her and knew he'd been wrong earlier when he'd said she was lovely. With the delicate porcelain of her skin, the baby-owl seriousness of her dark eyes, the shy smile that could easily go from innocent to smug, from sweet to sweetly satisfied, there was no doubt about it.

She was beautiful.

And he was damn lucky to have her.

By the end of the week, the temperature was in the seventies and the snow was just a memory. But not all that it had brought. Grace had had the most wonderful week of her life. Ethan had spent most of the days and all of the nights with her. He'd taught her things she hadn't even heard whispers about, and he made her feel alive in ways she couldn't explain. He had changed everything.

And nothing.

Though he spent time at the store, helping her out, everyone who saw him seemed to assume that he was working for her. No one, not even Reese Barnett, suspected there was anything between them. Of course, Ethan gave them no reason to suspect a thing. He kept his distance whenever there were customers around. He was friendly, reasonably polite, reasonably wary. He was so good that at times he could almost fool *her* into wondering whether their relationship really was strictly business. But that was what she wanted, wasn't it? No suspicion, no gossip, no speculation that could come back to haunt her baby. *Wasn't* it?

Or did some foolish part of her want him to publicly stake a claim? To acknowledge to one and all that he was having an affair with her, was maybe even—please, God— learning to care about her. Surely he must care. Surely he couldn't kiss her so gently, hold her so tenderly, make love to her so passionately, if he didn't care just a little.

Of course he could. Men did it all the time. He'd done a wonderful job of it last summer when they were strangers, when he'd felt nothing for her but lust.

Besides, the secrecy was her idea, remember? It was one of her terms that Ethan had agreed to uphold until she decided differently. And she was being pulled in so many directions by so many conflicting needs that she couldn't decide anything.

With a sigh, she forced her attention back to the open books on the desk. Ethan was finishing the inventory she'd barely started then forgotten when he'd come home, and she was supposed to be working on accounts, but she couldn't concentrate. When he came around the counter, turned up the volume on the radio, then claimed her hand and pulled her to her feet, she gave up trying. "What are you doing?" she asked with a laugh.

"I'm dancing with my girl."

"Dancing? In the hardware store? My father would have a fit."

"But your father's not here, and we are." He pulled her into his arms, holding her firmly enough that she couldn't get away if she tried...not that she had any intention of trying. She'd learned well that in his arms was where she wanted to be. Closing her eyes, she rested her cheek against his chest to enjoy the moment.

The song was slow, the lyrics romantic, about making

love and the world standing still. She could relate to that. In those wonderfully intense moments, it was as if time stopped and nothing in the world existed but the two of them. It was incredible.

When the music ended and a commercial began, their movements slowly stopped, too. But Ethan continued to hold her, and she continued to let him, until a voice boomed across the counter.

"Well, I'll be. Gordon James's boy and Jed Prescott's girl dancin' in the hardware store in the middle of the day," Pete Davis said with a cackling laugh. "Now I've seen everythin'."

With a flush heating her entire body, Grace would have jerked away from Ethan, but he didn't let go so easily. As a scowl tightened his features, he slowly released her, holding on to her hand until she forcibly pulled it away. "Pete," he said stiffly. "I figured you'd died years ago."

"Funny. I figured the same thing about you, son. Too much booze, too much cheatin', another man's wife…" Pete laughed again, then reached out one bony hand. "How long you back for?"

"Don't know." Ethan shook hands with him before giving Grace a sidelong look. "I'm thinking about staying this time."

Pete looked at her, too. "It's a good thing none of us ever put our money where our mouth is, son, 'cause you weren't even on the list. You never fail to surprise us, do you, boy?"

"You need something today?" Ethan asked levelly. "Or did you just come in here looking for gossip?"

"I actually did need something, but durned if it hasn't plumb escaped me what it was. I'll be back when I remember."

For a long moment after he left, Grace couldn't even look at Ethan. She didn't know where to look, how to stand, what to say. She'd even forgotten what to do with her hands, and so they just fluttered nervously, helplessly, before she laced her fingers tightly together. Of all the people who could have walked in on them, Pete Davis was the worst. Along with the old men who hung out at the café, Pete was the biggest gossip around. Within an hour, it would be all over town that he'd caught them dancing in the store—an even sillier notion now than it had seemed when Ethan had first suggested it. For their inventive minds, it was only a leap from the dance to the idea that there might be something going on between them, and a tiny jump to the possibility that he could be the father of her baby. Everyone would know by sundown.

Ethan turned the radio down again, then grimly faced her across the desk. "Your secret's out now."

She clenched her fingers tighter to keep from gasping in dismay. "Do you think he guessed…?"

"Guessed what?"

"That you…that this…about the baby?"

A puzzled look crossed his face. "Sweetheart, he didn't guess. He *knows.* Didn't you hear him?" When she blankly shook her head, he grimaced. "'It's a good thing that none of us put our money where our mouth is, because you weren't even on the list.' He was talking about bets. They were making bets on who the father is, but they hadn't considered me. Darlin', if ol' Pete talks like he used to, everybody's gonna know by closing time at the café."

Grace numbly shook her head from side to side. "It was one stupid dance. It doesn't mean anything. All they can do is guess, and we'll tell them they're wrong."

Now Ethan shook his head. "I know I told you I would keep your secret, Gracie, and I've already done it once, but I won't do it again. When Reese Barnett asked if I was the father, I told him no, and I felt like the worst bastard that ever lived. It was wrong, Gracie. It was wrong then, and it would be unforgivably wrong now. I won't publicly disagree with you. I won't tell anyone you're lying, but I won't lie myself, not again, not about that."

She thought about facing everyone once the truth was known—about the pitying looks she would get from some, about the looks Ethan would get from others. She thought about the gossip, the whispers, the disapproval and the scorn—thought about her baby being subjected to all that—and she felt sick inside.

And there *would* be gossip and scorn. She had no doubt about that. What had Pete's first words been? *Gordon James's boy and Jed Prescott's girl dancin' in the hardware store.* His tone had been mocking, teasing, just a little disdainful. That was kindness compared to what others would offer.

Damn it, for seven and a half months, she'd kept her secret without any problem, and in just a couple of minutes, with one stupid dance, Ethan had ruined it. Sure, she could insist that he wasn't the father, but she was a lousy liar, and when he was standing there refusing to confirm or deny her story, who would believe her?

Stricken, she sank into the chair. "You have no right to do this," she whispered.

"That's my baby!" he snapped. "I have every right!"

Before she could do more than shake her head in dismay, the bell over the door rang. Because the radio wasn't blaring, because she wasn't dancing around in Ethan's arms like a fool, she heard it, but even with advance warning, she couldn't pull herself together. She couldn't do much more than look when Guthrie Harris walked up to the counter.

"Grace. Ethan." He removed his Stetson and rested it crown-down on the counter. "I saw your truck out front when I dropped Liv and the girls off at the grocery store, so I thought I'd come by. We haven't seen you around much lately.''

Ethan sounded almost normal. "I've been keeping busy. I'm still painting over at Grace's house, and I help out here some."

"You must have painted the whole house, judging by how late you're there."

Ethan scowled at him. "I don't pry into what you and Olivia do at night. It's none of your business what I do."

Surprisingly, Guthrie didn't take offense. "Liv's about to pop that kid out any day now. We don't do *anything* at night." He hesitated, and when he spoke again, discomfort underscored his words. "Listen, can we go someplace and talk?"

"We can talk here."

Guthrie glanced at her, and Grace automatically got to her feet. She eased past Ethan without touching him and went into the break room because it was the polite thing to do. It only created the illusion of privacy, though. If she faced the door, she could see them both. No matter which direction she faced, she could easily hear them.

She took a bottle of water from the refrigerator and chose to face the wall while she drank it.

"Listen, Ethan, I don't want to pry into your business—"

"Since when?"

"But we've been hearing a lot of talk."

"Mama always said you shouldn't listen to gossip." Ethan sounded defensive, almost hostile, when Grace knew he didn't feel that way. He just wanted Guthrie's approval—and, in part thanks to her, he probably wasn't going to get it any time soon.

"Yeah, well, Mom liked a good bit of gossip as much as the next person," Guthrie said dryly. "As long as it didn't involve her family."

"I can't help it if people have nothing better to do than talk about me," Ethan said stiffly.

"I don't care if they talk about you. Hell, I was their favorite topic of conversation for a long time after Shay dumped me. They can talk about anybody in the county as long as it's not my family or me."

Well, hell, Ethan thought with an ache strong and deep. That made it pretty damn clear where he stood in Guthrie's life. He definitely wasn't family any longer.

"I just think I should find out a few things about your life from you and not from the gossip going around."

Ethan shrugged. "Ask whatever you want."

"All right." But now that he had permission, Guthrie looked uncomfortable, as if he'd rather let the subject drop. "Are you living over at Grace's?"

For all practical purposes, but not officially. Most of his clothing was still in the closet at the cabin, along with all his personal belongings. He'd moved only the bare necessities to her house—a few clothes, toothbrush, razor—because they were living on a day-to-day basis. Every night he was prepared to go home and sleep alone until she let him know that he was welcome to stay. The next night he waited for another invitation.

"I've been staying there," he hedged.

"Why?"

Ethan glanced at the break room. Grace's back was to him, but he had no doubt she could hear their conversation. He should have left with Guthrie when his brother had suggested it, should have at least stepped outside. Now he moved away from the counter and lowered his voice. "What kind of a question is that? She's a beautiful woman. I'm a single man."

At the "beautiful" comment, Guthrie's puzzled gaze shifted toward the break-room door. He was trying to envision Grace as beautiful, and failing. But what he thought of any woman in the world besides his own was irrelevant, less than pointless. "But she's a pregnant single woman, and you're…"

Ethan didn't prompt him, but waited silently, stiffly, to hear what his brother thought of him.

Guthrie took the easy way out, changing the focus. "She's not your type."

"You might think that," Ethan agreed as he gazed out the dusty window that overlooked the parking lot. "But you'd be wrong."

"So you're saying she *is* your type? That Ethan James, world-class heartbreaker at Heartbreak High, has suddenly developed an interest in very pregnant single women?" Guthrie shook his head emphatically. "Yeah, right. Unless…"

The silence drew out, and Ethan waited, anger and hurt and disappointment building inside until he couldn't wait one second longer. "Unless what?" he demanded. "I'm planning to rip her off? Maybe to con her out of her business, her house and her life savings? Because, after all, that's what I do, isn't it? I steal from people. I betray them. I take what I want and to hell with everyone else—"

His voice calm but louder, firmer, Guthrie cut in. "Unless you're the father of her baby."

Chapter 11

Ethan was startled, so surprised that Guthrie wasn't expecting the absolute worst from him that he had no answer to give. The first time he opened his mouth, nothing came out. The second time, he managed words, but the tone he meant to be brash and cocky was instead shaky. "Why—why would you think that?"

Guthrie took a moment to drag his fingers through his hair, ruffling it where the band of his hat had flattened it. "It took me a while to notice the coincidence of the timing. Grace's baby is due a month after Liv's, which means she got pregnant at the beginning of July, when you were home. Now you're back again, with 'personal' business to take care of, and from your first day back, you've been hanging around Grace. Now…we both know that you two weren't friends when you were kids, and you've been away too long to have business of any kind here. You don't have a thing for pregnant women, and you've never stayed with the same woman for two weeks in your life, so that leaves the baby. Is it yours?"

Ethan glanced over his shoulder, but Grace was out of sight. If she was listening, she was surely sending fervent prayers his way that, in spite of his earlier words, he would keep his promise and lie. He'd done it once, and hated it, but he could do it again. He could betray two of the people most important to him. He could do it for Grace.

With a sickly smile, he looked back at his brother. "You know me better than that, Guthrie. Don't you think if I were the father I would stay—" he drew a deep breath "—I would stay hell and gone away—" despite his best efforts, the smile disappeared "—away from..."

He couldn't finish, not even for Grace. Staring out the window, he knotted his left hand into a fist and muttered, "I'm sorry. I can't do this, not again." Steeling himself for disappointment, for condemnation, he met his brother's gaze and said flatly, "Yes, it's my baby. I came home as soon as I found out."

But there wasn't any disappointment. No condemnation. Guthrie's gaze remained steady, curious, nothing else. "What are you planning to do about it?"

"What makes you think I have any say in what I do about it?" He glanced toward the break room again and rubbed an ache pounding in his temple. "Life wasn't real easy for Grace, having her mother run off when she was just a kid and her father being such a bastard. It wasn't much fun being Jed Prescott's poor, pitiful daughter."

"Probably not much more fun than being Gordon James's charming, delinquent son."

Ethan gave him a long, wary look. He couldn't recall Guthrie ever acknowledging that he might have had anything to live down when he was growing up. His older brother had always been a black-and-white, no-excuses sort of guy. You took responsibility for your own actions. You didn't try to justify them, didn't lay blame anywhere but squarely on your own shoulders. Either you were honorable or you weren't. Period.

"No, probably not," he agreed before returning to the subject. "All her life, people have either ignored her or pitied her. She never had any friends, never had a *life,* until Jed left last fall. For the first time in twenty-five years, she's got friends, people who worry about her, people who respect her. She's afraid…" Breaking off, he drew a deep breath. It was harder admitting her fears to Guthrie than to Olivia. Of course, Olivia was just his sister-in-law. He liked her a lot and, given the chance, would probably come to love her, but she wasn't the half brother he'd grown up worshiping. He hadn't spent his entire life trying to win her approval or, failing that, trying to provoke her anger, just to satisfy himself that she felt *something* for him.

"She's afraid," he forced himself to repeat, "that if people find out the truth, they'll treat the baby badly because of it. Because of me."

"And you're afraid she's right," Guthrie said quietly.

Ethan shrugged. "Growing up here as Gordon's son was tough. After all the stunts I've pulled, especially what I did to you and Olivia, growing up here as *my* child might be impossible."

Guthrie came to stand beside him, gazing out the same window. "I wish I could say you were both wrong. But there are still people here who believe a James is a sure sign of trouble. There are some who will just be waiting for the kid to screw up, who will blame everything he or she ever does wrong on being a James. I—I'm sorry to admit that I've been one of them for a very long time."

Ethan turned his head just enough to make eye contact. "No kidding."

Guthrie's smile was embarrassed. "You figured that out, huh?"

"I'm not as smart as you are, or as capable or as perfect,

but after the first ten or twenty times you told me I was a loser, the message sank in.''

''I didn't—''

''You never missed a chance to tell me my father was a poor excuse for a human being, that he was lazy, no good, worthless, that you all were better off without him. And you never missed a chance to add that I was just like him. Since I couldn't convince you I was better than Gordon, I settled for convincing you I was worse.'' He grinned bleakly. ''Did a pretty good job of it, didn't I? It's the only thing I ever did that I didn't screw up.''

Guthrie gestured toward the break room. ''You haven't screwed this up.''

''I don't know. I want to get married, she doesn't. I want to quit hiding, she doesn't. Right now she doesn't even want to talk to me. We were dancing—my idea, my fault—and Pete Davis saw us together and guessed…'' He finished with a shrug.

His brother chuckled. ''Hell, the whole county'll know by morning. I'm glad I finally figured it out. It would have been a sorry thing to find out that I'm gonna be an uncle from ol' Pete .''

''I don't know. I found out I was gonna be a father from Olivia.''

Guthrie gave him a startled look. ''Liv knew? And didn't tell me?''

''So did Shay.''

He gave a long-suffering shake of his head. ''Women and their secrets. So…what are you going to do now?''

''I don't know.'' The answer didn't satisfy Ethan, but it was the only one he had. He supposed they would first deal with the gossip now that Pete had spread it around. Then maybe Grace would see that it wasn't so bad, that people weren't so shocked or scornful or narrow-minded.

Or maybe she would see that it was worse than she'd

feared. Maybe some people would wonder out loud what in hell he'd seen in her, or what in hell she'd seen in him. Maybe they would be petty, mean and cruel.

Maybe Annie *would* suffer for having him for a father.

"Bring Grace out to the ranch. She's always wanted a family, and Lord knows, we have a family. Maybe they can help change her mind."

"Maybe." She certainly liked Olivia. Maybe the idea of being sisters-in-law would help convince her to accept his proposal.

"Whatever you do, don't let her push you away. If she decides your reputation is too much to bear, she can turn that kid against you without even realizing she's doing it. Whatever happens, don't let her keep you from your baby. Trust me on this."

Ethan smiled faintly. "I've always trusted you on everything."

Guthrie started to walk off, then came back. "For what it's worth, Ethan... We almost lost the ranch when your father left. I was sixteen, trying to finish school, to hold on to property that had been in my father's family for generations, trying to keep a roof over our heads. Mom was upset and hurt, and I was furious with Gordon. We were in so much trouble because of him. But he was gone, and you were there, so I...I took it out on you. Hell, you looked just like him, with the same blond hair, the same blue eyes, that same damned grin. Even the way you walked and talked were perfect reminders of him. It was so damned wrong to blame you, but it was so damned easy. Later it became a cycle. The harder I pushed you, the worse you behaved. The worse you behaved, the harder I pushed. At some point along the way, I'd begun to believe my own insults—that you really were just like your father."

"And I began to act like him."

"I'm sorry, Ethan. I'm so damned sorry."

Even if there weren't a lump in his throat, Ethan wouldn't know what to say. He settled for clearing his throat, for blinking away whatever was making his eyes water, and shrugged. "It's okay."

"No, it isn't. But if you give us a chance, maybe we can make it okay."

One chance. That was what he'd asked for from Grace. It was easy enough to grant the same to Guthrie. "Sure," he said as if it were no big deal. "I'd like that."

"I'll have Liv call Grace and arrange dinner or something," Guthrie said as he headed for the door. "And come by sometime. The kids are missing you." Then he added just before he walked out, "I'm missing you."

Ethan gave a heavy sigh as he listened to the door shut. He'd never felt more hopeful—or less so—in his life. It looked as if things might finally work out with Guthrie.

Now, if he could just make them right with Grace.

It didn't take long for the curiosity to start. Before the close of business on Saturday, Grace had waited on at least a dozen customers who were there strictly to find out if ol' Pete's information was correct. Pastor Hughes's wife didn't come right out and voice her disapproval, but she kept shaking her head and clucking her tongue, as if she'd just found out that Grace's baby was the spawn of Satan.

She dealt with sly hints, outright nosiness, condescension, amazement and countless other responses. She told no one anything, but kept tightening her jaw until her teeth hurt. By the time she turned the Closed sign over on the door, she wanted nothing more than to go home and cry.

She was sitting at the desk, contemplating doing just that, when Ethan came up behind her and began kneading the tense muscles in her shoulders. Part of her wanted to push him away, to remind him that if he hadn't insisted on that stupid dance, none of this would be happening. Part of her wanted to turn around, crawl into his arms, hide her face against his chest and stay there forever.

Instead she did nothing and let him rub her.

"Run away with me, Gracie," he murmured as he leaned close to her ear.

The tension in her muscles doubled. "I thought you were through with running away."

"I'll take you someplace where it's warm all the time, where you'll never have to worry about cold or snow."

"I like winter," she said, being deliberately difficult.

"Then I'll take you to New England, where the seasons are just as pretty as you please. We'll find a little village on the coast of Maine and sell nuts and bolts and be handymen-for-hire."

"I like Heartbreak."

"Better than you like me?"

His teasing tone made her lips twitch with the urge to smile. She forced them into a thin line. "At the moment."

Kneeling on the floor beside the desk, he swiveled her chair to face him. "What about in the next moment when I kiss you? Or in the moment after I've made love to you? What about the moment when you're cranky and tired and I'm taking care of Annie Grace so you can rest?"

Her lip trembled, but she kept her frown. "Don't be charming, Ethan. I'm angry, and I don't want to be teased out of it."

"Okay." Leaning forward, he pressed his mouth to hers, tickled her lips with his tongue, filled her mouth with it. It was a sweet kiss, an it's-been-a-long-day-and-you're-tired kiss. It relaxed and soothed her and made her feel... Lazy. Lucky. Loved.

And obviously delusional.

But she liked the delusion too much to force it away just yet.

Finally, when he pulled back to take a breath, she gave

a soft little sigh. "Let's go home and pretend today never happened."

"There are parts of today that I don't want to pretend didn't happen," Ethan said stubbornly as he helped her to her feet. "Waking up with you this morning. Talking to Guthrie. Our dance."

She scowled. That damn dance. Her father had been right not to allow music in either his store or his house. It could seduce a person into bad decisions, could land her in an awkward position.

So could gossipy old neighbors.

They closed up and went home. Ethan suggested that they go out to dinner—not in Heartbreak, he was quick to add—but all she really wanted was to lie down. Between the baby and the drain on her emotions, she was exhausted. She felt as if she could sleep twenty-four hours straight through. Maybe if she did, when she awakened, life would be better.

And maybe she'd still be stuck in the same hard place.

Cassie had warned that she might get a bit emotional, thanks to her pregnancy hormones, but Grace had thought she'd escaped that fate. Now she knew she hadn't. Her hormones had just been waiting for Ethan to come along before they threw everything into turmoil. As she curled onto her side in bed, she couldn't decide whether she was mortified that the truth had come out or relieved. Whether she wanted to admit it *was* true or lie to protect the baby. Whether to cry and lay blame or accept it and get on with her life.

She didn't know whether she loved Ethan or merely felt grateful to him, whether he cared for her or merely felt responsible.

He closed the curtains, then tucked the covers around her before stretching out beside her. "Do you want me to wake you for dinner?"

She shook her head. "If I get hungry, I'll wake up."

"Do you want me to go home?"

After a brief hesitation, she shook her head again. It was the right answer for him. It made the corners of his mouth curve up just a little. He kissed her forehead, brushed his hand across her cheek, then rose from the bed. "I'll be downstairs or in Annie's room if you need anything. Good night, babe."

Lifting her head from the pillow, she stopped him in the doorway. "Ethan? Thank you."

"For what?"

"Everything."

"You're welcome." Then… "Get some rest, darlin'. I'll check on you later."

Knowing that he would check on her made it easy for her to follow his orders. She snuggled into the covers that smelled of him and dozed off.

When she awakened again, it was morning. The sun was shining, the curtains were open again, and music was coming from down the hall. She rolled over to see the alarm clock on the opposite night table, then sat bolt upright. Eleven o'clock! She'd practically gotten that twenty-four-hour nap she'd claimed she could use. She felt like a slug—though an incredibly well-rested one.

"Hey, sleepyhead." Wearing old jeans, a stained T-shirt and a smear of white paint across one cheek, Ethan stood in the doorway. "It's about time you woke up. How do you feel?"

"Lazy."

"Oh, yeah, that's you. Grace Prescott, slacker. Are you hungry?"

"Starved. Annie and I don't often miss one meal. We've never skipped two in a row."

"Then get up and get dressed. I'm taking you out for lunch today."

Feeling suddenly wary, she slid so she could sit with the headboard at her back and kept the covers over the lower half of her body. "Where?"

"I thought we'd eat at Shay's place."

"I don't think so." She didn't eat at the Heartbreak Café often under the best of circumstances. The small diner was more or less the heart of Heartbreak. Everyone with time to sit and talk passed it at the café. That was where you went if you wanted the latest news, weather or gossip, and since she *was* the latest gossip...

"I do think so. We've got to face these people, Grace. If we don't, they'll just keep talking."

"They'll keep talking, anyway."

"Come on, Grace. You can't hide out forever. Then they'll really have reason to talk about the crazy lady who lives at the end of the lane and never comes out in daylight."

She folded her arms across her chest and skeptically asked, "It really doesn't bother you?"

The teasing light disappeared from his eyes and grimness took its place. "Hell, yes, it bothers me, but you know what, Grace? It's a fact of life. Whenever your life is more interesting than everyone else's, they're going to talk about it. Whenever life is slow and dull, which in Heartbreak is all the time, they're going to look for someone to discuss. For large parts of my life, it's been me. Before that, it was my father. Guthrie's had his share of gossip. So have Shay and Easy and Reese Barnett. Hell, for that matter, so have you. The difference is, the rest of us ignore it. Maybe it's uncomfortable. Maybe it hurts. But we don't let it ruin our lives."

"Ignore it? If it were that easy, Ethan, don't you think I'd do it?" she demanded. "I'm not like you, Guthrie and the others. That's part of the problem."

Mindful of his paint-stained clothes, he crouched beside

the bed, pulled her hand free and laced his fingers with hers. "You're just like us, darlin', only a little more shy. You haven't quite mastered that go-to-hell attitude that you need to deal with these people."

She didn't want to smile, but she couldn't help it. The idea of her telling *anyone* to go to hell was just so ludicrous. She'd never been disrespectful to anyone in her entire life...even though they had, on numerous occasions, been disrespectful to her.

"Surprise 'em, Grace," Ethan urged. "They expect you to endure this new round of talk like the same shy little mouse you always were. *Don't.* Look 'em in the eye and tell 'em it's none of their damn business."

"I can't do that."

"Of course you can."

She shook her head. "Lightning would strike me dead if I even tried."

He grinned boldly. "Honey, I've been telling them that for fifteen years and I haven't been struck down yet."

Freeing her hand from his, she stroked his blond hair back his forehead. "I'm not like you, Ethan. I care what they think."

"I care, too. Don't ever make the mistake of thinking I don't. But you can't let what others think of you determine how you live your life."

"You're a fine one to talk. Everything you do can somehow be traced back to Guthrie. You came back here when you found out I was pregnant because Guthrie would have thought it was the right thing to do. You're willing to marry me—" she pretended not to hear the catch in her voice "—because that's what he would do."

His fingers tightened fractionally around hers, and his expression, for one instant, became distant and remote. Then he released her hand and stood up with a careless gesture. "I'm not making some great sacrifice in offering to marry that poor, pitiful Prescott girl, Grace. Even in the beginning, the first time I asked, I thought the sacrifice would be yours, not mine. I *want* to marry you. I want to live with you and raise our baby with you.''

''For how long?''

His jaw tightened, his mouth thinning in a frustrated line. ''I can't give you guarantees, Grace.''

''Of course not.''

He ignored her. ''I could die tomorrow.''

''But it's more likely that you'd get bored and pack up and leave. Life here is slow and dull, remember? You just said it yourself. And when things are dull, you move on. It's what you've done since you were fifteen.'' Watching the tension streak through him, she regretted her words— heavens, she regretted the entire conversation—but she couldn't take them back, couldn't soften them. His leaving was one of her biggest fears. She couldn't pretend it didn't exist. She couldn't pretend, as he did, that everything would somehow turn out all right if they just believed strongly enough.

''Sometimes people change,'' he said flatly. ''Unlike you. You've got everyone convinced that you *have* changed, but down inside you're still the same scared little Grace, and you're still living in a miserable little prison. It's different from the one your father kept you in, but it's a prison all the same. One where only you and your baby matter. Where you don't have to trust anyone. You don't have to believe in anyone. You don't have to take any risks, any chances.''

''I've taken plenty of risks with you!''

He shook his head stubbornly. ''How? By meeting with me only in private? By having an affair with me in secret? By only being seen in public with me an hour away from here where no one will know? By demanding that I deny my own child? By lying to all those friends whose opinions mean so damn much to you, telling them that I'm just an old friend, that I'm around only because I'm doing some work for you, that I couldn't possibly be important to you?''

Grace pushed the covers back and left the bed. Though her nightgown fell to her knees, she pulled on her robe, too, just for the extra comfort it offered. ''You—you *are* important to me, Ethan,'' she said quietly, awkwardly. ''Don't you see that that's part of the problem?''

His thin smile cut her. ''First I'm a stigma. Now I'm a problem. Well, hell, who said we weren't making progress?''

She wanted to crawl back into bed and cry, almost as much as she wanted to stamp her foot and shriek, or slap that cold sarcasm away. Instead, she went to the closet and yanked out the dowdiest of her old dresses. After taking underwear from the dresser, she turned to face him. ''Get cleaned up so we can get some lunch.''

The look he gave her was almost enough to make her wilt. ''I'm not hungry.''

''Well, I am, so get ready.'' With that she flounced down the hall to the bathroom, where she tried to slam the door but managed only a firm click.

When she came out, hair combed, teeth brushed, but without makeup, he was waiting at the foot of the stairs. He'd changed into clean clothes and scrubbed away the paint, but he was still coldly angry. Fine. So was she.

They arrived at the Heartbreak Café in time to join the other Sunday dinner early birds. Once the church bells started ringing, every seat in the place would fill up and the overflow would line up outside to await their own tables. Grace knew this from talk, not because she'd ever eaten Sunday dinner there. In fact, this was the first time she'd walked through the door in a long time—the first time she'd ever walked through with a man.

And the response was every bit as bad as she'd dreaded. There were a few diners who glanced up, only vaguely curious, then returned to their meal or their companions, and there were some who actually stared as she and Ethan walked past. She even caught a whisper—*The father of that baby…. Whoever would have believed it?*—from one booth, though she couldn't bring herself to look and see who had spoken.

Her face burning, she slid into the last booth, taking the side where she could face the wall. Ethan sat down opposite her and pulled the table closer to give her a little breathing space. She'd rather have taken her space under the table, out of sight of prying eyes.

The waitress who approached with a pot of coffee was as curious as the others. "Hi, Grace," she said, greeting her with a smile before turning to Ethan. "You probably don't remember me, but I'm Amalia Parker. Used to be Gibson. I was a year behind you in school."

She said it so easily, so naturally, that Grace was immediately envious. If she'd even tried to talk to Ethan like that in the bar that summer night, she would have swallowed her tongue.

"Hi. Uh, no coffee, Amalia," he said. Though Grace was staring at her menu, she knew he was smiling, just a bit, just to be polite.

"So…Grace, we all heard the news." Amalia smiled broadly as she brushed her fingers over Grace's arm. "I told those old men there was no way it was Leroy. Even you had better taste—I mean, even the old you—I mean…" Taking a noisy breath, she rushed on. "I'd better make the rounds with this coffee. I'll be back in a minute to take your orders. Special today is roast with all the trimmings. I'll be back."

In the unusual silence that had settled over the dining

room, Grace could hear the buzz of whispers, along with a few soft murmurs. For all she knew, they could be talking about the weather or personal business of their own, but she couldn't stop the nagging fear that she and Ethan were the topic of every whisper, every murmur. When she got proof a few minutes later in another loud-enough-to-carry comment—*Any girl he wants.... What in the world did he see in her?*—she wanted to duck her head and slink out.

Ethan glared fiercely at the woman who'd spoken, then reached across the table to grab Grace's hand. "Hold your head up," he demanded in a low voice. "Don't you dare let them make you cry."

"I'm not going to cry," she said, but with her chin on her chest, he had to strain to hear. But when the woman's companion responded—*Well, we* know *the only reason he's coming around now*—a tear escaped the corner of her eye.

His first impulse was to confront both women, but rudeness in response to rudeness rarely accomplished anything. His second was to pull Grace to her feet and walk out, but that wouldn't accomplish anything, either. He was saved from having to come up with a third option by an unlikely source.

Sometime in the last few minutes, Reese Barnett had entered the café, and apparently he'd heard the remarks. He hung his Stetson and uniform jacket on the rack behind the door, then strolled the length of the dining room, making a show of greeting diners left and right. "How are you doing, Mona? Everything going okay, Jake? Earl, I hear your prize mare delivered a fine filly." He stopped at the next-to-the-last booth. "Miz Taylor. And the other Miz Taylor. Church let out early this morning? Or did you figure you could do your souls more good gossiping here at the café?"

One of the women sputtered. The other didn't waste a

moment's breath. "You know, Reese Barnett, we put you in the sheriff's office. We can take you out."

"Now, don't go adding to your list of sins this Sunday morning, Miz Taylor. You didn't vote for me, and the whole county knows it. It was an honor not receiving your vote." Amid chuckles from a few other diners, he came to their booth and nudged Ethan on the shoulder. "Slide over there. Let me join you for a cup of coffee."

Ethan watched Grace dab embarrassedly at her eyes as he moved to sit beside her. When she thought she'd covered the evidence of her teariness, she looked up and offered the sheriff a wan smile. It wasn't much—she'd given Ethan better ones a hundred times—but it still affected him like a kick in the gut.

"Hi, Reese."

"Grace." Barnett fixed his gaze on Ethan. "You lied to me."

"Oh, gee, a James lying to a cop. Who would have expected it?" The sarcasm made Ethan feel about six years old. The jealousy made him feel about a hundred and six. But hell, Reese Barnett was exactly the sort of man Grace wanted and needed. Doing nothing more than sitting there, he was a living, breathing reminder to Grace of how short Ethan fell of every mark.

"I didn't expect it," Barnett said. "I thought you were telling the truth."

"I was telling you Grace's truth. Mine is a little different."

"So whose truth is true? Yours, hers or Pete's?"

"Pete's pretty accurate. You can probably go with his."

In the silence that followed Ethan's reply, the two women behind them left. Once Barnett had mentioned their name, Ethan had been able to place the outspoken one. She considered her family Heartbreak's social elite and the arbiters of class and good taste. But Inez Taylor wouldn't know class or good taste if it bit her on the butt, his mother had always claimed. Once again, time had proved her right.

After the waitress brought coffee for the sheriff and took their orders, Barnett directed his conversation to Grace. "You can't listen to anything the Taylor sisters-in-law say, Grace. No one else does, not even the Taylor brothers. They're petty, small-minded and mean-spirited. Inez wanted to make a complaint last fall against Easy because he wasn't appropriately grateful for her daughter's sympathy for the poor Indian cripple."

And it was a fair bet Easy had told the daughter so in plain, simple terms an idiot could understand. But Grace couldn't do something like that. She'd tried to crawl inside herself to hide. Ethan wished she was less sensitive, then immediately rephrased it. He wouldn't change a thing about her—except to give her faith in *him*. He wished he was less worthy of gossip and more worthy of her. He wished he'd aimed for less notoriety in his past and for more anonymity. He wished he was a man she could be proud of.

"Back when people ignored me, I thought it would be nice to be the center of attention from time to time," she said, trying to sound as if it were no big deal. "But being ignored really wasn't so bad. I could go back to that again."

"You will," Ethan assured her, daring to reach under the cover of the table to clasp her hand. He half expected her to pull away and was grateful when she didn't. "Something more interesting will come along and they'll forget all about you. Even I can't stay front and center in the gossip for very long and, believe me, I've tried."

She smiled that weak little smile again but didn't look convinced.

After that, Barnett changed the subject and kept the con-

versation going, but neither Ethan nor Grace had much to
contribute. Neither of them had much of an appetite, either.
She merely picked at her meal, wishing, he knew, that she
was anyplace else but there, probably with anyone else but
him. But when the time came to leave, she suddenly looked
as if she planned to take up residency in the booth.

It was the line of people waiting for a table, he knew,
that made her nervous. He wanted to slide his arm around
her shoulders, to clear the way for her and block anyone
from even looking closely at her, much less speaking to
her, but in the end, it was Barnett who cleared the way,
who blocked everyone's view of her and distracted anyone
interested in chatting with his own conversation. He walked
to the truck with them and helped Grace inside before
Ethan had a chance. Barnett even made her smile again
with something he said as Ethan circled the truck to climb
behind the wheel.

As he waited for a chance to back out of the parking
space, he asked, "You like him a lot, don't you?"

"Reese? He's been a good friend. When my father threw
me out, he found me a place to stay. He and the lawyer
down the street persuaded Jed to give me the store and the
house when he left town."

"And how did they do that?" Ethan asked, struggling to
control the sarcasm. Barnett was just damn near perfect, as
far as she was concerned. He'd given her nothing but help,
while Ethan had brought her nothing but trouble…and the
baby.

"Blackmail, I think, is the technical term for it." The
memory lightened the worry that seemed permanently
etched on her face. "They went to my father and pointed
out that, in hitting me, he was guilty of assault, and the fact
that he was so much bigger than me and I was pregnant
made it felony assault. They reminded him of all the people

who witnessed it, and suggested that the best way to avoid arrest and certain conviction was to leave town and leave the store and the house to me.''

"And he did. Just like that.''

"He took all the money, but he left everything else. So at least I had a home and a way to support myself.'' She was silent for a moment, then she answered his question. "Yes, I like Reese a lot.''

The response left him feeling inadequate and hopeless. He didn't notice the people on the sidewalk, didn't notice the cars on the street, until a horn tap alerted him to someone wanting his space. Numbly he pulled out and had covered half the distance home—to her house—when she spoke again.

"I like you a lot, too.''

"Yeah,'' he agreed bitterly, thinking it was definitely too little and just might be too late. "I'm your number-one guilty pleasure.''

"Ethan, please don't—''

"Don't what, Grace? Don't remind you? Don't take offense? Don't take the fact that you're ashamed of me the wrong way?''

"I'm not—'' Unable to finish the lie, she broke off and stared out the side window until he parked in her driveway. Then she faced him again. "I have to consider what's best for my child.''

"Our child! You never quite grasped that concept, did you?'' Without waiting, he went on. "You get to decide what's best for *our* child—you, who never had a normal life before now, who never knew a normal relationship until now. And you've decided that one of the lessons you'll teach her is that public opinion is more important than having a father. That what strangers think about her matters more than what she thinks of herself. That how much some-

one loves you doesn't matter a damn unless he's got everyone else's approval first.'' He looked away for strength,
then back again. ''God help you, Grace, if some of these
people in town decide that you're not fit to be her mother—
because with everything you're going to teach her, she'll
believe them.''

He opened the door, slid to the ground and breathed in
deeply of cold, sweet air. A couple of breaths put him back
in control enough to walk around the truck to help her out,
then follow her onto the porch.

She unlocked the door and went inside and halfway
down the hall before realizing that he hadn't crossed the
threshold. She turned back. ''Aren't you coming in?''

He wanted to, wanted it more than his pride could admit.
But he gathered his courage, shook his head and said, ''No.
I—I don't see much point in it.''

She looked stricken. Stunned. ''But— You can't—you
can't just—''

''Leave?'' he finished for her. ''That's what I've been
doing since I was fifteen, remember?''

''But what about— What about the painting and the—
the inventory? What about setting up the crib?''

The sadness that settled over him was unlike any he'd
ever felt before. ''Is that all you need me for, Grace? To
do things?'' Hopelessness changed to despair. ''Don't
worry. They'll get done. And if you come up with anything
else that needs doing, you can call me over at Guthrie's—
or, even better, call Reese Barnett. I hear he's a real good
friend.''

He stepped inside to catch the doorknob, then stepped
out again, closing the door firmly. For a minute he just
stood there, not certain he could walk away, even if it was
the best thing he could do for her, for Annie, hell, even for

himself. Not when he wanted more than anything in the world to stay.

He was pulling his hand back from the knob when he heard footsteps on the hardwood floor inside, then the faint creak of the door as she leaned against it. Even through the wood, her tears were audible. So were her plaintive words.

"What about me, Ethan? I need you, too."

Steeling himself, he walked away.

It was too little. And much too late.

Chapter 12

Deep in her heart, she'd known he wouldn't stay.

Grace tried to comfort herself with that, but it didn't work, thanks to that nagging little voice in her head that kept insisting maybe he would have if she'd given him half a chance. If she hadn't driven him away. If she hadn't been so damned afraid.

She moped around the house all day Sunday, hoping he would return, but bedtime approached without any sign of him. Considering how few nights he'd spent there—only seven—her bed felt incredibly empty and cold without him. Her heart felt empty and cold.

He would come back on Monday, she told herself as she dressed for work. She would open the door and find him waiting out there to give her a ride. And when she opened the door and found no one waiting, she told herself he would come along somewhere between the house and the store. When she reached Main Street with no sign of him, she insisted he would be waiting at the store. And when he wasn't…why, he'd probably had a restless night, like her. He would come in sometime before lunch.

When she sat down in the break room to a solitary lunch delivered from the café, she finally admitted that he probably wasn't going to come in at all today. Maybe he would show up tonight, before they had to spend another night apart. Maybe he would wait a couple of days, just so she could have a taste of what life without him was going to be like, so she could appreciate him more when he finally did come.

But she knew what life without him was like—sad, bleak, depressing. She'd lived twenty-five years of it. And she *did* appreciate him. He was one of the two best things to ever happen to her.

Not that anyone would have guessed from the way she'd treated him.

In spite of her best efforts, she still hoped to see his truck parked out in front of the store when she closed up, or in front of her house when she got home, but there was no sign of him. The instant she stepped inside the house, though, she knew he'd been there. She could feel him, could practically smell him. Nothing was out of place, and there were no notes, but she *knew*.

Had he used the key she'd given him to pick up the few belongings he'd brought over? she wondered as she trudged up the stairs.

The answer was in the small room at the top of the stairs where she'd slept for twenty-five years. Last week he'd cleaned it out, stripped the wallpaper, repaired the wallboard and sanded all the wood. Sunday morning, before everything fell apart, he'd applied the first coat of white paint to the trim and the built-in shelves. Today he'd applied the second coat and gathered all the painting supplies so he could start on the walls.

She stood in the middle of the room, hands clasped beneath her stomach, and cried.

She played her little game again on Tuesday. When she opened the front door, he would be waiting. When she got to the store, he would be waiting. When she got home, he would be waiting.

On Wednesday morning she couldn't help pausing in front of the door, closing her eyes and whispering a fervent prayer that when she opened the door, she would see him. But she wasn't surprised when she opened the door and he wasn't there. Just very sad. And she didn't expect him to be waiting at the store, or to saunter in sometime that morning, or to show up for lunch. Though some small hope remained every time the bell over the door rang and every evening just before she took that one step that would bring her house into view, the constant disappointments were so hard to bear. She couldn't live that way. She had to accept that, if left to Ethan, she wouldn't see him again.

And she couldn't live that way, either.

"So *you* go see *him*," Ginger advised over lunch on Thursday. "You know where he is."

Grace picked at the sandwich her friend had picked up at the café on the way over without much appetite. "I wouldn't know what to say to him."

"How about the truth?"

"I don't even know what that is."

"You know the important parts of it. You know he's the father of your baby. You know that he'd be a great father, and you know that every kid needs a great father." Ginger leaned across to pluck the dill pickle spear from Grace's plate. "You know that you love him."

Yes, she loved him. It was amazing how easily she'd managed to pretty much avoid facing that fact until he'd gotten fed up with her and left.

But love might not be enough, because she also knew that she'd hurt him deeply. She'd never meant to—Lord, all she'd wanted was to give her baby her absolute best— but regardless of intent, the results were the same. She'd hurt him, told him she was ashamed of him, told him that he wasn't good enough to be his daughter's father.

As if she were any sort of prize herself.

"Is it really so important what people think?" Ginger asked.

"I always thought so." But these past few days she'd begun to wonder. Customers continued to give her curious looks, and the more forward among them asked sly questions about Ethan, but she'd been so distracted by other, greater problems that she'd hardly noticed. And the less she noticed, the less attention they paid.

Of course everyone wanted to be well thought of. No one wanted to be the subject of gossip, especially when much of it was mean-spirited. But what really mattered, she was learning in a painful demonstration, was what the people close to you thought, and the people close to her, few though they were, thought she was nuts. Ginger hadn't hesitated to say so. Neither had Reese, when he'd come by for coffee yesterday morning.

Ethan, of course, wasn't saying anything at all.

"All my life, Ginger," she said quietly, "I've been different, and there was always someone around waiting to point that out to me. The kids at school used to make fun of me because my clothes were secondhand and never fit and I always wore these damn thick glasses and I was too shy to talk even to the teachers. They heard their parents talking about my parents, and they tormented me with how mean and hateful my father was and how spineless my mother was and how she ran off and left me behind. How she didn't love me enough to take me with her. I was this…freak, this oddity. Half the people ignored me, and the others didn't want anything to do with me because I was different. I don't want that for my baby.''

Ginger's tone was less than sympathetic. "Well, jeez, Grace, are you planning to dress her in ugly clothes and treat her like property instead of a child? Are you going to raise her the way your father raised you? Are you going to neglect and abandon her the way your mother did you?"

"Of course not!"

"So…what you're really worried about is the torment-ing-you-because-of-your-parents part. Exactly what is it you think they're going to say? 'Oh, that poor child. Keep your kids away from her. Her mother wears glasses and doesn't have much fashion sense. And her father…jeez, he was a wild one growing up. Do you know, when he found out she was pregnant, he came halfway across the country just to help her out, knocked himself out trying to prove he deserved her and fell in love with her along the way? Oh, no, we don't want our children playing with *their* child.'"

Grace glared at her. She wanted to argue, wanted to point out all the things people really might say, all the little whis-pers she and Ethan had heard for themselves. She wanted to set the record straight, that Ethan had never said, had never even hinted, that he might love her. That would have made all the difference in the world.

But hadn't he, in his truck outside her house Sunday? *How much someone loves you doesn't matter a damn unless he's got everyone else's approval first.* Wasn't that a pretty strong hint?

"I haven't lived in Heartbreak long," Ginger continued, her voice gentle, her touch on Grace's arm gentler. "It's only been about a year. But working at the only grocery store in town, I've met just about everybody. I've heard their good news and their complaints. They've told me all about their kids and their grandkids. I've worked with a lot of those kids. And you know what I think most of these people would say about your baby? 'She's got a mother and father who love her dearly and each other as well. How lucky can one child get?'"

How lucky, indeed, Grace thought tearily.

"And you know what else, Grace? I think most people in this town would be thrilled to see you and Ethan together. Because your childhood was difficult, because his wasn't much better, I think they would think it was no more than the two of you deserved, and they would be happy for you."

Grace had also thought that people would probably think they deserved each other, but in her poor-Grace way of thinking, she'd managed to put a negative spin on it. But she liked Ginger's positive outlook better. She could appreciate it much more.

"Why don't you call him? Better yet, go see him."

Go see him. After four days, she was hungry for the sight of him. She missed the sound of his voice, that damned grin, the quiet strength of his presence. *Go see him.* Close up the store, go to her house, surprise him at work.

She smiled faintly. In the entire twenty-years-plus history of Prescott's Hardware, it had never been closed up in the middle of a business day. She'd often thought nothing short of his own death could make her father do that.

But some things were more important than death. Like life. Love. Living happily ever after.

A set of keys landed on the table in front of her with a clatter. She looked up to find Ginger grinning broadly. "Take my car. Go on. I'll stay here and mind the store."

"What do you know about minding a hardware store?" Grace asked even as she picked up the keys and got to her feet.

Ginger patted her hair, pursed her lips and smiled prettily. "I know that most of your customers are men. I know that if I open my eyes wide and pull my shirt down a little lower—'' she demonstrated ''—and say, 'Why, I don't know nothin' 'bout hardware,' they'll wait on themselves and all I'll have to do is collect their money and keep their change.''

"Gee. And here I've spent my time actually doing the work myself." The dryness disappeared from Grace's voice as she paused in the doorway. "Wish me luck."

"Good luck."

"I won't be gone long."

"You will if you have good luck. Don't worry about me. I'll be fine here." Jumping to her feet, Ginger began rummaging through her purse. "Ooh, wait a minute. Pucker up."

Grace waited patiently while she applied lipstick, then blusher, then dusted her face with powder. When she reached for her mascara, Grace caught her wrist. "This is enough. Ethan's seen me plenty of times without makeup."

"And he kept coming back. God love him." Ginger's smile softened the words. "Go on. Find the poor guy and tell him *you* love him."

Grace pulled on her coat before stepping outside. There was a nip in the air, but spring was definitely on its way. She felt a sense of relief, though often Oklahoma's fiercest winter weather came in March or even April. She was ready for spring, for the baby to be born, for new life to begin.

Ginger's car wasn't much bigger than her Bug, but there was ample room behind the steering wheel. She settled in, started the engine, then took a minute or two to breathe deeply. What if Ethan wasn't at her house? What if he'd gotten tired of waiting for her to come to her senses and he'd left town again? What if he didn't love her at all, if everything he'd done had been done for the baby? What if—

She forced herself to stop. She could drive herself crazy

with what-ifs. Her time would be better spent thinking about what she was going to say to him, finding words sincere enough to express everything she felt.

But she didn't have time to come up with a single thought, because in the next block, parked in front of the Heartbreak Café, was a familiar old pickup truck. Next to it was Guthrie's truck, and next to that was Easy's. Of course Shay was inside—it *was* her café—and probably Olivia, too.

Grace deflated like a child's balloon. She would wait until later this afternoon, when she could find him alone, when she would have the privacy they needed to resolve this mess.

But wasn't privacy one of the problems? Not too little, as most couples found, but too much. Hadn't they lived out enough of their relationship alone, hidden from curious eyes, and friendly ones, too?

Though her hands were trembling, she pulled into the first empty parking space she came to and shut off the engine. Praying she wasn't making a mistake, she climbed out, ran one hand over her hair in a gesture she'd seen other women make a thousand times, then started toward the café. A half dozen times she thought about turning back. A half dozen times she kept walking.

The bell over the door announced her arrival to a roomful of diners. Business at the café varied greatly. Breakfast was always a busy time, lunch may or may not be, and dinner was slower. Today was a busy lunch day. It didn't appear, in the instant she allowed herself to skim the room, that there was an empty seat in the place. If she wanted an audience, she had one.

The door slipped from her nerveless fingers and slowly closed again. Some people were looking at her. Maybe they'd heard the gossip, or they were aware of the problems between her and Ethan and wondered if she knew he was there. Frankly, what they'd heard or thought just didn't matter this afternoon, not the way it used to.

Too bad she hadn't stopped caring five days sooner.

Ethan was easy to locate in the crowd. He wasn't the only blond in the place, wasn't the only handsome man, but he was the only one who mattered to her. He sat in a booth back in the far corner, with Easy beside him, Guthrie and Olivia across from him. Shay was standing next to the booth, one hand resting on Easy's shoulder.

Even from across the room, she could see the weariness on Ethan's face. She knew he wasn't working too hard, though he had almost finished the baby's room. Last night when she got home, she'd gone upstairs to see what progress he'd made, and she'd cried again, not because he cared enough to do this for Annie, but because he'd been nearly finished. The walls had been painted a sunny yellow, and the quarter-century-old carpet had been taken out and replaced with a wood floor in warm yellow oak. All that was left was some final detail work—replacing the overhead light fixture, adding new switch and outlet plates, setting up the crib. He could finish in an hour, and then he'd have no reason to come back again until the baby was born.

Did she dare hope that his weariness stemmed from the same source as hers—sleepless nights, heartbreak, loneliness?

After a long moment, she turned her attention to the other diners. The faces she was searching for were among those who'd fallen silent to watch her with an expectant air. The old hens, most people called them. They shared a table in the center of the room—Pete Davis and Bill Taylor, whose bones predicted snow, rain, a cold front moving in or a warm spell. Bill's son Velt, one of the elderly Smith brothers and Max Owens rounded out the group.

As she started across the room, a shiver raced down her spine. She knew without looking that Ethan had finally noticed her. He was watching her, no doubt wondering why she'd come. Please, God, not wishing she would leave. If he was, the next few minutes were going to be the most humiliating of her life.

She stopped at the middle table and looked at each of the men before her gaze settled on Pete. He was grinning as if he knew why she was there and was going to relish every minute of it. "Mr. Davis," she said softly. "Would you and your friends come with me, please?"

"Why, we'd be delighted, Miss Prescott." He stood up, gathered his cronies and followed her across the room to the back booth.

By then everyone in the restaurant was watching, their lunches forgotten in front of them. When she stopped at the table, the five old men gathered behind her. Guthrie, Olivia, Easy and Shay all seemed to know, or at least suspect, what was coming. The two women were trying to contain smiles. The two men offered no sympathy for Ethan. Ethan was the only one, she thought, who truly didn't seem to know what to think.

Pushing her glasses higher onto her nose, she stalled by saying a polite hello to the others. That took all of ten seconds, and then there was nothing to do but face Ethan. "Hello, Ethan."

"Grace."

"I—" Her cheeks grew warm. She'd never had such an audience in her life, had never spoken to more than probably four people at one time in her life, and certainly never about anything so important, so personal. But not private. They'd been private for far too long. "I wanted to tell you I like what you did with the nursery."

He looked confused. "Thanks."

"I also wanted to tell you that…you were right. That I cared about the wrong things, even if it was for the right reasons. That I was too afraid of the past repeating itself. I was an idiot.''

"He called her an idiot?" Bill Taylor asked loudly.

"Of course he didn't," Shay responded, then darted a suspicious look at Ethan. "Did you?"

"No, he didn't." Grace glanced at the people behind her, and the people behind them. "The idiot remark was my own, okay?" Turning back, she clasped her hands together, then dried her palms on her jeans before clasping them again. "It was so hard for you to be a James in this town, for me to be a Prescott. I was afraid that it would be even harder for our baby. She's already stuck with all my problems, and I thought if people knew you were her father, she'd get stuck with yours, too. But that's not the way it works. Yes, she'll be a Prescott, but she'll have things I never had—a mother who loves her, a father who would do anything for her, a family...." She gestured with both hands to include Guthrie and Olivia, Easy and Shay. "If I'd had those things, it would have made a world of difference. I wouldn't have lived my whole life as 'poor Grace.' And with them, she'll never be 'poor Annie.'"

"Who's Annie?" someone behind her asked in a stage whisper. He grunted when someone else, she suspected, poked him with an elbow.

"Her baby," that someone answered.

"But she hasn't even had it yet. How can she know it's a girl?"

"There's tests." That was Bill's ninety-some-year-old voice. "Doctors can tell pert near anything now. I seen it on TV. With that satellite dish, we get all sorts of programs."

"Hey," Shay said loudly enough to get their attention. "Grace is doing the talking here, okay?"

She tried to refocus her thoughts, to find the words she needed so badly. Nothing would come, though—no magic.

No easy sentiments. No easy anything. "What I'm trying to say is I—I…" Painfully aware of the witnesses she'd deliberately invited, of the lack of privacy she'd deliberately sought, she swallowed hard. This was a mistake, she thought with a sudden panic. The first time a woman said "I love you" to a man shouldn't be shared with half the town.

Unless she'd treated him the way she'd treated Ethan.

Pete didn't give her a chance to gather her courage once again. "What she's trying to say is that she loves you, boy. Ain't you got nothin' to say to that?"

"You pushy old man," a woman said from the back. "She don't want you saying it for her, and *he* sure don't want you saying it. Give her a chance."

"Aw, she'll be standin' here stumblin' around the subject for the rest of the day," Velt Taylor scoffed. "Pete's just givin' her a little help."

At some point in the conversation—Ethan wasn't at all sure when—Easy had moved to stand behind his wife, with his arms around her, leaving the way clear whenever Ethan wanted to stand up and put an end to this. Knowing how hard it was for Grace, he'd been tempted from the beginning. Knowing how important it was for her to finish, he'd kept his seat.

He did put an end to the current bickering. "You're a nice guy, Pete, but you're not my type." Amid the old men's laughter, he slid across the bench and got to his feet, then looked around the crowd. "I've waited a long time—" his gaze returned to Grace and stayed "—all my life for this. The next person interrupts her, we're taking it outside, and then you'll have to settle for making your best guesses about what's said."

Immediately they quieted down.

"Grace?"

Her fingers nervously worked together. She was embarrassed, uncomfortable, afraid, and yet she gathered the courage to continue. He loved her for it.

"I've waited all my life, too," she said quietly, "and I've been scared all that time. Scared of loving, of not being loved in return. Scared of being loved and being left. I was so afraid of losing you that I wound up pushing you away. But alone is no way to live. Our baby deserves better. I deserve better." She tried to smile, but her mouth wouldn't cooperate. "We deserve you. We—I love you, Ethan, and I want you in my life, in our daughter's life, for as long as I can have you."

For a moment, he was too choked up to speak, then pure emotion dissolved the lump in his throat and propelled him a step closer to her. "What about my reputation?"

Tears glistened on her lashes as she took a step, too, propelled by a nudge of Pete's elbow. "A reputation's just talk. Besides, it'll provide you with stories to tell our grandchildren on cold winter nights."

He took the last step and reached for her, the way he'd been aching to do for five unbearable days, drawing her into his embrace. "Why would I want to entertain the grandkids when I could entertain their grandmother instead?" As the last word faded, he kissed her with every bit of sweet, tender emotion he could muster. It was enough to make her knees weak, to make her lean heavily against him and cling to him as if—well, as if she loved him. And she did. Almost as much as he loved her.

"Well?" someone spoke up. "You gonna kiss her all day or ask her to marry you?"

"Yeah. It's not like you've got all the time in the world. You gotta get it done before Alice—"

"Manny," someone else corrected.

"*Annie,*" a third one said, then snorted. "What kind of people would name their little baby girl Manny?"

Ethan ended the kiss to take a badly needed breath, then

gazed down into Grace's hazy brown eyes. "You wanna marry me, Gracie?"

"More than anything in the world."

"Are you prepared to be stuck with me for the rest of our lives?"

"I can't think of anything I'd like more."

"I love you. You know that, don't you?"

Looking wide-eyed, innocent and amazingly beautiful, she nodded.

"Then would you tell me something I don't know?" He waited for another nod, then gestured toward the old men. "Why are they here?"

She looked at Pete and the others, then graced Ethan with an incredible smile. "Because if they're going to gossip about us—and they will—I want them to get the details right."

Probably for the first time in their lives, the old men looked chastened, but not for long. "Gossip?" Pete echoed, then began shepherding his group back to their table. "Now, why in the world would we want to gossip about them? Two young people in love and about to have a baby... There's nothing new in that. Happens all the time. It's just normal."

And that, Ethan thought as he kissed Grace again, was all either of them had ever wanted to be.

Just normal.

A perfect Oklahoma spring was difficult to come by. The season came late, was often chilly and damp, and gave way too soon to summer's heat. But the perfect spring day... Those weren't so rare. There were always a few of them, and the second Sunday of April was one.

It was also one of those nostalgic family days that for too long had been missing from Ethan's life and, until recently, had never been a part of Grace's. They'd gone to church that morning, sharing a pew with Guthrie and his family and the Raffertys, and then they'd all driven out to the Harris ranch for dinner. After the meal, Ethan had taken advantage of the warm afternoon to go outside and sit on the porch swing.

The chain creaked with every movement, but it didn't bother him. It certainly didn't bother Annie Grace, asleep in his arms. She was a heavy-duty sleeper. Of course, it was easy to sleep well when you wanted for nothing. He'd never felt more rested himself, even with middle-of-the-night feedings.

Last night she hadn't awakened at the usual time, but he had. He'd gone into her room anyway, just to stand and look at her in the pale moonlight. For such a tiny little creature, the feelings she roused in him were amazingly powerful.

After a time, he'd returned to bed and gazed for a while at his wife. The feelings *she* aroused were pretty damn powerful, too. He'd never imagined loving someone, needing someone, the way he loved and needed Grace.

She made his life complete.

As if summoned by his thoughts of her, the screen door opened and Grace came out. She was wearing her first after-Annie dress, soft pastels that suited her coloring. The fabric clung to her breasts and her waist, flared over her hips, then ended mid-calf. The first time she'd put it on, she'd gazed at her reflection with such wonder. She'd decided right then that there would be no more baggy, poorly fitted, secondhand clothes for her.

Although there was a baggy deep purple sweater that they both had an extraordinary fondness for.

"Is she asleep?" she asked as she eased onto the swing beside him.

"Of course. She never misses a chance to snooze in my arms."

"That's because she feels so safe there."

He shifted the baby, freeing one arm so he could slide it around her shoulders. "She gets that from her mama."

"Yes," she agreed. "I feel safe there, too."

They sat in sweet silence for a while, simply enjoying the day. With the same thought apparently in mind, after a time Guthrie joined them, sitting in one of the two rockers with six-week-old Taylor Vernon Harris napping on his shoulder. Taylor seemed twice Annie Grace's size, but in Guthrie's big hands, he looked fragile. In Ethan's own not-so-big hands, Annie Grace felt fragile, but he would always, always keep her and her mama safe.

In another minute Easy joined them, drawing the other rocker near. Soon after the twins drifted out, Elly bringing a coloring book and Emma carrying a prissy-looking doll. They sprawled on the floor between the rockers and gliders.

After a little more time passed, Ethan looked at Guthrie, then Easy, then all three men turned to the door. As if on cue, the screen door opened and Shay and Olivia joined them. Olivia took the empty space at the other end of the swing, and Shay sat on her husband's lap.

Gradually Elly became aware of the silence and looked around the group. "Anyone wanna play a game?"

All she got were head shakes.

"Wanna talk?"

More head shakes.

She scrunched up her face. "Well, then, whaddya wanna do?"

"Exactly what we're doing," Olivia said with a contented sigh.

"What's that?"

"Being a family," Guthrie answered.

"Oh." Satisfied with the odd reply, Elly returned to her coloring book.

Ethan looked from Annie Grace to Grace, meeting her

dark gaze, and they shared a smile. That was all either of them had ever wanted—to be part of a family. He'd looked for it everyplace in the country but the one place where he could find it, and she'd stayed right there, believing she would never find it.

Sometimes he thought it was nothing less than a miracle that they'd managed to meet at exactly the right time. Most of the time, though, he knew it was simpler than that. It was because they were family.

And meant to always be.

*   *   *   *   *

*For more of Marilyn Pappano's
masterful storytelling, watch for*

BIG SKY LAWMAN,

*Marilyn's riveting contribution
to the exciting miniseries,*

**MONTANA MAVERICKS:
WED IN WHITEHORN,**

*only from Silhouette,
available October 2000!*

Look Who's Celebrating Our 20th Anniversary:

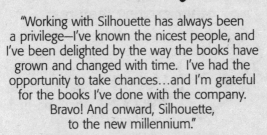

"Working with Silhouette has always been a privilege—I've known the nicest people, and I've been delighted by the way the books have grown and changed with time. I've had the opportunity to take chances...and I'm grateful for the books I've done with the company. Bravo! And onward, Silhouette, to the new millennium."

—*New York Times* bestselling author
Heather Graham Pozzessere

"Twenty years of laughter and love... It's not hard to imagine Silhouette Books celebrating twenty years of quality publishing, but it is hard to imagine a publishing world without it. Congratulations..."

—International bestselling author
Emilie Richards

INTIMATE MOMENTS®

Silhouette®

and

BEVERLY BARTON

bring you more riveting romantic stories in
the exciting series

THE PROTECTORS

Ready to lay their lives on the line, but unprepared for
the power of love

Available now:
MURDOCK'S LAST STAND
(Intimate Moments #979)

Available in July 2000:
EGAN CASSIDY'S KID
(Intimate Moments #1015)

Look for more books in THE PROTECTORS series in 2001!

Available at your favorite retail outlet.

And don't miss these past Protectors titles, which you can order now:

DEFENDING HIS OWN, #670, 10/95
GUARDING JEANNIE, #688, 1/96
BLACKWOOD'S WOMAN, #707, 4/96
ROARKE'S WIFE, #807, 9/97
A MAN LIKE MORGAN KANE, #819, 11/97
GABRIEL HAWK'S LADY, #830, 1/98
KEEPING ANNIE SAFE, #937, 7/99

Silhouette®
Where love comes alive™

SILHOUETTE'S 20ᵀᴴ ANNIVERSARY CONTEST
OFFICIAL RULES
NO PURCHASE NECESSARY TO ENTER

1. To enter, follow directions published in the offer to which you are responding. Contest begins 1/1/00 and ends on 8/24/00 (the "Promotion Period"). Method of entry may vary. Mailed entries must be postmarked by 8/24/00, and received by 8/31/00.

2. During the Promotion Period, the Contest may be presented via the Internet. Entry via the Internet may be restricted to residents of certain geographic areas that are disclosed on the Web site. To enter via the Internet, if you are a resident of a geographic area in which Internet entry is permissible, follow the directions displayed on-line, including typing your essay of 100 words or fewer telling us "Where In The World Your Love Will Come Alive." On-line entries must be received by 11:59 p.m. Eastern Standard time on 8/24/00. Limit one e-mail entry per person, household and e-mail address per day, per presentation. If you are a resident of a geographic area in which entry via the Internet is permissible, you may, in lieu of submitting an entry on-line, enter by mail, by hand-printing your name, address, telephone number and contest number/name on an 8"x 11" plain piece of paper and telling us in 100 words or fewer "Where In The World Your Love Will Come Alive," and mailing via first-class mail to: Silhouette 20ᵗʰ Anniversary Contest, (in the U.S.) P.O. Box 9069, Buffalo, NY 14269-9069; (In Canada) P.O. Box 637, Fort Erie, Ontario, Canada L2A 5X3. Limit one 8"x 11" mailed entry per person, household and e-mail address per day. On-line and/or 8"x 11" mailed entries received from persons residing in geographic areas in which Internet entry is not permissible will be disqualified. No liability is assumed for lost, late, incomplete, inaccurate, nondelivered or misdirected mail, or misdirected e-mail, for technical, hardware or software failures of any kind, lost or unavailable network connection, or failed, incomplete, garbled or delayed computer transmission or any human error which may occur in the receipt or processing of the entries in the contest.

3. Essays will be judged by a panel of members of the Silhouette editorial and marketing staff based on the following criteria:

> Sincerity (believability, credibility)—50%
>
> Originality (freshness, creativity)—30%
>
> Aptness (appropriateness to contest ideas)—20%

Purchase or acceptance of a product offer does not improve your chances of winning. In the event of a tie, duplicate prizes will be awarded.

4. All entries become the property of Harlequin Enterprises Ltd., and will not be returned. Winner will be determined no later than 10/31/00 and will be notified by mail. Grand Prize winner will be required to sign and return Affidavit of Eligibility within 15 days of receipt of notification. Noncompliance within the time period may result in disqualification and an alternative winner may be selected. All municipal, provincial, federal, state and local laws and regulations apply. Contest open only to residents of the U.S. and Canada who are 18 years of age or older, and is void wherever prohibited by law. Internet entry is restricted solely to residents of those geographical areas in which Internet entry is permissible. Employees of Torstar Corp., their affiliates, agents and members of their immediate families are not eligible. Taxes on the prizes are the sole responsibility of winners. Entry and acceptance of any prize offered constitutes permission to use winner's name, photograph or other likeness for the purposes of advertising, trade and promotion on behalf of Torstar Corp. without further compensation to the winner, unless prohibited by law. Torstar Corp and D.L. Blair, Inc., their parents, affiliates and subsidiaries, are not responsible for errors in printing or electronic presentation of contest or entries. In the event of printing or other errors which may result in unintended prize values or duplication of prizes, all affected contest materials or entries shall be null and void. If for any reason the Internet portion of the contest is not capable of running as planned, including infection by computer virus, bugs, tampering, unauthorized intervention, fraud, technical failures, or any other causes beyond the control of Torstar Corp. which corrupt or affect the administration, secrecy, fairness, integrity or proper conduct of the contest, Torstar Corp. reserves the right, at its sole discretion, to disqualify any individual who tampers with the entry process and to cancel, terminate, modify or suspend the contest or the Internet portion thereof. In the event of a dispute regarding an on-line entry, the entry will be deemed submitted by the authorized holder of the e-mail account submitted at the time of entry. Authorized account holder is defined as the natural person who is assigned to an e-mail address by an Internet access provider, on-line service provider or other organization that is responsible for arranging e-mail address for the domain associated with the submitted e-mail address.

5. Prizes: Grand Prize—a $10,000 vacation to anywhere in the world. Travelers (at least one must be 18 years of age or older) or parent or guardian if one traveler is a minor, must sign and return a Release of Liability prior to departure. Travel must be completed by December 31, 2001, and is subject to space and accommodations availability. Two hundred (200) Second Prizes—a two-book limited edition autographed collector set from one of the Silhouette Anniversary authors: Nora Roberts, Diana Palmer, Linda Howard or Annette Broadrick (value $10.00 each set). All prizes are valued in U.S. dollars.

6. For a list of winners (available after 10/31/00), send a self-addressed, stamped envelope to: Harlequin Silhouette 20ᵗʰ Anniversary Winners, P.O. Box 4200, Blair, NE 68009-4200.

Contest sponsored by Torstar Corp., P.O. Box 9042, Buffalo, NY 14269-9042.

ENTER FOR
A CHANCE TO WIN*

Silhouette's 20th Anniversary Contest

Tell Us Where in the World
You Would Like *Your* Love To Come Alive...
And We'll Send the Lucky Winner There!

Silhouette wants to take you wherever
your happy ending can come true.

Here's how to enter: Tell us, in 100 words or less,
where you want to go to make your love come alive!

In addition to the grand prize, there will be 200
runner-up prizes, collector's-edition book sets
autographed by one of the Silhouette anniversary
authors: **Nora Roberts, Diana Palmer,
Linda Howard** or **Annette Broadrick**.

DON'T MISS YOUR CHANCE TO WIN!
ENTER NOW! No Purchase Necessary

Silhouette®
Where love comes alive™

Visit Silhouette at www.eHarlequin.com to enter, starting this summer.

Name:

Address:

City: State/Province:

Zip/Postal Code:

Mail to Harlequin Books: **In the U.S.**: P.O. Box 9069, Buffalo, NY
14269-9069; **In Canada**: P.O. Box 637, Fort Erie, Ontario, L4A 5X3